JUST CALL ME
SPAGHETTI-HOOP
BOY

JUST CALL ME SPAGHETTI-HOOP BOY

LARA WILLIAMSON

USBORNE

TO DAVID AND JOSIE – MY SUPERHEROES

First published in the UK in 2017 by Usborne Publishing Ltd., Usborne House, 83-85 Saffron Hill, London EC1N 8RT, England. www.usborne.com

Text © Lara Williamson, 2017

The right of Lara Williamson to be identified as the author of this work has been asserted by her in accordance with the Copyright, Designs and Patents Act, 1988.

Main cover illustration by Carlos Aón

Photography: buildings © takiwa/Shutterstock; Spaghetti-hoops © blammo/Alamy

The name Usborne and the devices 🔱 🌐 are Trade Marks of Usborne Publishing Ltd.

A CIP catalogue record for this book is available from the British Library.

ISBN 9781474921305   FMAMJJASOND/17   04083-1

Printed in the UK.

1

KAPOW

I'm Adam Butters and I love comics. My favourite characters are the Zorbitans, which are little green creatures that live on the moon. I don't live on the moon but on planet Earth; top floor flat, number 53, Pegasus Park Towers. I like sunshine, my old teddy bear, rolling down hills and eating spaghetti hoops (but not at the same time). I wear my bobble hat because it makes me feel safe. When it gets wet my classmates think it smells of dogs but I don't care. We do have a dog, although it doesn't smell of dog because it doesn't exist. It's an invisible dog called Sausage Roll and belongs to my six-year-old sister, Velvet. I've got an older sister too and unfortunately she does exist. She's called Minnie. But the most important things in my life are my mum and dad, and there isn't anywhere else in the universe I'd rather be than with them.

My dad is called Clark and he's the person who got me interested in comics – he also loves the Zorbitans. Sinéad, that's my mum, she's the best. She tells me that I am her heart, which is a bit daft because she's got her own heart. I think she means she's got me *in* her heart. And Mum's heart is big, at least the size of Mars (the planet, not the chocolate bar). She always says I take after her but that's impossible. Thing is, I can't take after Mum because she's not my real mother. Dad is not my real dad either.

Yesterday, my schoolteacher, Mrs Chatterjee, came up with the bright idea that we should make our family trees for a project. It made me remember I'm adopted. That was the first time I'd thought about my real mother since my last birthday. But Mrs Chatterjee said this project would help us discover lots of new things about ourselves and our loved ones, and, the thing is, I already know everything about my family. Instead, I want to know more about my *real* mother. So I've decided I'll do my family tree on her.

To be fair, there are tiny bits I already know about

my background because Mum told me. The first thing is that I was adopted when I was very little. Mum and Dad brought me home to the flat and they had a "welcome home" party for me, and Minnie – who was four years old then – gave me a gift. After that I started crying and, according to Mum, she reached out to me and I looked up at her, tears in my eyes, and she held me and then I smiled. It was a wonderful moment. "I held you in my hands," said Mum. "But really I held you in my heart."

Another thing, which Mum told me when I was seven, is that there's an important envelope for me and I can open it when I turn sixteen. An envelope didn't sound all that interesting then, but now I'm eleven I do wonder if there are answers inside. Like where I came from, where I was born, what my real mother was called, and why she had to give me up. Maybe Mum doesn't know these facts, but if I'm doing a family tree project I'll need to find out.

You see, Mrs Chatterjee likes facts when we're doing projects. She says facts are like anchors. And it was only when she said that that I realized... I've got no anchor. Because I don't know the facts about me, or where I came from. So I need to do something to change that.

Today is the Friday before half-term. At the end of school, Mrs Chatterjee sent us away with homework to do over the week we're off. Everyone groaned when she said, "Find out whatever information you can to start working on your family tree when we return." Then she followed it with: "This will be the best project you'll ever do."

So now I'm at home, looking down at my notebook, and it's as blank as snow without a footprint even though I've been holding a pencil for the last twenty minutes. Outside there's a storm whipping around the tower block. The wind rattles the letter box like an angry monster. I feel its cold breath sweep down the hallway and swirl around my bedroom and tighten its fingers around my chest. Shivering slightly, I rise from the bed and go and stare out of my window, my fingertips pressed against the glass making ten marbles of warmth. "Stupid project," I mumble. "Why am I the only person who doesn't know who their mother is and can't do the project properly? No gold star for me." There's a distant rumble and slivers of lightning ignite the clouds and that's when I realize: I just need to find the envelope.

Even though I'm not sixteen, Mum always said it was important and that she was keeping it safe for me. Right now I want that envelope more than a first edition comic with a free gift on the front cover. And I know I should just ask Mum if I can have it, but she's been a bit stressed and weepy recently – even though she's tried to hide it – and I don't want to risk upsetting her. So I turn away from the window, pad across the floor and open my door, before tiptoeing down the hall towards Mum and Dad's room. Logic tells me that the envelope is bound to be there. But as I reach for the handle, Velvet appears from nowhere and pokes me in the back, saying she's on the way to the kitchen. Then she asks me what I'm doing.

"I am looking for an envelope," I say. Sometimes the truth is a lot less likely to attract attention than making up a complete lie. It works, because Velvet is totally disinterested and she sticks her finger up her nose and begins digging around.

"I'm looking for chocolate milk," says Velvet.

"Well, you won't find it up your nose."

Velvet pulls the sort of face Grandma says will stick like that if the wind changes and then wanders away to the kitchen. As I open Mum and Dad's bedroom door and ease into the shadows, I can hear the distant drone of Minnie rehearsing her lines for her part in the school play. And I can hear Dad laughing at something on the TV and then Mum telling him he nearly burst her eardrum and Dad saying he can't help it if he's got a loud laugh. And Velvet is pulling open the fridge and rattling bottles. But another thing I can hear, and it's louder than everything else, is the *thump-thump* of my heart.

The envelope isn't under the bed or in their bedside drawers. All I can see in Dad's drawer is a load of badges advertising his key-cutting company, Surelock Homes. Dad loves working with his hands, from cutting keys at work to making models of comic-book characters at home. Mum's always complaining that the flat is too small to make life-size models of Batman, but Dad does it anyway. I've got a life-size Zorbitan in my bedroom that Dad made. Luckily a life-size Zorbitan only comes up to my knee.

Anyway, there's no envelope and it's not in Mum's drawer either. All she's got in there are lots of our front door keys that Dad cut for practice. I remember Mum saying she didn't need ten keys cluttering up the drawer, and Dad said at least she didn't have ten *mon*keys because they'd take up even more space, and we laughed for ages. I wish Mum would laugh like that again because when she's sad it makes me feel sad too and then I hide in my bobble hat. Dad's the opposite of gloomy. In fact, he's a right comedian sometimes, but even his jokes don't seem to be cheering Mum up at the moment. On top of the keys is a sign-up sheet for this place called Bellybusters that promises to turn you from *a couch potato to a glowing goddess* within months, but that's all.

My heart's still thundering when I turn to the dressing table, and I pull that drawer open and suddenly it's as if the whole thing shimmers with a golden light – because I can see an envelope in there and on the front it says: *FOR ADAM. DO NOT OPEN UNTIL YOU ARE SIXTEEN.* My hands tremble like they're holding invisible maracas and then I do what any sensible eleven-year-old would do: I ignore what it says and open it.

Lightning rips the sky in two outside and the bedroom flashes in negative as I pull out a piece of paper. My birthdate is on the left side – same date, same year. The place of birth is Pegasus Park and I imagine that means Pegasus Park Hospital. But it's not my name on the paper. My mouth is as dry as a cracker on Mars as I lean closer, trying to read the words. My name is on the envelope and it's my birthdate, so it must be *my* birth certificate. But the name inside says Ace Walker. As the penny drops on my head from the height of the Eiffel Tower, I realize that *I* must have been called Ace when I was born.

There's another name on the paper too: Rose Walker. That must be my real mother's name. There's a whooshing inside me and it feels like my blood is racing around my body in a super-fast car. My real mother called me Ace. Why would she do that?

I think about the word. It's kind of a strange name. Pretty different to Adam. But pretty cool as well. I mean, if something is ace it's excellent. So if I'm called Ace then I should be excellent too. It even sounds a bit like the names of the superheroes in my comic books. "Adam" isn't a superhero name – Adam is the sort of name a boy who hides under his bobble hat would have. But Ace... Could I really be an *Ace*?

There's a thunderous crack outside and it sounds like biting into a chocolate-coated ice cream. To say I'm excited about all this is an understatement. My name is Ace...like a superhero... I give this some further thought and find myself grinning like a loon. That's because when I read my superhero comics I always smile. Superheroes make everyone happy. If you're happy then you're not fed up and moody. And the one person who needs cheering up most of all is Mum and now I know exactly how to do it. I'm going to *be* a superhero! Yes!

Mum's not the only one who is going to be happy after this. Everyone is going to love me. I'll get picked first for the football team instead of last. This is *sick*, but sick in a good way, not sick as in vomit. I'm ready to punch the air I'm so happy. And not only am I going to be a superhero, but I've also found out my real mother's name, which means I'll be able to do the best school project *ever*. I can see it all. There will be the biggest, brightest gold star, perhaps even a constellation, above my name. Mrs Chatterjee will say my tree is incredible and I'll say that's because it's a superhero's tree. Of course, I'll be humble too. I'll say I was simply trying to make everyone happy. It was my destiny.

Meanwhile, lightning snaps me out of my daydream and bathes the room in electro-silver again. There's another rumble and when I glance up I swear there's a shadow at the bedroom door, but when my eyes focus there's no one there. I'd like to hold onto the envelope and take it back to my bedroom to study it, but it's too risky in case Mum notices it's gone. After a final look inside the envelope to check there isn't anything else, I push the birth certificate back inside and try to seal it up again with spit before shoving it in the drawer and heading back to my bedroom.

My notebook isn't blank any more. In the last twenty minutes I've started my homework and written *ACE* in capital letters and I've drawn lightning bolts coming from behind it. Underneath I've tried to draw a long-stemmed rose to represent Rose, my real mother, but it looks more like a big smudge on a stick. I've written my birthdate and that I was born in Pegasus Park Hospital (I think). The page is filling up nicely with information, especially since I wrote Pegasus Park in big bubble letters.

I'm going to be Ace, I keep telling myself.

Everyone loves a superhero, because they're excellent.

When I am a superhero, everyone will be happy – including Mum. As I'm drawing Ganymede – which is Jupiter's largest moon – next to all the Ace stuff in my notebook, Mum knocks on my bedroom door and when she enters I feel a fireball whoosh up my cheeks. I'm sure I've got guilt written all over my face, except it must be in invisible ink because Mum doesn't seem to notice – and she doesn't mention the opened envelope in her drawer, so it's obvious she doesn't know what I've been up to. Instead she says, "Your room, Adam..." Mum looks at the Zorbitan in the corner and shakes her head. "It's small, isn't it? I think it needs decorating. We could get rid of the comic-book wallpaper."

"I like the wallpaper," I argue. Dad tore lots of pages out of old comics and we put it up together. When I'm bored I can read the stories, and it doesn't matter how many times I read them, they still cheer me up. My favourite is a story about the Zorbitans. They're looking for their creator, The Grand Moon Master. When they find him, their emerald hearts will glow red and they'll live together for ever. Mum says the comic wallpaper is nice but we've got to make the most of the small rooms and the whole flat is due a makeover.

The flat is small, Mum's right. Mum and Dad have a room, I have one, and Minnie and Velvet share – although Minnie has put a red line across the floor and no one is allowed to step in her half. But even though the flat is small, it's still amazing, because it's like living on top of the world and being able to look out and touch the stars. "I don't want my room to change," I reply. "I like it the way it is."

Defeated, Mum nods and says it's just a thought she had. Then she trots over to look at my notebook and I have to close it quickly because I don't want her to see everything I've been drawing. And I definitely don't want Mum seeing I've written ACE because she'd be suspicious. "It's nothing important," I say, the bobble on my hat nearly blowing back with the force of me slamming down the pages.

But it *is* important. When Mum's gone I pick up my pencil again and whisper, "Finding out about my family tree for this project *is* important. I want to know more and surprise Mrs Chatterjee and get a gold star – maybe even two." The pencil pushes into the paper. I let it dance in circles around the page. I know Mum would be hurt if she realized I'd gone searching for my birth certificate, but that's because she's had a lot on her mind recently. It's not just that she seems a bit sad and worried – she's always whispering to Dad and then shutting up when we come in the room too.

I look down at the page and see I've drawn a superhero. If I was this superhero, I'd be so excellent Mum would have to cheer up. Everything would be perfect and everyone would be happy. That's what I want most in the world.

The pencil tip snaps.

Mum always says that when you need to do something, "there's no time like the present" (although I am not sure this applies to homework). Next morning, I'm on the case writing notes about all the characteristics an excellent superhero should possess:

1. Superpowers
2. Courage
3. Being a clever clogs (that's what Grandma calls it)
4. Being honest and kind
5. Being special
6. A mission

As I scan the list I realize that number six is probably the most important. In my opinion, a superhero who doesn't have a mission isn't *actually* a superhero. Proper superheroes are trying to achieve a goal – I've learned that from my comic books. Well, my mission is to be the most excellent person I can be and make everyone happy.

I give the end of my pencil a chew as I glance down at the rest of the list, and then stop, realizing my gums don't like splinters. So number six is sorted: my mission is to be the most excellent kid on the planet. And I've got oodles of number five, being special. I once won a badge for a class quiz and Mrs Chatterjee said I was very special and it wasn't for having the highest score but for thinking "out of the box". To be honest, I didn't think I was in a box in the first place, but then teachers say strange things. I'm definitely numbers two and four as well, because I once told Minnie she looked like a Twiglet in her brown skinny jeans. That was a) honest and b) courageous, because she kicked me in the shins straight after. And she was wearing boots with studs on them.

Number one – superpowers – might be a touch more tricky and require more practice. This morning I've already almost broken my ankle trying to fly from my bed, and Mum's been shouting that it sounds like I've got a breakdancing hippopotamus in my room. Clearly flight is not my superpower at this stage. Neither is mind control, because after I'd had breakfast I tried to hypnotize Mum into letting me off washing the dishes, only she blinked rapidly to block my mind waves and then she threw the rubber gloves at me and told me to stop staring at her like I was constipated. Then I thought maybe my power could be mimicking animals, like the comic-book character Animal Man, but Velvet's already got that superpower because she really believes it is Sausage Roll barking, when it's actually her.

So I forget about superpowers for now, and instead I turn to a new page in my notebook and write down a list of things I think a superhero should do. If I can do any of these, I'll be a superhero for sure.

HOW TO BE A SUPERHERO IN FIVE EASY STEPS

1. Save a cat from a tree
2. Help an old person
3. Help an enemy
4. Save a life
5. Save the world

For the rest of the morning I try to work out how I can save the world, because if you're going to do a good deed you might as well go BIG. I watch the news to see if there are any local issues I could get involved in. But there's only a clean-up of Pegasus Park dog poop. And I'm not sure that dog poop is a global threat, unless you stand on it in flip-flops, and then I suppose it is the end of the world.

Next, I try helping an enemy. I tell Minnie she's looking particularly gorgeous this morning and she asks if I'm feeling okay and then she says it's a double-bluff and that I'm up to no good, and I say smugly that I'm actually up to a lot of good. Because superheroes are always up to good. It's a fact. Minnie tells Mum I'm playing games and Mum asks what I'm playing and Minnie says it's not Monopoly.

"He's being nice to me."

Mum looks at Minnie and says surely that's a good thing. Then she runs her fingers through her hair and sighs like she's carrying the weight of a baboon on her back. But I give a little smile because if my plan works and I become a superhero, then it's bound to make Mum one million times happier than she looks now.

"Do you think I could save your life?" I stare at Minnie, thinking I might be able to achieve number four of the FIVE EASY STEPS without too much trouble.

"OMG, Mum," wails Minnie, staring at me like a vampire caught in sunlight, "Adam's going to kill me!" She narrows her eyes to tiny blades and when Mum leaves the room Minnie jabs her finger towards me and says she knows I'm up to something and she'll find out what it is.

So it turns out helping an enemy was a bad idea and I'm glum that I couldn't achieve numbers three, four or five. It feels like my list is more HOW TO BE A SUPERHERO IN FIVE NOT SO EASY STEPS, also known as HOW TO END UP BALD LIKE DAD BECAUSE YOU'RE TEARING YOUR OWN HAIR OUT. I'm as miserable as Bigfoot with a sore toe, and I go and sit in my bedroom and try to figure out how I can help an old person (number two). Which is when I hear Mum and Dad talking in hushed tones outside my bedroom door.

"It'll be a big change," whispers Mum.

I stop, straining every fibre of my being to listen.

"I know, but it's worth it. And I know the flat is small but we can make sacrifices. Let's not mention it to the kids yet though." Dad coughs.

I swallow and it feels like I've got a goldfish swimming about in my tummy.

"Yes. Let's keep it as a surprise," says Mum. There's

a pause and then she says, "Oh, Clark, I'm really nervous about this appointment." I hear Dad soothing Mum but I don't hear the exact words, even though I've practically got my ear superglued to the wall.

I'm in shock. It's worse than when I scuffed my new shoes across the carpet and then touched the metal door handle and was nearly thrown halfway across the room. The reason I'm so surprised is that Mum and Dad are keeping secrets from us. Usually they tell us everything. I try to catch the rest of the conversation but it's all muffled and I can't hear anything else they say. Perhaps keeping the secret is the reason why Mum's moody at the moment. She's not being horrible or anything, but it's like she's on a roller coaster going up and down. One minute she's okay and the next she's staring out the window, her eyes glassy.

I don't know what Mum and Dad's secret is but I know if I'm a superhero it's going to make her less moody. I've just looked up the word "ace" in the dictionary and it says a person who excels; a genius, a master, first-rate, wonderful, outstanding, a star and a champion. It also says a playing card ranked as the highest card in its suit. I promise I'm going to be all those things listed (except the playing card – that would be tricky).

3

The half-term break is almost over and I still haven't found out what Mum and Dad's secret is. But in the meantime an opportunity to properly become a superhero has arrived and it's not a moment too soon, because Mum's as miserable as a wet weekend. Dad has booked me into a Saturday lifesaving course in the local swimming pool with the Pegasus Park Pool Piranhas, because he thought I might get bored in the half-term break (even though I never get bored doing nothing). I spend the twenty minutes before we need to go in my bedroom, which I've renamed SPAM HQ (Special Place of Ace Missions), making up a superhero motto to encourage me to be excellent. Because superheroes always have a motto – like Wolverine says he's the best there is at what he does, and The Thing says it's clobberin' time. I place my teddy bear, aka my sidekick, on the bed and tell him to prick up his furry ears under his bobble hat and listen. I've come up with: *I am Ace. I will start, righting wrongs 'cause I'm all heart.* My teddy bear stares ahead like he's not listening. Mind you, that's nothing new. After I've said the motto a few times and accidentally said fart instead of heart twice, I figure I'd prefer something easier like "Shazam", which is what Billy Batson says.

"Kazeem," I sing-song, running around the room with my arm held high. "Shazou, shezaam, kazoo."

Dad bangs on my bedroom door and says I need to stop shouting about a kazoo and get my wazoo out here or I'll be late for the Piranhas. Lifting my swimming bag, I fling open the bedroom door and say I'm ready. Dad is swinging his van keys around his finger and says he'll drop me off in the Surelock Homes van because we don't want the class to start without me. "Come on, champ," says Dad, scratching the clock tattoo on his bicep. "Time waits for no one." He pauses. "Except Minnie when she's in the bathroom doing her make-up and won't come out until it's perfect."

We walk down the staircase from our flat and past Mr Hooper's at number forty-eight. One level down we pass Mrs Karimloo's empty flat and Dad jerks a thumb towards it, saying she's gone to The Ganges.

"What, she's in India?"

"No, she's living with her brother above The Ganges takeaway. I cut her a new key. She'll stick that one under the flowerpot too, I suppose." Dad glances down at the flowerpot, touching it with his toe. "That's what she always did with the key for this flat. You know, whoever moves in here next will need a new lock, because that one's looking a bit damaged. Wait..." Dad reaches into his pocket and pulls out a leaflet for Surelock Homes and puts it through the letter box. "They need to talk to the best in the business."

Ten minutes later, Dad drops me off at the pool with a wave and shouts, "Do your best, sunshine." Then he zooms away in the red van like he's in a race and wants to win. I watch as the big silver key on the back glistens and then it disappears over the horizon.

"Superheroes always do their best, Dad," I whisper. The words flutter away like old chip papers on the wind.

So, I'm not going to lie, I'm excited that I'm about to save a life. Mum will be so happy she might even give me some extra pocket money. There's a Zorbitan comic called *The Zorbitans Take Over* that I want to buy if she does. I'll say, "Mum, no money is necessary because I did it to be excellent. But if you're offering, I'll take the cash." I might even say, "It was nothing really. I just want to make everyone happy, including you." Mum will smile and pat me on the bobble hat before passing me a fiver, and whatever mood she's been in recently will disappear as quickly as the last chocolate biscuit in the tin.

Fifteen minutes later the instructor introduces himself as Mark, chief Piranha of the Pegasus Park Pool Piranhas and we introduce ourselves. He says it's lovely we've joined him this Saturday to save a life. I don't hear what he says next as I'm watching a used plaster float past in the pool. Then Mark introduces Tyler, a gangly goon in flip-flops who I recognize from Minnie's class at Blessed Trinity. "He's my work experience for the half-term break," says Mark. Tyler grins and gives a tiny salute which looks so ridiculous that even he realizes it halfway through and pretends he was just scratching his head.

"Right, I see you've come in your clothes, as instructed – that's good. This is important because..." Mark waits for someone to answer.

A boy to my left whose name I forget says, "Because

you can only go naked on a nudist beach, my nana says."

Mark replies, "Um, right, let's just erase that image from our heads. The chances are if you had to save a life you wouldn't have time to get your swimming trunks on, so you'd jump in fully clothed." Mark looks at my bobble hat. Clearly, he is impressed that I've come more than fully clothed because I'm wearing a hat. I nod at him and my bobble wobbles. That's got to be a gold star for me. Mark tells Tyler to go and get the willing victim.

My mouth drains of saliva as I watch Tyler flippety-flop round the pool towards the spectator area. I half expect him to ask a spectator to come down, but instead he stops at a cupboard under the steps. At that point I swear a vision of Harry Potter floats in front of my eyes because he's the only person I know that lives in a cupboard under the stairs. Unfortunately, five seconds later, after a load of pool noodles fly from the cupboard, I realize it's not Harry Potter.

"It's Manny," exclaims Mark as Tyler throws a life-saving dummy on the floor at our feet. "Short for mannequin, if you're asking." Everyone looks at each other in confusion – nope, no one was asking. I'm so fixated on Manny that I barely hear what Mark says next.

All I make out is *blah-de-blah...jump in...blah-de-blah... find him...blah-de-blah...put your arm around his chest.* I watch as Manny is launched into the pool and Mark finishes explaining what we have to do. Thinking about HOW TO BE A SUPERHERO IN FIVE EASY STEPS, I realize saving a life is not the same as saving a dummy. This isn't looking as promising as it was five minutes ago. Mark looks over at me and says he likes my hat and then proceeds to tell me why he doesn't like it. "That'll get waterlogged immediately. It might weigh you down it's so woolly. It'll be like having a wet sheep on your head."

"I don't take it off," I reply bluntly. And I don't. I've been wearing a bobble hat since I was little and I love it. Mum says it's my security blanket, although that's crazy because it's nothing like a blanket. Even the school let me wear it – Mum cleared it with them. She said when I was little I liked to hide inside it when I was sad or angry and they said that was fine. There was no fuss and now the bobble hat is part of me, like my eyebrows and freckles. And I only still hide in it if I really need to.

"Okay, fair enough," says Mark, turning away. Next, he encourages us all to do a little warm-up before getting in the pool. And that's when it happens. A giant sabre-toothed beast clamps its jaws onto my calf – otherwise known as the twinges of a cramp.

"Who's going to jump in first?" asks Mark then, his eyes scanning us like heat-seeking missiles. Everyone is glued to the floor, probably by all those stray sticking plasters. "Come on, don't be a banana, be a piranha!" bellows Mark. Suddenly his missile-eyes hone in on me and he tells me to jump in: "Show us how it's done, Adam."

I remember that superheroes have courage, so I ignore the fact that my calf feels like it's a sheet of A4 going through a paper shredder, and I jump.

By the way, I have no idea where Manny is as I hit the water, which snaps around me like a cold bangle. Anyway, it doesn't matter where he's gone, because I'm distracted by the red-hot pokers jabbing my calf muscles. As I twist and turn on the surface of the water I hear muffled voices telling me I'm supposed to be a piranha not a curled-up prawn. Bubbles go up my nose and I clutch my leg and open my mouth to yell, but as I go under it fills with water and no sound comes out except *burble burble burble* (translation: *my calf is tighter than a jam-jar lid*).

"Cramp!" Blimey, someone up there is multilingual because they understand my bubble language. Bobbing up again, I hear, "He's got cramp!" As I thrash around someone shouts, "Look, he's not swimming properly."

I've no idea who says it but I suddenly see a flashing figure split the water like a knife through soft butter. I go under once more and Tyler appears in front of me, his fringe floating around him like a golden halo. Then he pulls me up, tells me not to struggle and drags me out of the pool. Spluttering and sodden, I flump down on the floor as applause explodes around me. I hear the spectators shouting "superhero" and I'm about to stand and give them a bow when I glance up and see Tyler doing a lap of honour.

No one remembers Manny has drowned.

Back at home in SPAM HQ I add *assess danger* to the list of qualities a superhero should possess. It was stupid and dangerous to jump in the pool when I had cramp and couldn't swim properly because of it. Disappointed by my attempt to save a life, I tell myself that I must try harder, and a little dose of good luck coming my way wouldn't go amiss. Anyway, saving a lifesaving training-aid dummy wouldn't have counted. I glance over at the certificate that I got at the end of the course.

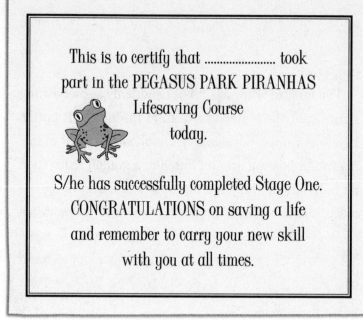

This is to certify that .... took
part in the PEGASUS PARK PIRANHAS
Lifesaving Course
today.

S/he has successfully completed Stage One.
CONGRATULATIONS on saving a life
and remember to carry your new skill
with you at all times.

Mark hasn't even filled in my name, which is probably because he was so preoccupied trying to stop Tyler giving autographs on swimming floats to the girls who were squealing about him being a superhero.

Fed up that I'm not as excellent as I thought, I take off my soggy bobble hat and give it a good squeeze. Pool water leaves a puddle on the bedroom carpet. If you squint really hard it could look like a superhero's broken mask.

4

ZING

The Monday morning after half-term arrives like a sneaky villain you're trying to avoid – bleak and grey and full of misery. Mrs Chatterjee ushers us into the classroom and I sit down beside my best mate, Tiny Eric.

"*Cześć*," says Tiny Eric. Tiny Eric's full name is Eric Kowalski-Brown and he's not tiny. In fact, he's about the height of King Kong's taller brother. He joined Pegasus Park Juniors in Year Five and he lives at 35 Kink Street, Pegasus Park with his mum and dad. I haven't visited him at his house yet but Tiny Eric says I should come over sometime soon. Tiny Eric's mum is from Poland

and Tiny Eric sometimes says things in Polish.

"Greetings," I reply, but I don't look up because I'm still miserable that I haven't got anywhere with being a superhero. It's harder than trying to get dried-up breakfast cereal off a bowl. If I was being truthful, I'd say I expected it to go more smoothly than this. I thought I'd be excellent straight away.

"What's with the long face?" asks Tiny Eric, in between getting out his pencils and notebooks. "You're in a right mood. And we've only been in class five minutes so you can't be bored to death already."

I don't want to tell Tiny Eric anything yet so I say, "I am drained of energy. What I need is some serious good luck to cheer me up." I take my notebook out of my bag and flick through the pages, stopping at my drawing of a rose.

"You want good luck?" Tiny Eric looks concerned and then his face brightens. "You've come to the right place." He taps his nose knowingly.

"What, school?" I mumble, looking around the classroom. I tap my nose unknowingly. To be honest, it doesn't look all that lucky to me.

"No," says Tiny Eric, leaning towards me and waving his arm dismissively. "Don't be daft. *Me*. I'm a master of good-luck charms." I look at Tiny Eric like he's got two heads and neither of them are making any sense. This is the first I've ever heard of Tiny Eric being interested in charms. "In Poland they carry *czterolistna koniczyna* and they'll bring you as much luck as you can handle." Turns out he's talking about a four-leaf clover. But when I ask him if he's got one on him, Tiny Eric says no, he hasn't been lucky enough to find one yet. Oh. I think my face says it all because Tiny Eric adds cheerfully, "I'll draw you one instead. It's almost as good."

Tiny Eric is a master of art. He got a gold star at the end of last term for his drawing of his dad. It looked really lifelike. You could totally imagine his dad was in the classroom with us and it was so good Mrs Chatterjee put it on the wall. I drew Velvet wearing her tiara, but Velvet insisted I also draw a castle and when I said we didn't live in a castle she said yes we did because we lived in the clouds. Anyway, I got a bronze star for that because Mrs Chatterjee said she loved my octopus and I said they were turrets and she quickly changed the subject.

Already Tiny Eric has drawn me a four-leaf clover and coloured it in, and now he tears it out of his notebook and hands it to me. I look at the drawing and it reminds me of four hearts joined together on one stem. "There, your luck will change. All you need to do is stare at this four-leaf clover drawing and believe good things will happen. Then they will."

How can a drawing bring me luck? If it was that easy, I'd not be sitting here like a melted welly worrying about becoming a superhero and cheering my moody mum up. "Okay," I mumble, staring at it. "I suppose it wouldn't hurt." I make a mental note to shove it in my bag and forget about it.

Tiny Eric grins and says we'll talk more about it in the playground and I can stare at the drawing properly then. I make a mental note not to shove it in my bag and forget about it.

Tiny Eric is insisting I stare at the four-leaf clover drawing for at least one minute to get myself in the right frame of mind to receive luck. We're in the playground next to the water fountain and I lean against the wall, pretending to stare at the drawing. Tiny Eric asks why I need good luck anyway. "I just want a bit of luck, it's no crime," I respond, blinking because my eyes are beginning to feel like tiny soldiers are pricking at them with bayonets.

Tiny Eric tells me my minute is up. That's sixty seconds of my life I'll never get back, I think. Then he proceeds to tell me all about lucky charms in Poland and how his grandmother (he calls her his *babcia*) wears red to protect her from evil, and how if they see a chimney sweep they grab one of their buttons and that brings them luck. When I ask Tiny Eric what happens if they don't have any buttons he tells me he hasn't a clue. I'm about to open my mouth to say he's hardly an authority on good luck charms then when he tells me to "button it" and I fall about laughing. Tiny Eric, who doesn't seem to think he made a joke, looks at me as if I'm crazy and then continues, "When you've got your good luck you can pass some on to the next person."

"Do they do that in Poland?"

"I don't know," replies Tiny Eric, leaning down and pressing the button on the drinking fountain so an arc of water rises up. "That bit about passing it on was just my idea." Tiny Eric leans down and takes a drink and then the arc splutters to a stop.

"But I can't draw four-leaf clovers to pass it on."

"Nah, you don't have to. You can draw something special to you and pass that on. It works, honest." Tiny Eric wipes small rivers from his chin.

Seriously, I think Tiny Eric might have lost his even tinier mind. Although, I have to say his drawing of the four-leaf clover is so good you could almost pluck it from the page. After looking at the four joined hearts again I ask Tiny Eric where all my good luck is since I've done my one minute of staring. Tiny Eric says I've probably done enough for *now*. Holy guacamole, am I going to have to do this again? Apparently, yes. According to Tiny Eric, I should start regularly staring at it for one minute and build up. Good luck is like a snowball that builds and builds, he tells me. I'm tempted to say then you find yourself in an avalanche, but I don't.

"Could you draw something else for me?" I say instead, putting the four-leaf clover drawing in my pocket. "I mean, if staring at the clover was lucky, could you do a drawing of who I want to be?" I've just had a clever idea. All I need is to get Tiny Eric to draw me as a superhero, stare at it every day, believe, get lucky, and then – *KAPOW!* – turn into a superhero.

Tiny Eric looks confused and I know this because his eyebrows are going up and down like they're on a spacehopper. "Do a drawing of who you want to be? What do you mean?" He pulls a piece of paper and a pencil from his blazer pocket as I tell him I'd like him to draw me as a superhero. "You what? Are you having a laugh?"

"Do I look like I'm having a laugh?" I reply matter-of-factly. "A superhero. I want a drawing of who I could be if I was *grrrreat*." I roll my rs to emphasize how great I could be. Tiny Eric shrugs and says okay, he'll draw what I'd look like if I was *grrrreat*. "Don't forget to make me look strong," I say, planting my hands on my hips. "And I need a serious outfit and maybe a cape fluttering behind me, and make it look as though I'm in Gotham City not a school playground. Oh, and I'd like a helicopter hovering above me." I pose, my nose in the air as I look towards the horizon (which is really the assembly hall and quite disappointing, unless you count the place where someone has scribbled in gold marker: *What food is okay in Mr McGammon's maths class? Pi!*).

There's a crowd building around us, kids craning to see what Tiny Eric is drawing and why I've got my arm in the air and am shouting "Kazoo!" at the top of my lungs (since that's my new motto). This is it, I tell myself. This is what it will feel like when I'm a superhero for real. People will surround me and go "Ooh" and "Ahh" and say I'm amazing.

"And don't forget lightning," I continue. "Make me look like a true superhero. I want to be the sort of person who is kind and caring and helps others. That's the sort of person who is loved and makes everyone happy."

One girl with a fringe is pointing at the drawing and

saying Tiny Eric has got it just right, and I feel a swell of excitement build up in my chest and I say "Kazoo!" again to make sure I'm totally channelling the superhero inside me. The Beast, who's almost as tall as Tiny Eric and from the other Year Six group, barges to the front of the circle and stares at the drawing, then says it looks like I've got a woolly mammoth on my head.

"That's me as a superhero," I snipe back. I've never talked to The Beast before, even though we've glanced at each other a few times in the playground. The Beast has milky-hot-chocolate-coloured hair and no friends and that's because there was once a rumour that The Beast pushed a girl into a bush in the playground. The legend goes it was a holly bush. To be fair, it was years ago and no one even knows if it was true but everyone still avoids The Beast.

Swallowing back laughter, The Beast then turns to Tiny Eric and says, "I like the huge nose you've drawn." Fringe Girl says there is no huge nose on the drawing and The Beast says, "Oh, I was looking at that big bobble on the hat by mistake." Excuse me while I split my sides laughing.

Tiny Eric ignores The Beast and keeps drawing, the pencil moving this way and that. When the bell rings, the crowd around us dissolves like candyfloss. "Hurry up,

Tiny Eric. I don't think I can shout 'Kazoo' again and my arm is aching from holding it up."

"I bet no one said that to Michelangelo when he was painting the Sistine Chapel," mutters Tiny Eric, putting his pencil back in his pocket.

"How long did that take?" My arm flops to my side.

"About four years," explains Tiny Eric, who knows everything about art.

"I'm not surprised," I reply. "It was probably the claws that slowed him right down. I mean, Teenage Mutant Ninja Turtles aren't good with paintbrushes."

5

CRASH

What the blinking flip is this? Tiny Eric has just handed me the drawing as we troop back into class. Where is the cape? Where is the helicopter and Gotham City behind me? And he's forgotten the lightning bolts too. All he's done is a simple drawing of me. I can't look at this picture and believe this is a superhero of the future. It's another load of rubbish to throw on the rubbish I was already feeling this morning. Oh, and hang on... Now there is a whole truckload of rubbish coming, because Mrs Chatterjee is saying that she'd like us to get out our notebooks so we can talk about all the work we did over half-term.

"We discussed the family tree project just before we broke up," says Mrs Chatterjee, her chandelier earrings swinging around. "I told you this was a chance to explore your family history. Now, I want to elaborate a little on what you'll be doing. We're going to do lots of research, before making our tree out of cardboard and then hanging tags on the branches. Each tag will represent something you've discovered about a family member you've been researching. I expect lots of tags."

I look at my notebook, knowing I'm not going to have lots of tags. I've found out three things in the half-term break: my birth name, my real mother's name and where I was born. Yes, I was excited about those at the beginning because they were three things I didn't know before. But thinking about it now, it's still going to be a pretty empty tree. I wish I had a bit more information.

Mrs Chatterjee explains that she understands if we don't have many tags to start with, but as we continue she will expect the tree to grow. I blow out a bubble of relief. She is calling this project the *Forest For Ever* project.

Nish in the front row hoists up his hand. "Will we go to a forest to study trees first, miss?"

"No, we will be staying in the classroom but it will be just as exciting."

Honestly, I am not sure how staying in this classroom could be as exciting as running around a forest, but then teachers say all sorts of strange things, like "You'll love this maths test" or "You'll really enjoy learning about amoebas". The upshot of this is you cannot trust everything a teacher tells you.

According to Mrs Chatterjee, this project is about researching information and going "from tree to me". Nish puts his hand up again and asks Mrs Chatterjee why our family trees are connected to her. There is a moment of confusion until Mrs Chatterjee says it's not from tree to *her*. "It's tree to *me*, meaning *you*." She points at us. Nish puts his hand up again and begins muttering, and Mrs Chatterjee says no one should be moving their lips when her lips are moving.

"Unless you're a ventriloquist," says Nish, slumping down in his chair.

After Mrs Chatterjee gives Nish the "hard stare", she tells us this is a great opportunity to find out about the past and the present and prepare for the future. It's about each one of us at the top of the tree. "We will have an exhibition of the trees in the assembly hall and this time we're doing something different. It's not simply a class project. We're going to share it with everyone." Mrs Chatterjee pauses, her eyes resting on every pupil at once.

"It's like she's the Mona Lisa," Tiny Eric once said, and when I asked why, he said because Mrs Chatterjee's eyes follow you no matter where you are in the classroom.

Nish's hand shoots up. "You mean family can come to this one?"

"Yes," says Mrs Chatterjee, perching on her desk. The chandelier earrings dance around. "Sisters, brothers, aunts, uncles, grandmothers and fathers – all relatives are welcome at Pegasus Park Junior for the *Forest For Ever* display. I will print out invitations and you can give them to your family."

Tiny Eric sighs and when I turn to look at him a bubble of saliva forms on his lips and then bursts.

"I expect you've already made a great start over half-term," she goes on, tapping her red nails on the desk. "You were supposed to ask questions and get information from the family around you. Well, now I'd like you to choose one person you researched over the half-term break and write down five things you love about them. This can be your first tag. You've got twenty minutes. Go!" Anyone would think we were poised at a starting line.

Mrs Chatterjee wanders down the aisles, giving us large luggage tags with white string on the ends. I'm not feeling particularly "Go!" so I look at mine and flatten it with my finger. That takes a few seconds. It's obvious everyone else has already taken off as they are chattering and writing. Then I sharpen my pencil – another few seconds. I still haven't managed to move from the starting line. After that I check the clock and it is one minute and three seconds since I last checked it.

The trouble is I don't know what I love about my real mother, because I don't know her. The only information I've got is her name and that's not enough to write five points on. Blowing out air, I rest my head on my hands. And then slowly I start to think about all the things my own mum is now and that I hope my real mother *could* be, and suddenly I feel a burst of energy and I'm off.

1. Loving
2. Kind
3. Thoughtful
4. Funny
5. There for me

Mrs Chatterjee wanders towards me and leans down, her face level with mine. I can smell coffee and digestives on her breath. "Adam," she whispers, her dark eyes like two chocolate buttons staring into mine, "are you happy doing this project? I wanted to make sure you were."

I nod, telling Mrs Chatterjee I'm happy about the project because it has made me think and it's given me the opportunity to explore my tree. "I've already discovered a few things I didn't know before," I add and a grin spreads over my face.

Mrs Chatterjee goes on to say that I can write about my mum and dad or Velvet (who's in the infant part of the school). Then she mentions Minnie and says she enjoyed teaching her a few years ago and I could put her on the tree too. Mrs Chatterjee looks down at my tag and says I've written a lovely list.

"They're about my mother," I reply.

Mrs Chatterjee trills, "Wonderful start, Adam." I get a closer look at the chandeliers on her ears. They look like dozens of little teardrops and each time Mrs Chatterjee speaks, they whoosh around like they're on the swings in a play park. Mrs Chatterjee points to my tag. "Loving, kind and always there for you – your mum is certainly very special, isn't she? I've always enjoyed meeting her at school events."

As Mrs Chatterjee straightens and walks towards Nish's desk, I think to myself, *My mum is special, but I already know that. For this project I'm writing about my real mother, because I reckon she must be special too.* And I feel a tiny smile spread across my lips.

A few seconds later, I look over at Tiny Eric's tag to see what he's doing and he's not writing anything at all. Instead he's drawn a picture. Although Mrs Chatterjee loves drawing, she says we're only allowed to do it when it's art class. What she doesn't like is everyone drawing when they're meant to be writing. Once, when we were doing maths, Mrs Chatterjee looked at Tiny Eric's maths work and asked why on earth he was drawing unusual plants. Tiny Eric said it was exactly what Mrs Chatterjee had asked for – a square root. Laughter exploded in the classroom and Mrs Chatterjee couldn't stop us, and after that she put up a large sign above the whiteboard saying: *Is it a doodle? Use your noodle. Before you start, are you in art?*

Well, we're not in art at the moment and Tiny Eric is supposed to be writing about his family. From what I can see he's drawing a monster with mean eyes and there are lots of angry dark scribbles around it. "Oi," I hiss, leaning towards him. "You're supposed to be writing five things about someone you love in your family. What's that?"

Tiny Eric explains, "It's *Tata*."

"Tata?" I blink. "What's that got to do with your family?"

Tiny Eric says it has everything to do with his family.

47

"It means Dad in Polish."

"But your dad isn't a monster," I reply, a smile disappearing from my lips.

Tiny Eric shrugs.

When I get home from school, Dad's back from Surelock Homes already and he's sitting in the living room among plastic bags and strips of wood. Velvet is playing with Sausage Roll. This basically means she's sitting in the corner pretending to have a conversation with an invisible dog. Velvet's always wanted a dog and when she didn't get one she just made one up. When Velvet's not around, Mum says Sausage Roll is her imaginary friend and we should embrace this for now as Sausage Roll will disappear eventually.

Dad picks up a thin rod and sticks it to another one. When I ask him what he's making he tells me it's a wish, which is ridiculous because you can't make wishes out of bits of wood. "You want to take it slowly and methodically when you're working with your hands. It would be easy to rush, but it's better not to. Granddad Fred taught me that. He was the creative one in our family." Dad lets out a tiny sigh that makes a piece of paper on the table flutter like the wings of a butterfly, and then he picks up the rods and checks they're sticking together.

Suddenly, I have a thought. What if this is part of the surprise Mum and Dad were talking about? I haven't given it much thought since I heard them, but what if the surprise is building a fortress for me? It would take up space, but Mum and Dad said we could make sacrifices. Superman had a fortress called the Fortress of Solitude. And Dad knows I've always wanted one. But either way, he's not telling me.

I don't like to think Dad's keeping secrets. Parents aren't supposed to do that. Then Dad asks me about my day at school and I realize I've got a few secrets of my own. I'm not telling him I'm working on a family tree project. I'm not going to say that I've found out information about my real mother. And I'm not going to tell him that every birthday I feel like a little bit of me is missing so I make a wish of my own that someone could tell me who I am and where I come from. And that when Mrs Chatterjee mentioned the project before half-term, it was like giving the birthday-wish candle some oxygen and then it went whoosh and now I can't think of much else but finding out all that information.

That's what I'm thinking about when Dad says, "You've gone quiet. Is everything okay at school?" My stomach twists like a broken Slinky and I stare at Dad's hands as he smoothes down the rods. Screwing up all my courage, I tell myself, *I'm going to ask Dad what the surprise is. I'm going to ask him if he's making me a fortress.* I inhale, knowing this is my chance to be honest. A superhero is always honest. That's number four on the list of a superhero's characteristics.

I ask Dad to stop what he's doing because I want to talk to him. "Have you got a surprise for us?" I mumble. "Or even for me?" My mouth feels like I'm doing one of those marshmallow challenges where you stuff in a load of sweets and then try to speak but it comes out muffled.

Dad looks at me. "What sort of surprise?"

Dad must be having a laugh, pretending he doesn't know.

Only Dad isn't having a laugh, because he looks genuinely perplexed. I'm about to say a fortress-shaped one, but Dad shakes his head and runs his fingers along the rods to check they're smooth. Then there's a silence and it's obvious Dad's not going to say anything else. After a moment of feeling more uncomfortable than when your pants go up your bum, and thinking it might not be a fortress after all, I ask Dad about superheroes instead.

Dad grins, happy to move onto a subject he knows something about. "Yes, I love a superhero. What I don't know about heroes you could write on the back of a key that would fit the lock in a doll's house," he boasts.

"So if, for example, I saved the world or saved a life or helped someone, would I be a proper superhero like in the comics? Or are there any shortcuts you've read about that could make it easier? Superheroes make everyone happy, right? They're top banana." I chew on my lip, hoping Dad can give me tips on how to achieve superhero status quickly. Dad knows everything. If you ask him questions, like "What ended in 1066?" he'll answer 1065 in a flash, or if you ask him "What is the highest frequency noise that a human can bear?" he'll straight away say Mum yelling when he's forgotten to put the bins out.

Dad runs his hand over his bald head like he's giving it a swift polish. "There aren't any shortcuts, son," he explains. "You've got to feel it here." Dad thumps his chest like a gorilla.

"In your nipples?" To say I'm surprised is an understatement.

A snort escapes from Dad and he shakes his head vigorously. I bet his brain is wobbling like a blancmange in there. "No, don't be silly. I imagine you'd feel it in your heart. It's a hard concept to explain." So much for Dad knowing everything there is to know about superheroes. He doesn't even know what he means. "Anyway," continues Dad, "there are lots of superheroes living right here in Pegasus Park."

I give my best goldfish impersonation. After a few further seconds' consideration, I realize that what Dad's just said is a load of rubbish, because I haven't seen a single person in a cape or wearing their pants over their trousers in Pegasus Park. Dad is no help. I'm just going to have to sort this out all on my own. Because if I don't Mum might not smile again. And I don't want to think about that.

6

SMASH

Dad was zero help last night and the lucky four-leaf clover drawing that Tiny Eric gave me is as much use as a chocolate kettle. I've brought it out of my blazer pocket lots of times and stared at it for ages. It has brought me nothing except sore eyeballs. As for Tiny Eric's drawing of me as a superhero which is actually just a boring picture of normal me, that's under the bed where it belongs, with a load of other rubbish. I looked at it earlier and it made me fume all over again. How is that supposed to inspire me into being my most excellent self? On closer inspection, I noticed Tiny Eric had roughly scrawled something in titchy letters below the picture, but it looked like the work of a broken-handed gibbon using a pen for the first time.

"You're not bringing me enough luck. I thought everything would be brilliant by now," I scold the clover. Gazing goggle-eyed at the drawing, I add, "Make me an instant superhero and I'll forgive you." I set down the drawing and run over to the mirror and stare at myself. Nope, it's still just me, wearing my Pegasus Park Junior uniform. Clearly I was pushing my luck. There's no special glow, and no gamma ray has turned me into a radioactive superhero. I'm still an ordinary school kid living an ordinary life in an ordinary flat in an ordinary town. And Mum's still fed up. "Fail," I retort, picking up the drawing again. My fingers trace each heart. "I wanted to be extraordinary. And I don't mean just extra *ordinary*. Come on. Make me excellent. Give me a sign that you're working and not broken."

Nothing happens. There's no lightning bolt from the heavens. I shove the four-leaf clover drawing back in my blazer pocket, close my bedroom door and make my way to the kitchen. Everyone's there when I plonk myself down for breakfast. Mum says we're starting a new healthy-eating regime because she thinks it'll make us all fit as fiddles, although I've no idea what she's on about. Her cheeks colour and she glances at Dad as she puts a bowl in front of me. Then she pats me on the bobble hat and says she's offering a menu of porridge this morning. Minnie is staring at her bowl in disgust and says we're not in a Victorian orphanage so why are we eating gruel? Mum says it's important for us all to keep our insides healthy. She's very firm about it and she rubs her temples and her eyes look misty. Meanwhile, Velvet's putting her bowl on the floor and telling Sausage Roll to eat it, and Dad's looking at his and asking for sugar, by the bucketload. Mum says sugar is the enemy and Dad asks what about fat then? Mum says fat is also the enemy. Dad looks hopeful when he asks about bacon. Mum shakes her head.

"Okay, bacon is the enemy," sighs Dad. "Especially if you're a pig. Eggs? Fried bread? What about a teeny-tiny hash brown hidden under some fried tomatoes? What about beans? They're not an enemy, unless you're full of wind afterwards and stuck in a lift with your work colleagues. Surely they've got to be one of your five-a-day?"

"Spaghetti hoops aren't the enemy, are they, Mum?" Spaghetti hoops are my favourite.

"What about chocolate?" says Velvet.

"Shush, everyone," warns Mum. She turns to Dad. "You already know why this is important, Clark."

There's a flicker of fire in Mum's eyes and Dad reels back and picks up his spoon. "Now everyone eat your porridge and not another word," adds Mum.

To be honest, no one could say another word anyway, because our teeth are glued together with porridge. If Mrs Chatterjee ever runs out of glue for the classroom, Mum could just mix her up a big pot.

When the bowls are cleared up, Mum tells everyone to stop, and everyone freezes like we've been playing musical statues all this time and we didn't know. Minnie is mid-rolling her eyes. I swear one is going one way and the other a different direction. Dad has a finger jammed in his ear. Velvet has one jammed in her nose. Mum says she has an announcement. My heart leaps up into my throat, along with what's left of the porridge.

I blink.

"Apparently, it's someone's birthday coming up." Mum winks, manages a smile for the first time in ages, and then lowers her eyes until her lashes tickle her cheeks. "To be honest, I didn't know about this birthday until recently."

Everyone else looks at each other. I'm totally confused. Is this the big surprise I heard Mum and Dad talking about? My birthday is in November so it's not mine. Dad's birthday is in December so he's saying it's not him, and Minnie's is in April and she's saying it's not hers, adding that she's a ram with a fiery personality. Then she tries to say that she should date a Leo as they're a good match, and Dad says she should date a saint, because that's the only person who could put up with the fiery personality.

"I knew there was a surprise. I just knew it!" I exclaim. There's a loose thread on my school jumper and I give it a tiny tug. It unravels in my fingers and then I end up trying to hide half a ball of wool under my arm, which isn't easy.

"You did!" shouts Velvet, hugging me. She lets out a little whoop of excitement that confuses me. Then she starts barking, which confuses me even more. "Sausage Roll says thank you for remembering his birthday. Mum says we're having a party later," explains Velvet.

Oh.

"You can come and bring presents," Velvet says, her eyes glistening with joy.

Minnie's eyes do a three-sixty and Mum glares at her. "Oh, did I just roll my eyes out loud?" says Minnie innocently. Then she adds, "I'm not sure about presents but I'm happy to bring my presence." Anyone would think the Queen was coming.

Dad looks at Mum. "Since when did we start having

birthday parties for a dog? It's the first I knew about it."
He shakes his head.

"A birthday party for an invisible dog," I'm muttering
to myself as I walk past Sharkey's corner shop on my
way to school. Why in the name of holy doughnuts are
we doing that? And Dad didn't know anything about it,
so that can't be the surprise Mum and Dad were talking
about.

As we left, Mum assured us it was important to
Velvet and there would be cake – lots of gooey home-
baked cake. Dad was drooling so much that he left a
snail trail of saliva all the way along the hall floor. I'm
wondering whether it'll be a chocolate cake when the
four-leaf clover drawing suddenly delivers a sign, just
like I asked. Right in front of my eyes I see a ginger cat
and it's up a tree. Now, you can't tell me that a cat
trapped up a tree isn't a job for a would-be superhero
to investigate.

There's a skip in my step and my school rucksack no
longer feels like I'm carrying the weight of a wildebeest
in it. In fact, I'm so light and cheery I could nearly
float up the tree like a helium balloon to save the ginger
cat that is eyeing me suspiciously. "Hey, kitty, kitty,"

I whisper, looking up into the branches. "I'm here to save you. I'm a superhero. No, you don't have to thank me." The cat narrows its eyes to slits and hisses. "Okay, like I said – no thanks necessary."

I begin climbing and it's obvious within thirty seconds that I'm nothing like Spider-Man. He could be up a skyscraper in no time and I can't even climb a small tree without huffing and puffing more than a man in a fancy-dress sumo suit running to catch a bus. When I eventually reach the right branch, the cat swipes at my hands. Who knew a cat could have a paw full of sharpened razors cunningly disguised as claws? There's a sharp sting across my knuckles and I'm about to shout something rude at the cat when I hear whooping and whistling below. When I look down I see a group of kids from Minnie's school, Blessed Trinity, looking up at me, and a few are saying the cat doesn't look like it needs saving.

"Looks can be deceiving." I wince, thinking I'll never be able to use my hand again.

"Why are you bothering?" shouts someone else. When I don't answer, they shout, "Cat got your tongue?" There's a ripple of laughter. Honestly, everyone's a comedian these days. My feet slide on the bark but I haul my body higher, because time waits for no schoolboy when the morning bell is imminent. The cat couldn't look less in peril if it tried though, because it's lifted its hind leg and appears to be casually licking its bottom as if it hasn't a care in the world.

"Come on, four-leaf clover, you gave me this sign. Now I need you to help me follow it through. We can do this."

"OMG," a voice shouts. I'd recognize that whiny, complaining tone anywhere. It's Minnie. When I glance down, she's draped over this boy and she looks at him and then at me. After that her lips are so tightly pursed you couldn't slip a penny between them. "Ignore him, Callum," she eventually says to the boy. "We've got rehearsals first thing." Only the boy is gawping up at me, saying he wants to see if I save the cat. Apparently I'm better viewing than TV, much to Minnie's horror. I hear her ask, "What about that decorating programme where you actually watch paint dry? He's not more interesting than that, I can promise you."

At this point I imagine clutching the cat in my hands and shimmying down the tree to set it on the pavement. Maybe I'll give a little wave to the waiting audience. Perhaps some of them will have filmed the rescue on their phones and they'll ask me who I am and I'll say, "Watch out world! I'm a superhero, just call me Ace." Of course, they'll agree and maybe the cat will snuggle up to me and purr happily.

But as I'm daydreaming I lose my grip on the branch.

There's an "Ooww" from the crowd.

There's an "Ahhh" from the crowd.

There's an "Ooof...ooof...ooof...ooof" from me as I hit the branches.

There's a *splat* as I hit the ground.

There's an "Ouch" from the crowd.

Then there's a soft *flump* on my belly.

Minnie trots over to me and says at least I provided a soft landing for the cat. I don't know what's worse – the pain in my coccyx or the humiliation of seeing the cat sitting on my stomach with a smug look between its whiskers. To be fair, it does purr happily, but only after it starts sharpening its claws on my school jumper.

The boy with Minnie asks her what kind of moron tries to help a cat and then falls himself. Minnie looks at him and says, "I have no idea. Oh, Callum," she whispers, "imagine the poor, beautiful girl who can act, sing and dance having a nut like him for a brother. I pity her, despite her being gorgeous and singing like an angel." She pulls a face at me and wraps herself around the boy like a boa constrictor before dragging him away.

I limp towards school, fearing that I've broken my

bum and may never sit down again without the aid of Velvet's inflatable rubber ring. I tip my head towards my pocket where I've got the four-leaf clover drawing and hiss, "Thanks for the sign, but next time can you try not to kill me in the process? I expect better from you."

Next thing I know The Beast pushes past me, snorting with laughter. "Hello hello, pocket. Come in, pocket. Are you receiving me?"

Ground swallow me up.

Mrs Chatterjee has set up a table at the back of the class with lots of cardboard boxes and she's telling us we can start making our family trees today. "Not only are we having an exhibition of the trees, but I felt it would be a nice touch if I gave a prize for the best tree too."

There's a big whoop.

"It's a certificate," says Mrs Chatterjee.

The whoop gets smaller.

"And there are sweets too."

The whoop gets bigger.

"A big bag of liquorice."

The whoop gets smaller.

"Okay, there's another prize."

The whoop gets bigger.

"A visit to the head's office."

The whoop gets smaller.

"For anyone who complains."

The whoop gets bigger.

"Great, thank you for that. So I take it from your whooping that you're all really excited about the project." Mrs Chatterjee claps her hands so loudly it's like she has ripped a hole in the galaxy, then she tells us we can go and collect some materials from the table. Everyone speeds towards the back of the room except Tiny Eric, who is drawing a picture in his notebook of a church with a tall spire and there's a house beside it with lots of windows.

"That's amazing," I say, passing Tiny Eric's desk. "Where is it?"

"It's just a house," says Tiny Eric, covering the drawing with his hand – but not before I've noticed something else. When I looked at the upstairs window of the house in the drawing, I swear Tiny Eric had drawn himself there, staring out with what looked like one tiny perfect teardrop on his cheek. I walk towards the table to collect some cardboard, thinking that something is wrong with Tiny Eric. Only I don't know what it is.

Later that afternoon as we leave school, I offer Tiny

Eric the four-leaf clover drawing back. When he asks me why, I say, "You look like you need some good luck and I've already had a bit of luck today." Tiny Eric looks up to the sky and blinks rapidly before looking back at me. "Honestly, have it back. I don't mind," I squeak. "It's yours, Tiny Eric. I can manage without it."

"Thanks. But it doesn't work like that. I can't take back the luck I gave you. That would sort of cancel it out and be unlucky." Tiny Eric sighs before shoving his hands in his pockets. "Anyway, the drawing was for a person like you." Tiny Eric emphasizes the word "you" like I'm an alien from another planet.

"A person like me?" I think for a second. My breath catches in my throat and my stomach feels like I've downed a sachet of popping candy. "What do you mean, a person like *me*?" I ask as we trudge through the playground and then out the school gates.

"A person who needs to believe and who needs a bit of magic in their life," says Tiny Eric, as if he's some kind of mystical guru. Pulling a face, I tell Tiny Eric I don't believe in magic. "Shame," says Tiny Eric, shaking his head. He stops suddenly, his eyes serious. "All it takes is for you to believe. Then, one day, when you least expect it, magic is everywhere and suddenly the world is as bright as the sun. And you realize you're happy."

"You're just like Yoda," I reply as Tiny Eric takes his turning at the end of Agamemnon Road. *Clever, but kind of hard to understand*, I think to myself as I wave goodbye.

I swing by Surelock Homes on the way home from school. When the bell tinkles, Dad looks up and smiles. He's wearing a T-shirt I bought him for Christmas that says: *Be yourself unless you can be a Zorbitan. Then always be a Zorbitan.* And I can just see his clock tattoo poking out from under the sleeve. Dad asks what he's done to get a visit from his son.

"I dunno," I reply, my fingers running along the rows of keys on hooks. Each one dances and sways as though moving to an invisible orchestra. "I just wanted to drop by."

"Don't we need to get home soon for the party?" Dad

laughs and puts a key he's cut on the counter in a clear plastic bag, along with a green raffle ticket number 368. "I'm going to shut up shop early because I'm working late tomorrow night. Plus there's cake and now Mum's talking about us eating healthily I need to stock up on as much food as I can get before I waste away." Dad jiggles his two bellies.

Slouching against the counter, I muse, "Do you think Mum's really into this health thing then?" Dad switches off his equipment and goes out the back and grabs his coat. As he pulls it on he nods and says she's got a point. "But why now? What's the big deal?" I wait for Dad to answer but he doesn't.

Instead, he ushers me towards the door and turns the sign to CLOSED. When I repeat myself, Dad stops and looks at me. "Because she's..." From where I'm standing I can see Dad's Adam's apple bob up and down like it's on a super-springy trampoline. It's as if the words are on the tip of his tongue but his lips are keeping them prisoner.

"She's what?" I stare at Dad.

"She's making sure we all keep well," says Dad and he looks away as if he's thinking about something else. "There's nothing strange about that." He glances back at me and then locks the door of Surelock Homes and tells me we've got to get to that cake before someone else eats it all.

There's a banner stuck on the front door of our flat. It says HAPPY 40TH BIRTHDAY in bright rainbow letters on foil and it gently flutters in the afternoon breeze. As we enter the hallway, Mum shouts, "We're all in the party zone." I think she means the kitchen. Dad zooms in, shouting that he's ready for cake, and then he stops and his head droops. "Carrot sticks and cucumber slices at a party?" Something just died in Dad's eyes.

Mum turns from the kitchen counter with a cake in her hands. She says there are only three candles because she doesn't know how old Sausage Roll is, but whatever age he is she's not multiplying it by seven to get dog years. She doesn't want to set the flat on fire. And apparently the banner on the door was one they had left over from Dad's birthday.

After we all sing "Happy Birthday" to Sausage Roll, Velvet blows out the candles and says Sausage Roll would do it but he's too busy.

"Licking his bum," says Minnie. She laughs until Mum says we don't want that kind of dirty talk at the table, and then Minnie says, "Muck, drains, cesspits," and asks if that kind of dirty talk is better. By rights I should be laughing because it was quite funny, but I'm not, because instead I'm thinking of my last birthday and how I sat at the end of the table and Mum made a rainbow cake that had five different colours of sponge. There were eleven candles on it and I blew them all out and I was happy, but for a split second I thought about who I was and where I'd come from and I felt as if a tiny bit of me was missing and I wasn't sure if I'd ever find it.

I feel Mum's gaze on me but I don't look at her and then she bustles around the table, cutting large slices of cake and asking Dad if he wants a big slab.

Do footballers dribble?

Do woods have trees?

Do superheroes wear their pants over their trousers?

Dad's already shovelling in the cake and he looks at Mum, his mouth full of crumbs and his eyes full of sadness.

"Beetroot cake," says Mum brightly. "I knew you'd all love it." Now, I'm no Isaac Newton, but anyone with half a brain knows that cake and beetroot should never be mixed.

Mum whizzes past us and out of the kitchen, before returning with a present wrapped in blue paper with a big blue bow on top. Right now, Velvet's eyes resemble those of a pop-eyed squid and she reaches out her hands.

If there was a page in the *Guinness World Records* for the child who could rip off wrapping paper in the fastest time, Velvet's picture would be there. There's already a small pyramid of scrunched-up blue paper by her feet and she's mouthing "Yay!" In her hands she's holding a pale blue collar and lead, and a rubber dog biscuit. Mum and Dad get a big hug and Velvet says Sausage Roll is going to love his collar. Then she squeaks the dog biscuit until Dad picks up a comic and says he's just got to go to the toilet and read it and he might be some time. Mum says it's only a comic, not *War and Peace*.

Velvet asks Minnie if she's got a present for Sausage Roll. For the first time ever, Minnie actually goes pale under her fake tan. "Are you serious?" says Minnie. Clearly Velvet is, because she nods and her mouth is set in a firm little line of determination. Apparently, Sausage Roll is one of the family, and you always buy presents for family.

Minnie disappears to her bedroom and returns with a pale pink nail polish, saying it's the best she's got. "It's called Sea Shells and it dries in sixty seconds to a mirror shine."

Velvet taps her finger against her lip. "It's not really his colour."

"Good, I'll keep it then," says Minnie, taking it back and zeroing in on me. "Where's your present, Adam? Surely you didn't forget to get Sausage Roll a present?"

Oh, for the love of all things comic book, I *did* forget. For a millisecond I think of giving Sausage Roll the drawing of the four-leaf clover, but then I figure, how much good luck does an invisible dog need? But then what *do* you give an invisible dog? I mean, does he need an invisible five-star kennel or a tower of invisible doggy biscuits? That's when the idea comes to me. I'll quickly draw a doggy treat and say it's for good luck. That's what Tiny Eric might suggest. Anyway, doggy treats are just circles and I can manage one of those. Racing to my bedroom and coming back with a sheet of paper, I hand it to Velvet.

"It's not much…" I say, giving a half-shrug.

Velvet hugs me and says it's the best present Sausage Roll's ever had. I'm about to say thank you when she holds up the blank side of the paper, and says it's a portrait of Sausage Roll. I don't have the heart to tell her I've drawn a lucky dog treat on the back, especially when she's so happy looking at the blank side. After that I offer to do a portrait of Sausage Roll's family and I hand Velvet another sheet of empty paper, but she asks why it's blank. When I remind her that it's Sausage Roll's family, Velvet says I'm stupid because we're his family and I haven't drawn us. Sometimes it's better not to try to get inside a six-year-old's head.

Later, when Mum has cleared the kitchen table and put the uneaten cake in the fridge, she asks me to sit down beside her. There's a big bark from the living room. That's Velvet pretending to be Sausage Roll. Then there's a squeak from the rubber dog biscuit. "Birthdays are strange days, aren't they?" Mum gives a tiny half-smile and shuffles some crumbs to the edge of the table before catching them in her hand and throwing them in the bin.

"Definitely if it's a dog's birthday," I mumble.

Shaking her head, Mum replies, "That's not what I meant. Birthdays can be…"

There's another distant squeak from the rubber biscuit.

"Funny," adds Mum. "Sometimes they're happy and sometimes they can feel a little sad. It happens at New

Year for me too. What I'm trying to say is…I thought you looked a little sad when Velvet was blowing out the candles." It seems Mum has her own superpower. She's like a human sticking plaster, knowing you're hurting and trying to make it feel better.

There's something in my eye. To be honest, I think it might be tears, so I have to blink furiously to make them disappear back inside before they make a break for freedom.

"We've been meaning to give you a little gift," says Mum as my finger does a sneaky sweep under my eyes. "We've had it for ages but the time wasn't right till now. Anyway, Dad and I both agree that you should have this." At first I think it's the envelope and I feel sick that Mum might have discovered I've already opened it. But it isn't, because Mum sets a blue box on the table in front of me. "Now, before you get too excited, it's old and it's broken."

Mum's really building this up.

I'm in a frenzy of mild interest.

Opening the box, I see a watch with a frayed and worn leather strap. The face is gold but there are tiny gaps where you can see the internal cogs and they're not moving. Mum says it might have been wound up too tightly. "I know it doesn't work but it's still special because it used to be Granddad Fred's. We thought you could keep it. We tried to get it mended years ago and it wouldn't go, but we still wanted you to have it. Perhaps we could try and get it mended again for you."

I take the watch in my hand and the strap feels buttery soft to the touch and I peer into the cogs and give it a tiny shake before placing it on my wrist.

"You don't have to wear it," insists Mum.

"I like it," I reply, deciding the inside cogs make it look like a gadget a superhero might have. "I will wear it." I twist my wrist this way and that, hoping the watch will start, but it doesn't.

"Granddad Fred would be happy for you to have it. He was special, just like you are. We thought it would remind you of your family."

I thank Mum and say it's a lovely gift and she squeezes my arm and tells me I deserve it. "Is this the surprise we're not supposed to know about?" I look up at Mum and her face is blank and she asks me what surprise I'm talking about. I don't get this at all. My whole family is bananas sometimes. There *has* to be a surprise, because they talked about it. I didn't make a mistake. But both Mum and Dad are acting like there isn't one.

The thing is, I can tell Mum's hiding something because her cheeks go red and she rises from the table and starts wiping the kitchen counter, even though she just did it a few minutes earlier. I ask Mum if she's okay and she stops but doesn't look at me. She says she's fine and that everything is fine. But when a grown-up says things are fine, it usually means they aren't. So I say, "I'm going to be excellent, Mum."

"You *are* excellent," replies Mum, turning around.

"But if I could be even better," I explain, "you'd always be smiling."

"You don't need to be better, because I'm already smiling," says Mum, giving me her biggest grin. But somehow it doesn't reach her eyes and it makes me feel sad and even more determined to be excellent in the future.

Five minutes later, when I'm in SPAM HQ and lying on the bed, there's a small *rat-a-tat-tat* at the door. "What's the password?" I mumble.

"Is it 'I like pink fluffy unicorns sliding down rainbows'?"

"Um...no."

"Is it 'I like dancing around wearing a tutu because I am a fairy'?"

"No way is it that one."

75

"Is it 'I like pink glittery cupcakes and strawberry milk and floppy hair bows and painting my nails pink'? Is it 'I like picking my nose and eating—'"

"Nope."

"Is it—"

"No, no, no. Just come in, Velvet," I offer, since she's never going to guess the real password, which is "Kryptonite kills". Velvet swings open the door, still in her tutu, with the blue bow that was on Sausage Roll's present on her head. She dances into my room, touching things with a long silver wand with a star on its tip. She says she's bringing magic with her and I say I'm not one hundred per cent sure about magic and Velvet stops, wounded.

"Is that why you have a sad ugly face at the moment that looks like it might cry? Because you don't believe in magic?"

"No," I reply, pulling an even uglier face. "You've got a way with words."

"Oh, I know. My teacher says I could get a gold star for talking," says Velvet proudly and she comes over and sits down beside me, her tutu fluffing up like a swirl of pink candyfloss. Her legs swing over the edge of my bed and she asks me why I'm sad then. I tell her I'm not and Velvet replies, "Okay, you're very sad, so you can borrow my best friend, Sausage Roll." Velvet waves her arms expansively into thin air.

"Um...oh," I breathe. "'Kay." It's easier not to argue.

"Sausage Roll is only staying with us for a bit," explains Velvet, picking up my teddy bear and playing with the bobble on his hat. "Mum told me he might have to leave us soon, because he's got other families to go to."

At this point I am trying to put myself inside a six-year-old's brain and...nope, I still don't understand what Velvet's on about. "Why would he go when he's happy here?"

Velvet smiles at me and says, "Because Mum told me he likes to make people happy. He's a special dog. He's staying here for a while to make us all smile, and then he's going to leave us." Velvet shrugs. "Mum says he's a very busy magic dog, and I might have to prepare for the day when he'll go. But Mum promises he won't leave until we're all happy. She promised me."

I grin and reach out towards Velvet and grab the wand and bop her on the head with it. *"You're* magic," I say. She drops the bear, jumps up and takes the wand back before reminding me that I'm borrowing Sausage Roll tonight. With a little pirouette, she leaves SPAM HQ and then I hear her shouting to Mum that she's eaten too many carrots and what if she turns into a rabbit? Mum shouts back that she's only just got used to the invisible dog and the last thing she needs is a Velvet rabbit in the flat.

Easing myself back on the bed, I fling my arms behind my bobble hat. "So, Sausage Roll, if you're staying with me tonight," I whisper, staring up at Batman fluttering gently from the superhero mobile that Dad made me, "can you make everyone, including me, happy like Velvet said? The four-leaf clover isn't working properly. I think it's malfunctioning. If you know how to turn me into a superhero and make everything okay, bark."

There's silence and it seems like Sausage Roll is as clueless about what I should do as me.

8

VABOOM

The following morning, Mrs Chatterjee watches as we all drag our feet into the classroom and take our seats. Clearing her throat, she says breezily, "So, the *Forest For Ever* project – you've started building your trees out of cardboard. And I'm impressed that, after a day's work, a few of you have managed to make the cardboard still look like cardboard rather than trees. I think we could all work on those trees a little more." Mrs Chatterjee adds, "And then they will be tree-mendous."

I watch as everyone shakes their heads and groans. Tiny Eric isn't even listening, because he's playing with his compass and making tiny holes in his notebook.

"But for today I think we should go back to writing. We need more tags to put on our trees." There's another collective groan and Mrs Chatterjee holds up her hand to halt it. "I know how much you all love art but, as I said, it's writing today. What we're going to do is write a letter on a tag to someone on your family tree. Now, it could be a close relative or a long-lost relative or your great-great-great-grandmother twice removed. Even if you don't know them, you could still write a letter telling them what you've achieved and asking them questions about their life."

Tiny Eric has punctured a big hole in his notebook cover and now he's moved on to the inside page and he's gently stabbing the paper. Mrs Chatterjee peers over her glasses, her eyes like tiny rabbit droppings in snow, and tells Tiny Eric there's going to be more holes in his notebook than in a Swiss cheese factory.

Tiny Eric puts down the compass.

"Right, you've got half an hour on this task and it doesn't matter how long or short the letter is but every word should count. Get cracking." Mrs Chatterjee makes it sound like we're a load of eggs waiting to be scrambled.

This exercise is hard because I'm supposed to be writing about someone on my tree. I've only got one person and that's my real mother and how can I write a letter to her? What would I say? I think about it for ages before beginning to scribble down my thoughts.

Dear Mum,

Is it strange to call you Mum? I'm not sure because I've never said it out loud to anyone before but my mum who I live with. My other mum is called Sinéad and she told me I was adopted. I think about you on special occasions like my birthday and at Christmas. Sometimes I even think about you on Sunday afternoons when it's raining and I stare out the window. But I'm very happy with my family and I love my mum, even though she seems a bit sad at the moment. I'm trying to make things better by being a superhero. Superheroes are excellent and they make people smile because they do good things and put the world right. I want to do that.

The reason I'm writing this letter is because my teacher, Mrs Chatterjee, told me to. We're making family trees and, seeing as I know everything about my family at home, I wanted to know more about the other family I have out there. That's you.

The thing is, when I was ten my sister Minnie

gave me a jigsaw puzzle of the Zorbitans, and it had one piece missing. Nine hundred and ninety-nine pieces and one piece missing and that missing piece had a Zorbitan's heart on it. A Zorbitan's heart is important. Well, I'm like that jigsaw. Everything is great in my life but there's a tiny bit missing and I can't help but notice it.

My teacher said when we write to our family member we should ask questions. So, I'm writing to you and these are mine:

Why did you abandon me?

Why didn't you come back for me?

Who is my dad?

Why did you call me Ace?

Did you love me?

I'm lost in thought after writing down the last question. *Did you love me?* echoes inside my head. Outside, shards of sunlight glint on the classroom window and I can see a spiderweb in the top corner and tiny droplets of rain glitter like teardrops on it. In the distance I can make out our tower block with clouds sailing past like white galleons on a never-ending blue sea. The words *Did you love me?* continue to bubble and melt inside my mind like molten cheese under the grill, and it's only when Mrs Chatterjee bellows, "Five minutes left," that I snap my attention back to the room.

Tiny Eric is staring out the window now too, his eyes planted on the horizon. He looks like he's got two glazed doughnuts for eyeballs. Under his bitten fingernails I can see the tag he's working on and today he hasn't drawn a picture. Instead he's written *DAD* and underneath in tiny letters he's written *WHY?* I know Mrs Chatterjee said it could be short, but that's ridiculous. How can every word count when he's only written two? I've got no idea what *WHY?* even stands for, but whatever it is, it has made Tiny Eric's eyes look all misty.

When I question him about it in the playground, Tiny Eric says he's got conjunctivitis. "What's that?" I ask and Tiny Eric says it's when your eyes go all funny and watery. I tell him I think my mum's got that too because recently her eyes have been misty a lot. Tiny Eric says he doesn't think my mum has what he has and then he shrugs. He does that a lot at the moment. He used to be so much fun, but recently he keeps moping about in the playground, and every time I ask him what's up, all he does is shrug his shoulders. I wish he'd just tell me. Friends aren't supposed to keep secrets from each other.

Trying to make conversation, I take Granddad Fred's watch off my wrist and hold it up. I tell him my mum gave it to me last night, and then I pretend to swing it in front of Tiny Eric's eyes. "Look deep into my eyes," I mutter. "You will see this watch belonging to my dead grandfather, and when I finish talking you will be hypnotized into telling me all your problems." I swing the watch back and forward until someone snatches it.

"I could tell you all *my* problems," says The Beast, looking at the watch, "but we haven't got all day. This is nice. The strap is a bit mangy though. That'll break if you don't replace it."

"Who made you an authority on watches?" I blink.

The Beast stares at the tiny internal cogs and tells me that they're not working. Someone give The Beast a certificate: *I HEREBY DECLARE THE BEAST HAS ACHIEVED A GOLD STAR IN STATING THE OBVIOUS.*

"My uncle repairs watches and sells batteries and second-hand jewellery. He's got a shop on Brolly Way, so that's who made me an authority." The Beast turns the watch over and says there's a picture of a heart on the back. I grab the watch and look at the tiny engraving on the reverse. The Beast continues, "My uncle said people used to say watches were like hearts because they tick. That's probably why it's been engraved."

"This one doesn't tick though," I reply, putting it back on my wrist. "I think the heart must be broken. Mum said she'd tried to mend it years ago but it couldn't be fixed. She might try and get it fixed again."

The Beast snorts. "Maybe it's got dust or sand or something in it."

I shrug. I don't care if it's not working. It still looks like a superhero's watch and it still belonged to Granddad Fred. That's good enough for me.

The next morning Minnie scowls at me as I take my seat beside her at the breakfast table. "Look, swamp boy in a grubby bobble hat rises from his pit." Then she stares down at the sawdust in her cereal bowl.

"It's organic muesli, in case you're wondering," says Mum, passing a carton of almond milk across the table. Minnie looks at it and says milk should come from a cow's udders and this is a travesty of nature. Gingerly, she brings the spoon to her mouth and sucks up the sloppy liquid. "Remind me why we're all eating sawdust clippings?" she splutters.

"It's important for your insides," says Mum. She pats her belly. "I've told you we should be healthy and we're sticking to it." Minnie says yes, it's important for your insides to be healthy if you're ancient, but when you're young it's important to eat burgers oozing with melted cheese and fried onions. I feel my mouth water, but it stops the instant I look in my bowl. Meanwhile, Minnie points and shouts that I've got the bonus prize.

"What?" I do a double take.

"You've got a raisin," she exclaims, tucking her hair behind her ear. "Don't eat it all at once."

Velvet is saying that Sausage Roll can't eat muesli because he likes chocolate cereals that turn the milk the colour of poop, and Dad is telling us all to simmer down, as if we're overexcited boiled eggs in a saucepan. When I glance at Mum she's staring into her sawdust and she says it'll make her feel good from the inside and Dad nods. He brings his spoon up to his mouth and nearly chokes but says, "Yum, yum, I can feel all my organs getting happy. Go, organs."

Mum says she's not as hungry as she thought. Maybe her organs aren't as happy as Dad's. I swear there's a tiny shimmer of a diamond in the corner of Mum's eye, but I think it must be conjunctivitis, like Tiny Eric has. When she blinks it's gone. Mum pushes her bowl away and says she's going to ring Grandma, and that everyone should finish eating their breakfast and think about getting to school. Dad says he'll drop us all off. Minnie says she's going to walk like she usually does, because she's not going to arrive at school in a van with Surelock Homes painted on the side – she'd rather be dead.

"That could be arranged," I mutter.

"Oh, I've just split my sides," says Minnie, pretending to laugh.

"That's because your skirt is too tight," I reply.

"Dad!" yells Minnie. "Adam is being a complete pain in the..."

"Bum," says Velvet helpfully. Minnie slaps her forehead and says that's not the word she was thinking of but good try. Unfortunately she doesn't slap her forehead hard enough, because she's still able to whinge on and on. And I'm about to argue back when Dad rises from the table, saying we need to stop fighting because Mum doesn't need all this hassle at the moment. He pulls open the kitchen drawer and takes out the van keys and asks who wants to come in the best vehicle in the world.

"If there's a Lamborghini downstairs I will," says Minnie, getting up. "If it's an old red van with a key on it, I won't bother." She pulls open the cupboard door, grabs a packet of biscuits and starts eating one before spitting it out. "What is this?" She reads the label. "A gluten-free dairy-free fat-free biscuit-free biscuit." In a huff she puts on her blazer and rushes past Mum, who's in the hallway on the phone. She kisses Mum on the cheek and slams out the front door, her feet click-clacking down the steps outside.

Meanwhile, Dad's urging Velvet towards the front door and I follow, saying goodbye to Mum as we head out. When we get to the end of the passage near the concrete steps, I realize I've forgotten my front door key. Dad gives me his and tells me to go back and find one. "There's one in Mum's drawer if you can't find yours," he says.

I use Dad's key to open the door. Mum's moved into the living room now and as I hurry down the hall towards her bedroom I hear her saying to Grandma, "I still can't believe it's happened to me. It's the size of a jelly bean and growing." I feel my breath catch in my throat. "I've got a scan soon and I hope it's all going to be okay. Last time I had scans at the hospital it was with Minnie and Velvet." There's silence so Grandma must be talking.

I feel my heart batter against my ribcage. *A jelly bean*. I think I know what the surprise Mum was talking about with Dad was. They're having a BABY! There's this programme about babies being born every minute that Mum loves, and it was on once and mums-to-be were talking about scans and babies being the size of a jelly bean or a pea or a watermelon. That's what Mum's saying to Grandma. The baby is the size of a jelly bean and she's having a scan and it's like the scans she had with Velvet and Minnie. And Mum's eating healthily now because she's having a baby. This explains everything!

Quickly I rush down the hall and open the door to Mum and Dad's bedroom. I can smell Mum's perfume and it is warm and comforting, like the scent of baking bread. Making my way to Mum's side of the bed, I pull open the drawer, knowing I can choose from about ten front door keys. But on top of the keys is a letter that wasn't there before. It's from Pegasus Park Hospital, confirming an appointment in a few weeks with a consultant, and it mentions the word *scan*. I know it's wrong to read things you're not supposed to, but my eyeballs aren't listening (although, to be fair, eyeballs don't really listen anyway).

As I rummage around, I also see a slip of paper torn from a newspaper. The top left-hand corner is missing, but I can make out most of it, and it's saying if you want to adopt or rehome then call this number.

It feels like I've got a gobstopper lodged in my throat. I stare at the number and my jaw plummets. Weren't

Mum and Dad whispering about our flat being small and that they'd have to make sacrifices? What if they meant they need my bedroom for a nursery? Mum wanted to redecorate my room – what if that was for the baby? What if the sacrifice is that I have to be *rehomed*? That's what that piece of paper is about, isn't it? They'd never ask Minnie and Velvet to be rehomed because they're not adopted. But I am.

Mum and Dad need my room for the jelly bean. There won't be any space here for me any more. I'll be sent somewhere else, probably to a strange new family I've never met before.

My legs are more wobbly than a jellyfish on Rollerblades as I take a key from the drawer and close it slowly. The key feels cold in my hot hands and I try to swallow down anger as I stumble towards the door. As I hurry back down the hallway towards the front door, I hear Mum saying, "Yes, it'll take our minds off everything else. It won't be long now."

As I close the front door, I wipe my nose with my blazer cuff and a tiny voice inside my head says, *"This changes everything. Information isn't enough. You've got to find your real mother now and you've got to find her as soon as possible. Perhaps she'll give you a home."*

9

POP

I can't concentrate on anything at school today. All I can think about is how I need to find my real mother. I can't live with complete strangers, I'd be scared. But if my real mother could give me a home, at least I'd be with my own family. Then I think about Mum and Dad and how they've been keeping this a secret and I'm as angry as a bumblebee trapped in a jar. Mrs Chatterjee keeps saying I'm not listening to her and asking me if I'm on another planet rather than planet Earth. Everyone laughs. When I tell Mrs Chatterjee I *am* on planet Earth, she says it would be nice if I could stay here until at least three thirty and then I'm welcome to fly to the moon or another planet if I wish.

"Uranus," says Nish, sniggering.

I don't even answer him because I'm already back to thinking about how I'm going to find my real mother.

I'm still thinking about it at home time when I spot Dad's red van outside school. Dad doesn't usually pick me up after school, but there he is, pulling faces and waving like an eejit from the other side of the road. Something fishy is going on. I pretend I don't know him to start with, as some girls from school are going past, but then he waves both arms and rolls down the window and starts shouting, "Hey, Adam, sunshine. Get yourself in Surelock Homes."

As I hurry across the road and climb into the van, Dad throws me a chocolate bar. "Here you go, champ, get your chops around that. Didn't you see me waving at you? You'll be needing glasses if you carry on like that. Right, strap yourself in and let's whizz off on an adventure. We're heading to Estermill town. I thought you could do with cheering up, because you had a face like a squashed rubber duck when you got into the van this morning."

I bite into the chocolate bar. "I was thinking about something," I mutter, spraying chocolate shrapnel over my knees.

Dad turns the key in the ignition and there's a funny splutter and we don't whizz so much as jolt and then trundle down Agamemnon Road. "Thinking is dangerous," he laughs.

I really want to say I've been thinking about the jelly bean and then ask him if it needs my bedroom, but Dad's too busy driving, eating four fingers of a KitKat at once and then rummaging in his jacket pocket. He stops at a traffic light and pulls out a piece of white card and hands it to me.

The ESTERMILL COMIC CON
invites you to an evening of
MAGIC, MAYHEM, MONSTERS and HEROES.
See the ZORBITANS and the grand
MOON MASTER.

Rare
COMICS
Fancy-dress PRIZES
RAFFLES

Out-of-this-world
CHILLI HOT DOGS
SWEETS

SPACE DUST
that'll take
you into
ORBIT

Come join us in our GALAXY
(The Estermill Warehouse).

"That's the adventure I was talking about," says Dad, as the light turns green. We continue, taking a right into Dover Street and then speeding along Carlisle Road. "It's just you and me on a proper lads' afternoon out. Now, you don't have to be so down in the dumps. I've cleared all this with Mum. We'll eat our tea there – I'm thinking chilli hot dogs. Mind you, Mum doesn't know about those." Dad takes the first exit at the roundabout. "What goes on at Estermill Comic Con stays at Estermill Comic Con, eh?"

"Dad..." I say, licking some melted chocolate off my fingers. I pause, not sure exactly what I want to say and then I mumble, "What would happen if I didn't live with you?"

Dad thinks for a second and shakes his head. "Why wouldn't you live with us?"

"Maybe if you needed space for something," I reply. Really I mean, If you needed space for *someone*. I'm trying to talk to Dad about the jelly bean, but it's harder than the time we talked about the birds and the bees and Mum had to step in because Dad nearly combusted.

Dad says we always need space because the flat is small. "It's a squeeze, but it's home, eh?"

That makes me feel worse and all the bravado I had in asking the question disappears like a magician's assistant behind a "poof" of smoke. I stare out the window and then press my nose against the glass. "What would it be like if I was a superhero like in a comic?"

"It'd be amazing," replies Dad, flicking the indicator. It clicks until he flicks it back again.

My breath makes a small cotton-wool ball of a cloud on the window. "If I was amazing, would everything be okay?" I lift my head off the glass and press my finger to the cloud and draw a question mark.

Dad grins. "If you were a superhero everything would be more than okay. It would be fantastic! The world would fall at your feet. It doesn't get better than that."

"Would Mum like it?"

"I'm sure she would, especially if you could hold up the traffic for her or fly her to the shops." Dad gives a throaty laugh.

"That's what I thought," I say. "Superheroes can live anywhere and still be the best, can't they? I mean, they don't have to live in one place. If they had to leave their home and go somewhere else they'd still be excellent." I can't help but think about having to leave the flat and, if I do, I want to make sure I'll still be amazing so I can make everyone happy. Once you start on a mission you can't just give it up when things get hard.

"Correctomundo," says Dad, who appears to have no actual grasp of the English language sometimes, but still makes me laugh. "Batman had Wayne Manor and the Batcave underneath. He was excellent in both places."

Sighing, I tip my head towards the four-leaf clover drawing in my pocket and whisper that things will be okay even if I do have a new home. Dad flicks his head towards me and then back to the road, before asking if I've got Tom Thumb in my pocket. I mumble something about talking to myself, which Dad accepts as totally normal. Mind you, that's not surprising when we've got Velvet, who is always talking to herself.

Dad swings the Surelock Homes van into the car park of the warehouse and shuts off the engine. "Here we go, Adam," says Dad, handing me ten pounds. "Go crazy and spend spend spend. Don't buy a Porsche, though."

I'm not sure what world Dad is living in, but in my world the only Porsche ten pounds will buy is one with plastic wheels that comes in a small box.

The Estermill warehouse is four times the size of our school hall and it smells of frying onions – or it could be sweat, because there are a lot of people dressed up in heavy costumes. Straight away, I spot Spider-Man queuing at the hot-dog stand. Batman is talking to Robin in the far right-hand corner and Doctor Who is talking to Dr "Bones" McCoy from Star Trek. Then Dad points out Ariadne, who is half woman, half octopus, and his favourite comic-book character. "Look," he hisses. "Can you see the tentacles? I've got to go over and talk to her and get her autograph."

"Have you got eight pens?" I mutter.

As Dad wanders off laughing, I head towards a stage where Frosty the Fearless from one of my favourite comics is just standing up from his chair. He's dressed in a long white cape and his face is covered in silver glitter and his lips are blue. There's a small crowd gathering as he steps towards the microphone and coughs. "Greetings, earthlings, monsters, aliens, superheroes, chubby guy at the hot-dog stand." Everyone turns around to see a man dressed as a galactic sumo wrestler shovelling a frankfurter into his mouth in one go. He waves a bread bun at us and mumbles that we should try one.

Frosty the Fearless waves back and gives him a frosty smile. "So, as I was saying, it is a pleasure to welcome you to the fifth annual Estermill Comic Con. What we read in comics gives us hope," he says, waving his finger in the air. "We can live out our dreams.

Thanks to these comics, we can be strong, we can be good, we can be worthy of our chosen superhero name. We can be special, braver than ever, true to our heart; we can find the right pathway and stay on it. Whatever struggle comes our way, we can overcome it. It's all in those comics. It's all in us."

There is a huge round of applause, mainly coming from Ariadne, whose eight tentacles are flapping all over the place. The alien next to me takes off the goldfish bowl he had on his head and lets out a *"Phew!* Ooh, he's good,"* he says, wiping some sweat from his brow. "He said just what I was thinking." I nod enthusiastically and the alien continues, "I was just thinking that I needed a hot dog. That chubby guy has the right idea." And he wanders off.

As I continue watching Frosty the Fearless, I feel a tap on my shoulder. "Look what I've got." Dad has appeared beside me again and he's holding up a piece of paper that says *Ariadne Ariadne Ariadne Ariadne Ariadne Ariadne Ariadne Aria...* When I ask Dad what happened to the last one, he shrugs and explains, "She got cramp in her tentacle." Dad's grinning and staring at the paper like he's just found treasure eight times over, mumbling on about how it was worth every penny. Then he says he's got to get a chilli hot dog before there's a run on them. He wanders off again, giving me a little salute and saying he'll bring me one back with extra chilli sauce.

Around me there are stalls and stands full of models, comics and badges, masks and lightsabres and gadgets. Above my head, stars dangle from the ceiling and there are giant planets made from papier mâché. One stand catches my eye and I trot over and rifle through a book about superheroes, before stopping at a page about Ace the Bat-Hound. The guy behind the counter glances over and says that Ace, the German shepherd dog, is the best. "He was an ally of Batman and good at tracking things down and finding missing people," he says.

"I'm Ace too," I reply. Misunderstanding, the man says he's also ace and everyone here at Comic Con is brilliant as well. "No, it's my name, my real name. I'm going to make everyone around me happy by being excellent. It's my mission." I pass over some money and take the book and the man says I've made him very happy by buying it. Then he wishes me luck, and I say I've got a four-leaf clover that I'm hoping will help so he doesn't need to worry. And I think, *I'm going to be as good as the Bat-Hound at tracking down my real mother.*

As I walk towards the hot-dog stand with the book under my arm, I see someone with milky-hot-chocolate-coloured hair poking out from underneath a shimmering blue helmet. I swear it's The Beast from school. But it's hard to tell and when I look again the blue helmet has disappeared into a crowd of aliens.

Slowly I wander past stalls, picking up comics and flicking through the pages. But I can't concentrate because all I'm thinking about is how I'm going to be rehomed because of the jelly bean. Earlier Dad acted as if he knew nothing about it and I wanted to ask him lots of questions but the moment passed. Just then, Superman wanders past me and I grab him by the cape. "Please, Superman, sir," I say. "I've got a question." If you can't ask your dad questions then Superman is the next best thing, right? Superman stops and looks down at me with his arms folded. His upper arm muscles look like two pork chops. "You know your mother, Lara?"

Superman nods and then I think it was a stupid question.

"What I mean is, you were adopted by the Kent family, right?" I say, bouncing on my toes. "So how did it feel not knowing your mother Lara properly?" Superman raises one eyebrow and says it was hard being adopted but it was the right choice and why am I asking? I reply, "You're adopted and you're special and you make the world happy. I'd like to do that. The thing is, I'd also like to track down my real mother. She's called Rose. I'm going to live with her. It's because the jelly bean is coming."

Superman looks confused. "Is the jelly bean an arch villain? Is the jelly bean going to destroy the world?"

"Sort of," I say. "The jelly bean needs my room." I shrug and tug at my ear before saying, "I want to be just like you, Superman, but they're big shoes to fill." I glance down and see that Superman has got tiny feet in little red boots. After a small cough, I add, "Can you give me any tips on being a superhero that might help me?"

"Have you saved an animal in peril?" asks Superman, scratching his chin. When I shake my head he asks if I've saved a life. I tell him I tried both but it was trickier than I thought. Superman nods and says never work with animals and saving a life is the hardest thing of all. "Help an old person across the road instead," says Superman finally. "That's a good one, young man. You could do that. That will make people happy. And my last bit of advice is to stay away from green things." I ask him if he means healthy vegetables because that will be tricky, thanks to my mum, and he says no, he means kryptonite.

"You're the best, Superman. I've got helping an old person on my list, but I haven't done it yet," I reply, rubbing my nose. "Just one more question before you fly off on your next mission – on your birthday when you were growing up, did you ever blow out the candles and think of Lara, even though you were happy with the Kent family? I mean, was there a tiny bit of Superman missing? In here?" I thump my chest.

Superman smiles and he's about to answer when a woman appears and shouts, "Hey, Colin, love, do you want a drink? I'm going to get one because I'm parched. My mouth's like the bottom of a budgie's cage." Superman Colin nods and tells me that he's got to go and replenish, because his energy is on zero and he's still got to do a book signing. He tells me to take care and then instead of flying away he walks, in his tiny red boots.

As I watch him go, I see a table set up with a starry tablecloth and there's a Zorbitan behind it and a queue in front. I crane my neck to get a better look. The Zorbitan is leaning down and I can see the top of his green head, and on his chest is a green emerald and there are three gold stripes on his sleeve. He's got the emerald heart and everything. I feel a big whoosh of excitement as I realize I'm close to an *actual Zorbitan*.

I push through a crowd of supervillains who are talking about how their costumes are so tight they'd better not eat or they'll need elastic waistbands. As I get through their group I catch a glimpse of The Grand Moon Master, which makes me stop in my tracks. He's the Zorbitans' creator, so I suppose you could call him their father. What's more, he's been missing from their lives for ever and they're desperate to find him and he's right here. Right under our noses. What's more, in real life he's really tall, even taller than Tiny Eric on stilts, and he's wearing a long black robe studded with stars and a glossy black mask that covers his whole face. Suddenly he walks into a pillar and then jerks backwards and rubs his mask before staggering off again. I think about going over and talking to him but he heads towards the Gents'. To be honest, I'd never considered The Grand Moon Master needing to pee. He opens the toilet door and gets his black cape caught in it as it closes behind him.

I shake myself and carry on towards the star-covered table, quickly joining the queue behind a girl with a hot dog, who appears to be trying to achieve the world record for boring a Zorbitan. The Zorbitan is looking up at her and nodding and he draws a squiggle on a photograph for her. You can't really read it because Zorbitans don't have actual names. It's probably more of a claw print. The girl leans over with her hot dog and she's breathing onion fumes everywhere. Zorbitans don't like onions. They eat zorbits – although this one appears to be eating custard creams. Eventually, the girl says thank you and disappears clutching the photo. When I look at the Zorbitan, he's rubbing his head.

"I saw The Grand Moon Master," I say.

"Right," says the Zorbitan. He doesn't seem all that bothered. I repeat what I've just said, only louder. "You want an autograph, kid?" he fires back.

"He's in the toilet."

"Great," says the Zorbitan, his pointy ears wobbling. "There's a queue building, so if you don't want a claw print you need to move on." I look behind me but there's no queue any more. It's just me and a furry wolf boy who's gone under the table for a sleep.

I open my mouth to speak but no words come out.

The Zorbitan blinks. "I know what you're going to ask me next, kid," he says. "When I find my creator will this emerald heart glow red, and when will that happen?" He points a claw to the emerald heart. "Do you know how many kids ask me that?" I shake my head. "Bazillions!"

"That's not even a word," I say.

"It is on my planet. Look around you, kid. Everyone here is going to ask me that same question about when

104

I'll find my creator. They're all obsessed with my heart glowing. You know, this one doesn't glow though, so even if I see The Grand Moon Master coming out of the toilet it won't work." He nudges me in the belly and then winks. "I got the cheap costume."

I hear myself muttering "Oh" and my heart droops a little. I wanted to see the Zorbitan's heart glow when he finds his creator. It's supposed to be perfect and they're supposed to find each other and hug and the Zorbitans will have a home with The Grand Moon Master and they won't be roaming around looking for him. I want to tell the Zorbitan that I'm adopted and looking for my creator too, but the Zorbitan is too busy flicking his pointy ears, and then a bit falls off and lands on the table.

We both look at it.

"You've lost the tip of your ear," I say, staring at it. The Zorbitan doesn't respond but I suppose he can't hear without it. Eventually I pick it up and hand it to the Zorbitan, who puts it back on again before continuing: "So, yeah, you can get costumes that glow, but they're hard to find." He laughs. "A bit like The Grand Moon Master. But keep reading the comics, eh? You never know when the Zorbitans will connect with him." He mumbles something about it probably being on the last page of the last ever issue, not that he's cynical. "So, kiddo. Thanks for the heads up about The Grand Moon Master being in the toilet and it's five pounds for a signed photo."

I pass the last of my money across the table and the Zorbitan picks it up and puts it in a cash box before picking up a pen and a photograph. He does a squiggle on it and passes it to me. I pick it up, making sure not to smudge the signature. "Mr Zorbitan, one last question..." I look down at him. It's the most important question in my head at the moment. "Why did The Grand Moon Master leave you in the first place? I mean, it's never explained in the comics. He was the person who made you and he should have loved you. Without him, you must feel like a piece of you is missing."

"Great question, kiddo. And one I've never been asked before. I have no idea. Why would anyone leave someone as loveable as me behind?" The Zorbitan points his claws to himself and shakes with laughter and the tip of his ear falls off again.

"I don't know," I whisper. "I really don't know."

10

BANG

The rest of the evening could be described like this:

• Dad appeared five minutes later and handed me a chilli hot dog and after a few seconds asked me why my eyes were watering, and I said the chilli nearly took the roof off my mouth. Then Dad looked down at my hot dog and said I hadn't even had a bite yet. After that I scoffed half of it in a hurry and it was as if a volcano erupted inside my head. "See," I said to Dad, pointing to my face, which I guessed was as red as a baboon's bum. "Even my eyeballs are sweating." The thing is, the tears had nothing to do with the chilli and everything to do with Mum and Dad wanting to rehome me and the Zorbitan not knowing why his creator left him.

- We looked at all the comics on the stands and Dad spent ages speaking to a stall owner who sold these wish kites shaped like superheroes, and I watched as Spider-Man strolled past. I thought about stopping him for a chat but I felt so fed up after talking to the Zorbitan that I didn't bother.

- On the way back to the car park to go home, I spotted an old lady with a Bag for Life trying to cross the road on a mobility scooter, and I remembered what Superman aka Colin said about helping an old person across the road to be a superhero. I could do this with ease. But as I ran after her, shouting that I was going to help her, she took off like a rocket, weaving in and out of the traffic to escape me. Then I noticed she'd dropped the Bag for Life, which must have been an accident because you're supposed to keep those for ever.

- Shouting, "You've dropped your Bag for Life," I picked it up and it nearly broke my arm. I looked inside and it was full of old tins and dirty clothes. When I got back to Dad he said we should leave the bag where she'd dropped it. But as we flung it on the ground, a man who came out of Comic Con carrying an ironing board on his back pointed to the wall, where a sign said: *NO FLY-TIPPING*. Dad squared up to him and said who did he think he was, interfering? The bloke said he was Iron Man and Dad nodded and said he'd take the bag straight to a bin.

• Later that evening I stood in my bedroom with my whole face pressed against the glass. And I saw a million stars blinking across the night sky and they were like all my birthday candles put together and I imagined blowing them out and making a wish. Actually two wishes, which I hoped wasn't cheating. "I wish I could be a superhero and put a smile back on Mum's face." Even though I was annoyed that they were rehoming me, I couldn't sulk for ever. Superheroes aren't like that – they want to make others happy. Anyway, Mum still looked sad and I didn't want to make things worse for her. That's how a true superhero would behave. "And I wish I could find my real mother and live with her," I whispered and my warm breath left a cloud on the cold window and I traced a heart in its centre. "And while I'm at it, I wish I could make a great family tree." Oh, that was three wishes. I've never been any good at maths. And through the heart I saw stars that went on for ever and lit up the darkness and it felt like anything was possible.

The next day at school Mrs Chatterjee gives us a permission slip for a trip to the library to get signed. Then she goes on to tell us there's been a miracle. Everyone stares at her like she's baby Jesus. "No, I haven't got twenty-eight fully correct maths homework exercises in my possession. But I have secured us a front page article in the *Pegasus Park Packet*." I don't know how Mrs Chatterjee imagines miracles, but I was expecting a bit more, to be honest. "A reporter will be coming to our exhibition and they'd love to take photos and feature someone's family tree, so that means you could be in the paper with your family. They'll want heart-warming, interesting stories though," she continues, "so make sure your tree is the best it can be."

I glance around the class, thinking that I've probably got the most interesting story of all. I could tell the reporter about how I decided to become a superhero to make everyone happy and how I also went looking for my long-lost mother and she gave me a home when I needed one. And that she came along to the exhibition to see the family tree I'd done specially for her. I can imagine it now: a photo of us together on the front cover. Only, in my head, my real mother's face is fuzzy.

No matter how much I try to imagine her, I don't know what she actually looks like. And no matter how many times I try to think of my real mother, Mum's face keeps popping into my mind instead.

Mrs Chatterjee gives us each a new luggage tag and says she'd like us all to imagine we are the person who has our story on the front page of the *Pegasus Park Packet*. "Now, let's try and make it exciting. I want you to write a headline. Perhaps your dad has won an award or your mum has an exciting job or there's a sporting achievement in the family that you could highlight. I want a headline and not the whole story, please. This is simply a quick exercise."

I think about Dad, because he's won Best Key-Cutter in Pegasus Park every year since 2010 – there's a silver key award on the counter at his shop. Then again, Dad's the *only* key-cutter in Pegasus Park. Mum used to work at the Broken Egg Cafe and they once won an award too, for being the best greasy spoon cafe in the local area – the prize was an actual greasy spoon.

Then I think about my real mother and I start chewing the inside of my mouth, before I realize that it doesn't taste all that great. I don't know what her achievements are but I know she's done something incredible because she had me. Smiling, I write on the tag: AN ACE

SUPERHERO TRIES TO FIND LONG-LOST MOTHER. WHAM!

I tap my pocket, hoping it'll make the drawing of the four-leaf clover spread more good luck to help me in my search for my real mother. That's when I have a thought.

I hoist my hand up in the air and Mrs Chatterjee glances towards me. "Miss," I say, "what do you think about believing in something even if it's hard to achieve? I'm asking for a friend." Mrs Chatterjee perches on the edge of her desk and says that's a good question. There's a flush of heat in my face as Tiny Eric glances my way.

"Okay, well, in my opinion, believing in something is important. And the fact that it's hard to achieve makes it sound like it's something..." Mrs Chatterjee pauses. "...Your *friend* really wants." I scratch under my bobble hat as Mrs Chatterjee continues. "I have a little saying: if you believe you can do something, then you're already halfway there." Mrs Chatterjee rises up off her desk and adds, "But there's one thing I think the whole class should believe in. Does anyone know what that is?"

Everyone shakes their heads until Nish pipes up, "Believe in making money and having a good job and being famous? So, if you believe you're famous you're halfway there."

A tiny cough escapes from Mrs Chatterjee's lips. "Um...it's a little simpler than that. Believe in *yourselves*. You can change the world if you believe in yourself."

Mrs Chatterjee's right, if I think about it. If I believe in myself changing into a superhero, then I can change the world. When Mrs Chatterjee asks if she's answered my question, I nod and say, "Yes, miss. I'm going to change the world one day."

"I'm sure you will," says Mrs Chatterjee, smiling. "But can you concentrate on your schoolwork before then?"

I nod. After what Mrs Chatterjee's said, I believe I'm going to be the best superhero ever, so that means I'm already halfway there. I look down at my tag and rub out my headline and instead I write: AN ACE SUPERHERO FINDS LONG-LOST MOTHER AND SHE GIVES HIM A HOME.

Mrs Chatterjee says she's so happy with the work we've done today that she's going to get us to do more over the weekend. I'm not sure that's much of a reward.

"For homework, pick a special person close to you – one you've mentioned on your family tree – and write a poem about them," says Mrs Chatterjee. "And write it from the heart."

I think about Mum for a second and there's a warm

feeling in my tummy like I've just eaten a steaming hot bowl of spaghetti hoops. But then I think about my real mother and how it will feel when I've got a home with her instead. This poem about a special person is going to be important, and I've got to consider exactly what I'm going to say. I chew on the wrong end of my pen before realizing I forgot to put the lid on it.

11

ZONK

"Everything's a catastrophe at the moment," I mumble to myself as I lie on my bed after scrubbing the ink off my lips and nearly taking all the skin with it. I've finished writing the poem for homework and I pull out the four-leaf clover drawing and stare at it. "And you're not much good either. You really haven't done much recently. Lazy four-leaf clover. You were meant to help make me a superhero, but a fat lot of good you've been, because I'm still not one. My lifesaving was so useless that I was the person who needed saving." As for saving the world...well, in desperation, I pushed Mrs Chatterjee's globe off the desk and then tried to save it, but I wasn't quick enough and it broke and she gave me lines saying *I MUST NOT DESTROY THE WORLD*, which is the precise opposite of what a superhero wants to do. "And now I have to find my real mother to give me a home, so I need even more luck than ever."

"OMG, talking to yourself is a sign of madness," says Minnie as she walks past my bedroom door. She pauses and comes back, lounging against the door frame. When I tell her I'm not talking to myself, I'm talking to a drawing, she says, "It's worse than I thought then – you're talking to a piece of paper! What is it you're looking at, *The International Book of Stupid*?"

"You're hilarious," I mutter.

Minnie stops. "Oh, I know." She undoes her ponytail and her dark hair spills onto her shoulders. "Seriously, though. Why are you talking to a piece of paper?" When I tell Minnie it's a four-leaf clover and it's going to bring me lots of good luck, she says, "And you think it can?"

"Well, it hasn't worked properly yet," I mumble. "I think it needs some new batteries."

Minnie laughs. "So, you've got a piece of paper that's supposed to bring you luck but it hasn't worked. Dad says the same about his lottery ticket – that's never going to work either, the odds are like a billion to one." Minnie comes into the bedroom properly and looks at the drawing. "It looks like a shamrock," she exclaims.

"It's a four-leaf clover, I told you. Anyway, I think it looks like four hearts joined together," I say, squinting at it. "For your information, it is going to work eventually. All I have to do is keep staring at it until my eyeballs hurt and nearly fall out."

Minnie is doing some staring of her own but it's at her fingernails and it's as if they're the most interesting thing she's ever seen and then she casually sashays towards my desk – before suddenly snatching my homework notebook which is sitting open on top of it. *Ambush! Ambush!* I tell her to give it back to me because it contains valuable information, but she holds it out of my reach and flicks through the pages.

"Ooh, that's a soppy poem... And what the heck is this big ball?" asks Minnie, flashing my drawing in front of my eyes and away again before I can catch it.

"It's Ganymede," I fire back, flinging myself forward like a human cannonball. "It's the largest moon of Jupiter." Minnie ducks and steps back, flicking to another page. With a puzzled look on her face, she asks what the big dark monster thing is. "It's a rose," my voice is brittle. "A beautiful rose."

Minnie bursts out laughing, her braces glinting in

the light. "That's no rose. That's a big ugly black blob. And if it is a rose, it's missing something important."

Fury bubbles inside me as I say it's not missing anything, thank you very much. Then I lunge for the notebook again, but I'm too slow and now Minnie has seen the word *ACE* in big letters and read my birthdate and where I was born. Desperately I manage to grab Minnie's hands and finally, as she screams about me damaging her freshly painted seashell-pink nails, the notebook is mine. I've got it between my fingers, but as I pull it away from Minnie there's a sickening rip. The page with the rose is torn in half. "Look what you've done," I spit. "You've wrecked my drawing, you dough ball."

"You did it yourself," says Minnie, her cheeks fiery. "Anyway, why are you drawing roses? And what's with writing your birthday? We all know when it is. And what does ACE mean? What's going on?" From the look on Minnie's face, I can tell she's guessed I'm up to something – and if I know my sister, she isn't going to stop until I've spilled the beans.

That's the thing about Minnie. She's older and she likes to know everything and boss me around. To be honest, it wasn't always like that. When we were younger we were the best of friends and we'd walk home from school together. But when she turned thirteen and I was nine, Dad got me interested in comics. After that everything went as wonky as a donkey in zero gravity. Minnie didn't like Zorbitans, villains and heroes, and Dad wasn't interested in listening to her talk make-up and fashion. Before long, Minnie stopped being nice to me.

Idly I flick through my notebook, trying to look as casual as a pair of jogging bottoms. I stop at the torn page and declare, "There is nothing you should know. And there's nothing strange about me drawing roses or writing down my birthdate. As for being ACE...well, that just means you're the best. Look it up in the dictionary. I have. Nope, all this is perfectly normal behaviour in my humble opinion."

"What flipping planet are you on?" Minnie gapes at me.

"The same planet as you, unfortunately," I reply.

Minnie lets out a little pig-like snort and then asks why I've written *Pegasus Park Hospital* in my notebook and put a question mark beside it.

I shrug. "I was born in Pegasus Park, so I was probably born at that hospital."

"Oh yeah?" says Minnie, sucking all the air from my bedroom through her braces. "And how do you know

119

that exactly?" There's a second before I realize I've been rumbled by my big sister. She says she doesn't know where I was born, so how do I? "Mum hasn't mentioned it to us. She's never discussed where they adopted you from. I didn't think anyone knew which hospital you were born in." Minnie's eyes are like two tiny subtraction signs and I feel my stomach go wobbly like the jelly in a pork pie and I'm back-pedalling so much I could be on a bike heading backwards.

"Um..." That's the best I can manage, as I'm already weighed down under Minnie's stony gaze.

In the end, Minnie says she's going to stage a sit-in in my bedroom until I tell her everything. She throws herself on my bed and flings her arms behind her head, closing her eyes. So eventually I tell Minnie I'm doing a school project about family trees. Opening one eye, Minnie tells me to continue.

"Well, I know all about this family, so I thought I'd do my real family. I needed information, so I found an envelope with a certificate that told me my name, my mother's name and where I was born. But that was it. That's all the information I have. Nothing more, I promise. I just needed some facts for school."

There's a pause and I swear I can almost see Minnie's brain working. "Since finding the envelope, you haven't gone looking for your mother, have you?" She's sitting up now.

I shrug again. "No." I'm not lying because I haven't looked for her *yet*. And I wouldn't even be thinking of looking for her now except for the fact that Mum and Dad need me to go to make space for the jelly bean. I don't think Minnie or Velvet know about the jelly bean yet and I can't say anything because I'm not supposed to know either.

"Put all this out of your head," says Minnie, her eyeballs searing holes through mine and then destroying the wall behind me and burning through the Earth's crust. "You've already got Mum and Dad. What more do you need? Mum and Dad are the best. They're the most brilliant parents on the planet." Minnie glares at me defiantly.

I tell Minnie I know that. And she's right, Mum and Dad *are* the best and I feel bad for wanting more. But I can't help it. It's impossible to forget that you've got a mother out there who you don't know, especially when you need to go and live with her. Minnie will never understand how that feels. How could she, when she's got a for ever home and knows that she won't have to leave? Plus, unlike me, Minnie knows what her mum and dad look like. Mum and Minnie are like mirror images, except Minnie's got more fake tan and bigger eyebrows. Oh, and she wears skinny jeans and crop tops. Mum doesn't like crop tops. She says they draw attention to your muffin top. Velvet looks a bit like Dad, without the bald head and tattoo. But I look like no one. I've got red hair and everyone else in the family has brown. Even Dad's was brown before it disappeared. "Your hair is like the finest spun copper thread," Mum used to tell me. She said it was special, but I didn't want special hair, I wanted hair like everyone else's.

I explain more about the project to Minnie and how we're going to make our trees. "It's about us more than anything and how we fit at the top of our tree. It wasn't about me finding anyone in real life. That's not what Mrs Chatterjee said. It's just a project."

Quiet descends and it feels like we've just walked into the chiller aisle at the supermarket. After mulling it over, Minnie breaks the silence. "You'd better not be thinking about anything else. And even if you do find out any more information for this daft project, then you can't act on it. Just because you found out your real mother's name, that doesn't mean she's wonderful, you know. Don't you go around thinking she's Mrs Perfect."

"But she could be," I mutter indignantly, suddenly protective of a mother I don't even know.

"Don't ever think you're going to go out and find her and she'll welcome you with open arms. You're completely bonkers if you get into all this. It's a can of snakes." Minnie's voice gets higher.

"Worms." I instantly regret correcting Minnie because now she's got a face like a bulldog chewing a wasp.

"No, Adam. It's a can of snakes. It's so much bigger than worms. But like you said, it's only a project and you haven't looked for her and you're not going to bother." With a flourish, Minnie adds, "I knew you were up to something that night of the storm because I saw you rummaging about in Mum and Dad's drawers." I swallow because I did see a shadow at the door that night. "You were looking for the envelope, weren't you?"

I squirm as bossyboots Minnie rises from my bed and sashays over to the door. "Promise me that what you're telling me is true. This is just a project and you're not looking for this woman. If you don't, I'll tell Mum you were snooping."

I promise but my hands are in my pockets and my fingers are crossed. Everyone knows that if you cross your fingers it cancels out a promise.

That evening, as I'm trying to put the two pieces of my torn rose drawing together, I think about my real mother again. Roses are beautiful – it's true what I said to Minnie earlier. I stand up and pad over to the window.

"Roses are beautiful," I repeat, pressing my nose flat against the glass. Outside there's a full moon rolling across the sky like a giant pearl sliding over black velvet. Stars prick the darkness and I reach out and imagine catching one in my hand. The lights in the windows of the other tower blocks wink and I know the lights in our tower block are winking back. Pegasus Park stretches out before me and I can see the high street with Dad's Surelock Homes shop, Sharkey's corner shop and Good Buy, Mr Chips. My school is in the distance and then I spy the hills that surround the town like a protective green lasso.

As the moon washes my bedroom in liquid silver I glance back at my drawing of the rose and I realize what Minnie meant earlier when she said that it was missing something important. At the time I didn't give it any thought because I was angry, but now, looking at the drawing, I know Minnie's right. There *is* something missing. Thorns! A rose always has thorns.

Monday morning starts off just like the last. There's sticky paste pretending to be porridge for breakfast, Minnie's giving me dagger-eyes over the table because she's angry about something I've said, Dad's talking about how it'll be a busy day because he's offering a Monday special – ten per cent off keys. Velvet is whispering to Sausage Roll under the table and after Mum has signed my permission slip she stares into the distance for ages. I think she's in one of her moods again. It's only when I ask for a spoon that Mum snaps out of it. She says she's sorry and it's because she's got a lot on her mind. "Ignore me," adds Mum.

Minnie takes Mum at her word and begins talking about how her drama rehearsals are going and that the boy playing her husband is lovely. "He's called Callum and he's a brilliant actor," gushes Minnie. "I think we're the perfect couple. Mr Bravo says we're like two star-crossed lovers."

"I thought you were doing *Macbeth*, not *Romeo and Juliet*?" says Dad, picking some fluff off his T-shirt. Minnie gapes at Dad and everyone can see how much porridge is in her mouth. "You don't call it that," she gasps. "You call it 'the Scottish play'." And she gets up and turns around three times and spits, much to Mum's horror. We all look at the tiny wet patch of porridge dribbling over the edge of the kitchen counter. "It's to counteract the bad luck from saying—"

"Macbeth," interrupts Velvet cheerfully.

Mum holds up her hand and says Minnie can go outside if she wants to spit again. Minnie pouts. "Doesn't anyone understand how this is a story of tragedy? There's a storm one night..." Minnie's gaze falls on me. "And it's as if the main character of the Scottish play's fate is sealed. Yes, he's ambitious and he wants more than he's already got. Even though what he's got is good and he should be content with it. Anyway, he gets what he wants in the end but he pays a big price. Oh, silly man." Minnie's shaking her head like a dog with a flea in its ear.

"Whoah," exclaims Dad. "That's a bit deep for breakfast time."

Minnie gives a rueful smile. "Well, Dad," she says, like a world authority on the entire works of Shakespeare, "this is a classic story that has parallels with our lives today. I simply thought I would share this knowledge with you all." Once more, Minnie stares at me as I shift uncomfortably in my seat. "What I'm trying to say is, sometimes we should all consider what we have in our lives without looking for more. Looking for more can end in catastrophe."

There's an awkward silence.

I just stare deeply into my watch, which still isn't working. I give it a little tap and then hold it up to my ear. Minnie glares at me and asks where I got the watch from. When I tell her it was Granddad Fred's, she looks at Mum and Dad and then back at me. There is the feeling of impending doom as Minnie grimaces, rises from the table and stalks towards the door.

Dad gives a tiny round of applause, saying, "Great performance."

It's obvious from Minnie's face that she wasn't giving one. She slams the door – and if Dad had any hair, it would have blown right back.

Mum sighs, picks up her cereal bowl and takes it to the sink, before taking a dishcloth to the spittle on the work surface.

I don't care what Minnie has said about Macbeth. Minnie doesn't know what it feels like to be adopted. She doesn't know what it's like to be happy but always feel like a tiny bit of you is missing. Minnie doesn't understand anything. And that's why nothing Minnie says is going to stop me.

It happens by surprise. I suppose all superheroes could say that. They don't expect to be eating fish-finger sandwiches when the Batphone rings, or to come across a person trapped under a car while they're out walking the dog, or to be in the bank getting some money out for a new pair of pants when a group of crooks in balaclavas appear, holding a swag bag ready to be filled with cash.

Anyway, I'm walking to school and there's a fine grey veil of mist over everything. As I make my way along the pavement I can hear the *thump-thump-thump* of music. In the distance I see the lights of a car and as I turn to my right I can make out Tyler, the guy who jumped in to save me at the swimming pool.

From the corner of my eye I see the car is now hurtling towards us. Suddenly Tyler steps down from the pavement and I swear he's going to be hit and, without thinking, my arm shoots out and I grab him by the neck of the blazer and pull. He falls backwards as the car whizzes past us both, honking its horn. I look down at my feet and Tyler is lying there in a heap. He stares up at me, slack-jawed, before taking off his massive headphones. "What the heck did you do that for?"

"I saved your life." My voice wobbles. My fingers are trembling. "You were nearly hit by a Mini."

Tyler blinks and says he heard nothing, and I tell him that's because he had two big cushions on his ears. No one would hear a Tyrannosaurus rex coming with those on. Scrabbling to his feet, Tyler says I might have a point, but he's sure he would have seen the car eventually. And I agree, yes, he would have seen it – a second before it hit him. Begrudgingly Tyler says okay, I've saved his life, but he saved mine too so it's quits. His mouth is set in a firm line.

"Quits," I say, smiling. And it's like a light bulb has just gone on inside my head. All I can think is, *I'm a SUPERHERO! I'm ACE and I DID IT! I'm EXCELLENT.* There's a whole fireworks display going off inside my brain. Everyone is going to love me. Mum's going to be over the moon when she hears this – she's going to smile so much her jaws will ache. And when I find my real mother, I can tell her what a great human being I am too, and she's going to think I'm so brilliant that she'll want me to move in with her.

As Tyler crosses the road safely, I let out a tiny whoop of joy and then I stick my arm in the air and shout "Kazoo!"

A man gives me a funny look as he walks past, and I drop my arm quickly before continuing, "A kazoo is an instrument." I whistle as I cross the road, taking care not to step out in front of any oncoming traffic. The last thing I need right now is to be hit by a speeding car myself.

As I walk into the school playground I'm convinced that I'm surrounded by a golden glow of greatness – I'm swimming in a sea of super, ecstatic about my own excellence, floating in a fog of fabulousness. Basically I *am* a superhero now. I'm one hundred per cent certain I'll look different. To prove this, I wave at Mrs Chatterjee, who is on playground duty, and she waves back. See, she can tell I'm excellent. She knows. I salute the kids in Year Four and they salute me back. I give a tiny smile to The Beast who is standing near the holly bush and The Beast looks confused but then smiles back and waves at me. Like I always thought, everyone loves a superhero. It's excellent being this excellent.

Unfortunately, nothing changes in class, because no one mentions the golden glow. In fact, after she's collected the library permission slips, Mrs Chatterjee is busy giving us a test on history and telling us to get on with it, and no matter how many times I try to smile at her she's ignoring my brilliance.

"What's with the goofy grin?" asks Tiny Eric, staring at me. "Did you get some good luck in the end? That's the only reason I can think of for that silly smile."

"I might have," I whisper mysteriously. "Hey, what's the answer to *By population, which is the largest city in Scotland?*"

"Pegasus Park?" hisses Tiny Eric. When I say that's not in Scotland, he adds, "Okay, Edinburgh then. And what was the good luck? You haven't told me yet and best friends are supposed to tell each other everything."

"Can't you see?" I puff up my chest and feel my school shirt strain. "I'm a superhero now. It happened this morning. You won't believe this but I saved a life. What's the answer to *What is the longest river in the world?*"

"Huh? You saved someone? I think it's the Amazon," says Tiny Eric. "It sounds like the lucky four-leaf clover did the job. You believed." When I say I stopped someone getting hit by a car but still need some more luck, he tells me not to exhaust the magic. And he asks me why I wanted to be a superhero in the first place.

"Everyone loves a superhero," I reply, like it's no big deal and I'm used to it already. "That's why I asked you to draw me as a hero. I was born to be one and now I've achieved it, everything will be perfect. Mum will be happy. Everyone will be." Tiny Eric lets out a little snort and Mrs Chatterjee looks over at us and then down at the test questions, saying that this is the last one. After a few seconds I lean over and whisper to Tiny Eric, "Russia, Lithuania, Belarus, Slovakia, Ukraine, the Czech Republic and Germany all share a border with which country?"

131

"It's Poland," says Tiny Eric, turning away.

Mrs Chatterjee thanks Tiny Eric for giving everyone the answer. "When I give a test, I ask the questions and you write down the answers. What you don't do is whisper the answers to each other. Tiny Eric, since you are already an expert on Poland, perhaps you could share a few interesting details about it with the class."

Tiny Eric glares at me and then stands up. Mrs Chatterjee tells everyone to pin back their ears, as if that's going to be easy. "Warsaw is the capital of Poland." Mrs Chatterjee nods. "The national symbol is the white eagle and Marie Curie was Polish. One of Poland's most popular dishes is gołąbki, which means little pigeons."

"*Eeeww*," shouts Nish, waving his arms around. "They eat little pigeons."

"They're not made of pigeons," says Tiny Eric, looking around the classroom. "They're cabbage stuffed with meat cooked in tomato sauce and spices. My *babcia* makes *gołąbki*. I'll be having some soon." He pauses. "Very soon." The words drift away and Mrs Chatterjee thanks Tiny Eric for his enlightening talk about Poland. As he sits down he says, "I don't like little pigeons."

"I don't like cabbage either," I whisper back.

"No, I just don't like little pigeons," says Tiny Eric, folding his arms.

I look at Tiny Eric but he turns his back on me. I don't think he remembers he's talking to a proper superhero now. No one would turn their back on a superhero, would they?

12
ZLOSH

Later that same afternoon I'm in ICT and I have this bright idea about how to find my real mother, Rose. So when Mrs Chatterjee tells us to use the computers to research designs for water bottles, I search the name Rose Walker instead. While Mrs Chatterjee is going on about style and convenience, I'm looking at three people by the name R Walker who mention they live in the Pegasus Park area. When I squint at the photos on the Internet I know the first R Walker can't possibly be Rose, because it's a man and he's aged about eighty. He lives on the outskirts of Pegasus Park with his wife, Mabel, and twenty cats. I couldn't live with twenty cats, not after what that cat did to me when I tried to help it. I've still got the scars. The second woman is about twenty and is waterskiing (not in Pegasus Park because we're not near a beach). Too young, I tell myself. The third woman looks about the right age and there's a photo of her wearing a pink vest saying *Lettuce Eat*, which is a grocery shop in the precinct. *She* could *be my mother*, I think.

As Mrs Chatterjee begins a circuit of the room, I quickly close down the pages I've been looking at and pretend to be interested in a water bottle design, but all the time I'm thinking I might have seen my real mother in that picture. But there's only one way to be sure, and that's to go to Lettuce Eat and see this R Walker lady face-to-face. If she is my real mother, it'll be amazing. I'll tell her who I am, she'll hug me and I'll ask if I can live with her. Of course, she'll say yes. This couldn't have worked out better if the four-leaf clover had arranged it for me.

As soon as the bell rings for the end of the day, I'm up and ready to rush out the door, when Mrs Chatterjee hands each of us a white card. I glance at it and put it in my school bag, then I'm out and running towards the school gate. I'm going to visit the precinct on the way home. Excitement builds up inside me as I run down

Agamemnon Road and take a right into Primrose Grove. As I near Lettuce Eat, I keep telling myself that I might be five minutes away from meeting my mother. Four minutes. Three minutes. Two minutes. In fact, I've been in Lettuce Eat a few times with Mum recently when she was buying vegetables and I might have passed my real mother and not realized.

When I reach Lettuce Eat, I decide to press my face against the glass and look in first. Unfortunately it's one of those doors that opens automatically when you get close enough...

After picking myself up off the floor I wander around, pretending to be interested in watermelons, but the whole time I'm looking out for R Walker. As I'm walking past the fish counter I'm stopped in my tracks and it's nothing to do with a giant cod eyeballing me. Someone is standing behind the counter with their back to me, wearing a bright pink tabard, their long hair pulled back in a ponytail. I can see the rainbow glint of scales as they lean over a fish, and I think, *This could be Rose*. My stomach somersaults, flips and rotates so much I imagine it winning its own Olympic gold medal.

I look down and see a crab in the glass cabinet with a label that says it's dressed, and it's really expensive, and my mouth suddenly goes off on its own, squealing,

"Holy doughnuts, what's that crab dressed in? A golden cape with diamond pants?"

My stomach is still doing gymnastics and then it falls flat on the floor with a splat as the person behind the counter turns around. "What's that you said about diamond pants?" the man says in a deep voice. He blinks and his ponytail swings gently like a horse's tail flicking flies on a lazy summer's day. There's so much shock on my face, the man asks if I've seen a ghost. "No, no," I say as I shuffle away. "You've got to be squidding. I mean kidding."

I'm in the frozen potato aisle looking at the potato shapes, when I hear a voice over the tannoy saying:

"Could Mrs Walker please come to the till?

Could Mrs Walker please come to the till?"

It feels like all the potato shapes have exploded from the freezer and have spelled out *THIS IS IT* in the sky. My real mother is in this shop. And I can see a woman walking towards the till and she's in a pink Lettuce Eat vest and she's smiling and, oh, she's got the loveliest smile. My heart is ping-ponging inside my ribcage and I'm skidding towards the tills like I've got banana skins on my shoes. R Walker is taking a seat and turning a key and smiling at a customer in front of me, who incidentally must be like Old Mother Hubbard who had nothing in the cupboard, because her trolley is piled so high.

Ten minutes later when I've nearly lost the will to live and I'm slumped against the energy drinks, I hear R Walker say, "Thank you," and watch as the receipt spills from the till. Suddenly I spring up and face her.

"Rose." The word is soft on my tongue.

"You'd like some roses?" The woman looks around and is about to press a buzzer when I say it's a pretty name. "Oh, yes, it is." She looks a bit confused and now *I'm* confused, because I thought she'd say she was called Rose and I'd say I was Ace. And then it would be like fireworks going off in my head. "Do you know anyone called Rose?" I blink.

"I don't," she replies. "Do you?" At that moment I see she's wearing a name badge and it says *RAMONA WALKER*. I'm so deflated I feel like a whoopee cushion that just had a giant bum sit on it.

I am not her son.

Today is not the day I find my real mother.

When I get home, Mum and Dad are sitting at the kitchen table and there's a piece of paper in front of them. I get a glimpse of what they've written: *THINGS WE NEED – BED, BLANKET, TOYS...* When they see me standing in the doorway, Mum quickly puts her hand over the paper and her cheeks go as pink as a flamingo's bum. She asks me how my day was. I tell her *gołąbki* means "little pigeons", and Mum says she's never heard baby pigeons called that. Then she says she's never actually seen a baby pigeon.

"It's a Polish dish," I say, looking away, swallowed up by hurt. My stomach feels like there's a bowling ball in it but when I hear Mum sigh softly I remind myself how superheroes want what's best for others. But deep down I still can't help how I feel. It was bad enough not finding my real mother today, but seeing the list of things they need for the jelly bean has made it one billion times worse. I glance at Mum saying, "Tiny Eric was talking about it. It's not baby pigeon pie though, it's got cabbage in it." Mum's hand doesn't move and there's a strange atmosphere in the kitchen and I feel like it's somehow my fault for interrupting their talk about the new baby. Slowly I turn and slouch away to SPAM HQ, muttering that I've got homework to do.

I can almost hear Mum's sigh of relief from my bedroom.

When I pull my notebook out of my school bag, the invitation Mrs Chatterjee gave us to the *Forest For Ever* exhibition falls out too.

You and your family are cordially invited to our Forest For Ever exhibition in two weeks' time (Tuesday 29th). We have made our individual family trees. Come and see what we've learned and marvel at our trees. Tea and biscuits will be served. All proceeds are going to the Pegasus Park Family Support charity.

£3 per person.

I'm not telling Mum and Dad about the exhibition. It would be too awkward now and anyway, I don't want to upset Mum by telling her I was snooping. As it is she's like the human equivalent of Atlas (who Mrs Chatterjee says is a titan who carries the weight of the world on his shoulders). I've decided I'm just going to invite my real mother, once I've found her. Anyway, Mum and Dad will be too busy buying toys and baby blankets for the jelly bean to worry about it. I push the invite back into my bag and slide off the bed, then grab a torch and make my way to the window. Outside I can see cars whizzing past. I switch my torch on and off. "If you're out there, Rose," I whisper, "I'm sending you a sign, so we can connect. I want to live with you and have a future with you. I can't stay here any more because everything is changing around me. I don't want it to change but I can't stop it. Thing is, I'm trying to be a superhero about the whole situation – I want others to be happy." I pause. "Even if I'm not. So, like I said, I'm sending you a sign because you're my future now." To be honest, I don't know what the signal is supposed to be, but I'm sure my heart is sending a message out into the world.

Unfortunately no message comes back.

At six thirty precisely (because my stomach is rumbling and telling me it's dinner time), Mum announces she's going out to her first Bellybusters weight-watching class in the Pegasus Park Parish Hall. She's wearing a slouchy grey tracksuit and a zip-up hoodie. To Minnie's disgust, Mum says she's going to go from a couch potato to a goddess in a few weeks. From the look on Minnie's face, there's only room for one goddess in this flat and it's Minnie herself. Mum says she's going to learn about how to take care of her body both inside and out. I swallow and look at Mum's belly. It doesn't look any bigger. Not yet anyway. "There's a quinoa, lentil and sweet potato stew in the oven," says Mum, throwing her bag over her shoulder and making for the front door. "Help yourself."

When the door closes, Dad looks at me, Minnie and Velvet. "Anyone for keen-wah?" Silence descends like a heavy blanket. "Um...anyone for pizza? We could order a Hawaiian. That's got pineapple on it and I'm certain pineapple is healthy. It's got to be one of your five-a-day, along with cheese, tomatoes, bread and thick crust." Dad is nearly deafened by us screaming, "Yes!" Dad rings up Slice of Heaven and orders a giant Hawaiian and potato wedges (which he says are extra vegetables).

It arrives fifteen minutes later and the kitchen is full of the scent of melting cheese. I ask Dad if I can have some spaghetti hoops with my slice. Since Mum's been on this health kick, I've missed eating spaghetti hoops. I used to eat them from the tin cold, or I'd have them on a jacket potato with cheese, or on toast. Mum used to say I'd turn into a spaghetti hoop one day and we'd all laugh. Dad opens a tin of hoops and heats them in the microwave, then sets the bowl in front of me as everyone helps themselves to slices of pizza.

Hot tomato sauce dribbles down my chin and I wipe it away with my hand. I look around the table. Dad's laughing and I can see pineapple chunks between his teeth. Minnie's rolling her piece of pizza up like a carpet and saying the smaller the slice, the fewer the calories. Then I glance at Velvet and she's stretching a piece of cheese between her fingers like it's yellow snot. There's a pebble of sadness lodged in my belly when I think about how soon I won't be eating at this table. Forcing the thoughts away, I think of my real mother. I'll be at her table instead and I won't be living with complete strangers. This is a good thing. I'll have my own bedroom again and, just like my bedroom here, I can decorate the walls with pages from comics. It's going to be okay, I tell myself.

I don't know why, but it feels like there's an even larger pebble in my stomach now.

As soon as Mum gets back from Bellybusters she sniffs the air. "Can I smell fat?" she asks, her nose twitching like a rabbit's. "Has someone been eating pizza?" Dad's shaking his head and wiping a string of cheese off his lip. Mum wanders into the kitchen and sniffs, saying she's certain it smells of unhealthy food. It's lucky she hasn't looked under the table, because that's where Dad has hidden the boxes. Then Mum launches into this big talk about what she learned at Bellybusters and how she needs to get healthy for the future because the future is important. Her eyes water when she says "future" and suddenly I blurt out that she'd be better seeing a doctor than going to Bellybusters.

I can't believe my mouth went and said that.

Mum stops and it feels like all the air has been sucked from the room. Dad looks at me, his mouth hanging open. I swear there's still some pineapple stuck between his molars. Minnie and Velvet look confused, although Velvet usually looks confused anyway. Minnie asks why Mum needs a doctor. I can hear my heart beating and my fingertips tingle. Everyone is waiting for me to speak and when I do my voice is all shaky. "Um...I meant for your eyes. I think you've got conjunctivitis 'cause your eyes are always watering. Tiny Eric has conjunctivitis too. You've got to look after yourself, Mum."

Mum relaxes and she rubs away a tear, mumbling that I'm probably right. She promises she's looking after herself and then offers everyone some pudding she's left in the fridge. Apparently, it's called chia pudding. Mum brings out a big bowl and we all look at it in horror.

"Since when did a frog start laying spawn in the fridge?" Dad asks.

I excuse myself, saying I've got something important to do. To be honest, I don't actually have anything to do, but I'm not eating anything that looks like it belongs in a pond, even if it is as healthy as Mum says. When I get to SPAM HQ, I stare at my comic wallpaper. A tiny corner is peeling away. I poke at it. It comes away easily. *I'm a superhero.* I pull at another bit of paper. *Everyone should be happy.* A big strip of paper comes away in my hand. *Mum will smile any time soon now I'm a hero.* There's a rip as another bit of paper falls away and lands on my foot. *I'm even helping Mum get this room ready for the jelly bean by taking down the comics.* I feel the wallpaper between my toes. *I'll be okay because I'm invincible.* I stop, feeling my nose beginning to run. *I'm unstoppable.* I swallow. *I'm also worried about having a place to call home with someone who loves me.* There are lots of curls of wallpaper surrounding my bare toes by now. I've helped Mum and Dad start the nursery. It's a nice thing. Something a superhero would do. But why does it feel so awful?

Later on, as I'm heading to the bathroom before going to bed, I sense a tiny movement to my right. Mum's bedroom door is open a crack and I see her standing in front of the mirror, wearing the saggy tracksuit from earlier. She's staring at her reflection and her eyes are misty again. Suddenly she reaches out and grabs the dressing table and her knuckles are white and bloodless. A sob builds up inside her chest and silent tears flood her cheeks.

Ducking into the bathroom without a word, I lift the toilet seat and stare into the water. Mum's still sad about something and I don't know why. Why would she be sad when she's got the jelly bean on the way?

When I get back to my bedroom I pick up my bobble-hat-wearing teddy bear. "Second-in-command," I say, saluting. "You have a mission. Mum has written toys on her list. You are the best toy in this house." Dad won me this teddy bear years ago when we went to an amusement arcade. Minnie had won a toy on her first try on a claw crane machine, but I hadn't. I thought I was different and asked Dad why I couldn't be as good as Minnie. Dad said I wasn't different, that his children were all as special as each other and he tried the claw crane over and over again until he won a toy for me too. He says he probably spent about fifty pounds to win that bear. I pet the fur on the teddy's tummy and when the coast is clear I make my way down the hallway. Mum's not in the bedroom any more. I hate Mum being sad – she's the best mum ever, and even if I have to leave home, I want her to be happy after I've gone. Now I've achieved superhero status I'm putting others' happiness first and I'm not going to stop. I wipe away a small tear as I place the bear on Mum's pillow.

"Sorry to let you go, little bear," I whisper. "But you're going to get a new owner who will love you. They won't care that you wear a dirty bobble hat and your fur is a bit saggy. They won't care that you started off with someone else. They will hug you and tell you that you're amazing every day, I promise. That's the sort of parents they are."

I close the door behind me.

13

ZAP

The following day, Mrs Chatterjee welcomes us to the class but tells us not to park our bums, as though our bums are types of cars. "We're going out this fine Tuesday morning," states Mrs Chatterjee, jiggling her foot from side to side. I watch as the tassels on her shoes do a little tango. "Gather together your notebooks and pens, because we're off to the Pegasus Park Library to do more research on our family trees. There you'll find out anything you need to know."

It feels like I've swallowed a moth and it's fluttering inside my belly. My head prickles under my hat and my breath quickens. Find out everything you need to know? Maybe even your real mother's address? This is going to be epic. I pat the four-leaf clover in my pocket, thinking that it's bringing me more luck at last.

"The library has access to old newspaper files containing stories of local residents, and they've got local notices and electoral rolls," continues Mrs Chatterjee. "They've got shelves of historical documents about Pegasus Park too. They have books on genealogy, so you can look up family names. Plus the librarian can help you with any questions you might have. Everything you need for research on your family and the local area will be at your fingertips. And before you think you could find all this information on the Internet yourself, you can't. The library has so many more local archives than you'd ever find on the net." Mrs Chatterjee snaps her fingers and Nish suddenly wakes up. "Gather yourselves together and those of you still half asleep, stop drooling on the table."

Everyone laughs as Nish wipes his chin.

We line up like ducklings and as we waddle towards the school gates, Mrs Chatterjee says she's hoping we'll find out something exciting at the library. "Wouldn't it be fabulous if you were related to a pirate?" I'm thinking that's not likely in Pegasus Park. "Or what if you were related to a famous person or an astronaut who walked on the moon?"

Memories stir inside me of how, when I was much younger, I sometimes imagined my real mother was an astronaut or a queen and that I was a prince. I was sure she had to be someone incredible, which would make me incredible too. But I always kept my thoughts to myself, because I worried that they might sound stupid.

Mrs Chatterjee, assisted by Mrs Finch from the school office, herds us out of the school grounds and cautiously steps out into the road, halting all the traffic so that we can mooch across. Then she carefully follows us, nodding to all the motorists, who are bleeping and waving her off the road because she's so slow. One bloke leans out of his car and shouts that he wasn't expecting a herd of snails travelling through peanut butter, and then he zooms off before Mrs Chatterjee can give him a piece of her mind. He's lucky, because when we get a piece of Mrs Chatterjee's mind, it takes for ever.

The library is a fifteen-minute walk from the school and it's in a large brick building with five storeys. Inside there are lots of books, bunting, posters and comfy armchairs. Nish runs over to one and flops down into it and the leather makes a funny squeaking sound like new shoes. "Pardon me," he laughs.

"Get over here," says Mrs Chatterjee sharply and she puffs out her chest until the buttons on her floral blouse strain. "We're in a room on the right."

The room we're directed to by Mrs Finch is full of documents and shelves spilling over with newspapers and desks with banks of computers. There are lots of hard plastic chairs that give you pins and needles in your bum. Mrs Chatterjee tells us to be seated and Tiny Eric sits down, rolling his tie up and then letting go of it like it's a yo-yo.

After Mrs Chatterjee explains how to begin our research, she tells us to get digging. Nish's eyes light up and Mrs Chatterjee says it's not actual digging. Nish's eyes dull down and he clicks on his computer mouse. Mrs Chatterjee gives us details of a newspaper archive we can access. The first thing I do is go to the *Pegasus Park Packet* site and type in *ROSE WALKER*, hoping I'll find more about her. Like Mrs Chatterjee said, perhaps there will be a story since she was a local resident. My body is tenser than the time I had to play the recorder at prize-giving. Nothing comes up and I sip in tiny breaths. Perhaps it was stupid to think I'd find out something so easily.

Mrs Chatterjee bellows, "I expect at least one tag to be filled by the time you finish here. At *least* one.

If at first you don't succeed…"

"Give up?" whispers Nish, and Mrs Chatterjee rushes towards him with a face like thunder. I bet he's about to get a piece of her mind.

Next I type in *ADAM BUTTERS*. There's a small pause, which I know means there is some information coming, and I straighten up, my eyes glued to the screen. Keywords flash up: *Adam Swimming Pool Water Baby Sinéad Butters*. At first I'm confused why my name and Mum's name have come up along with the swimming pool. This isn't what I'm looking for. But I click on the article anyway and hold my breath as the screen flickers. Then the world shifts around me and it's as if I'm standing still in the middle of it. No one notices that I'm frozen because they're all moving as if nothing's happening. But it is. It's happening inside me. I stare at the words on the screen:

THE PEGASUS PARK WATER BABY

SINÉAD BUTTERS, 29, FOUND HER VERY OWN WATER BABY YESTERDAY ON THE WAY TO AN EVENING SWIMMING LESSON AT PEGASUS PARK POOL.

Last night, Sinéad Butters of 53 Pegasus Park

Towers, heard a baby crying as she neared the pool. According to Sinéad, the crying came from a dark area with no street lamps near the rubbish bins. "I could have easily passed by or stood on the baby if I hadn't heard it crying." Sinéad went on to say, "It was as if I was supposed to find the baby and I'm so glad I did. It was a cold night."

Sinéad accompanied the baby to Pegasus Park Hospital, where it was checked over by doctors. The baby, a boy, was in good health and showed no signs of hypothermia. He was wrapped in a pale blue blanket and beside him was a plastic bag containing clothing.

The police have located the baby's mother and are discussing options with her regarding the baby's future. When asked by our reporter why the baby was left there, the police said they weren't at liberty to discuss the exact details and that social services would be dealing with the case. The baby, who has been named Adam by the nurses at Pegasus Park Hospital, is being cared for.

"He was the sweetest boy," said Sinéad Butters, on finding Adam. "I'm so glad I found him. I reached out and he gripped my hand, but really he captured my heart."

I feel tiny spots of sweat building on my forehead and my brain is so muddled up I can't think straight. My head turns, and it feels like it's in slow motion. Tiny Eric is frowning and drawing in his notebook and Nish's hand is up and I can see Mrs Chatterjee walking towards him, but my bum cheeks are stuck to my seat. My eyes swivel back to the screen.

I was dumped by the bins, I tell myself over and over again. This is epic, but not the type of epic I'd hoped for. Slowly I read the article once more and words jump out at me, particularly the ones about how the police were discussing options. "Why didn't you take me back?" I whisper dully.

"Huh?" Tiny Eric looks over at me and then twirls his pencil around his fingers as though it's a baton.

"Sorry," I mumble, looking back at the screen. "I was talking to myself." Tiny Eric says he does that sometimes too. As I stare at the article, I try to squeeze down a million feelings, but they keep popping back up. With shaking hands, I pull the tag towards me and write, *Why didn't you take me back?* in sharp black letters.

The rest of the morning passes in a blur. I just can't stop thinking that I was left at the pool by my real mother. And that it was Mum who found me.

In the afternoon, when we're back in class, Mrs Chatterjee says she hopes we all had a productive morning at the library. "Raise your hands if you discovered something that surprised you." No one does, but inside I'm thinking, *Is discovering you've been left by the bins at the pool surprising enough? It certainly surprised me.*

Teacher alert! Mrs Chatterjee is zeroing in on me. The hairs on the back of my neck are standing to attention like miniature soldiers. My eyes swiftly drop to the floor, but looking away doesn't stop a teacher when her mind is made up. "Adam, what did you discover?" I can feel my head shake and twenty-eight pairs of eyeballs latch onto me like zombies at feeding time. Mrs Chatterjee continues, "Well, if you didn't find out anything in particular about an ancestor, why don't you tell us about one of your family? Your mum, for example. I was impressed by the list you wrote about her previously. Elaborate on that."

It feels like my brain is torn in half. One half is trying to think of Rose, my real mother, but the other half keeps pulling me back to Mum. And when I think of Mum, I think of the fun days when she was all sunshine and happiness. "My mum..." I say, rising from my seat. The classroom is mine but the words won't come.

My throat dries and I struggle as my mind goes to Rose and the swimming pool. Stumbling over the words, I manage to remember the list I made before about what I thought my mother would be like. I say, "She'll be loving – she's going to love me and her hugs will be so incredible that it'll be like getting lost in a giant duvet and never wanting to come out... She'll be thoughtful." My eyes stray towards the window and out to the horizon. I continue haltingly, "She'll remember every birthday and she'll bake me a cake and it won't matter how busy she is, she'll be there celebrating it with me... She'll be kind and take care of me and she'll make me laugh, even if she doesn't like comics." Mrs Chatterjee doesn't say a word but I can sense she's nodding. "And she'll be there for me. When it's dark she won't leave me and it'll be okay. She'll give me a home where I'm safe." I sit down to silence.

There's a slow clap from Mrs Chatterjee and it builds until everyone else in the classroom is clapping too. "I'm so impressed by the relationship between you and your mother," says Mrs Chatterjee. "From what you've just told us she sounds like the perfect parent, and I'm sure she would love to hear what you think of her." Mrs Chatterjee says I deserve a gold star and she takes one from her drawer and puts it on the board next to my name. "One little thing," adds Mrs Chatterjee. "Remember your tenses. You meant to say your mother *is* loving, she *is* thoughtful, she *is* funny and she *is* there for me. Not that she *will be* – that suggests you haven't met her yet."

I didn't get the tenses wrong at all. I think again about how my real mother left me by the bins and my stomach does a somersault. I'm nervous about looking for Rose now, but Mum and Dad need to make sacrifices, they said so. It was Mum who found me and I feel like I owe her. She did something amazing for me eleven years ago and now it's my turn to return the favour. It has to be me who goes.

The rest of the afternoon I stare out the window, and the time passes so slowly I swear I've aged about one hundred years by the time the school bell rings. On the way home I'm dragging my feet like a clown in big shoes wading through jelly. Being a superhero hasn't been as much fun as I thought it would be. Perhaps I was stupid to think I could make everyone happy and the world would be perfect just because I saved one person's life. I can't even make myself happy and the world is definitely not perfect at the moment. Even the gold star I was given for talking about my mother hasn't made things better. But at least things can't get any worse.

Wrong. They can and they do thanks to Mum. She's dashing out the door with Velvet when I get home from school. She says she's got to get to the shops for some gluten-free bread, but she'll need a lottery win soon, considering how much this healthy food is costing her. I think that I could ask the four-leaf clover for a windfall of cash later on if that would help. "Where's Minnie?" I mutter and Mum says she's at rehearsals. Apparently the Scottish play is on Tuesday in two weeks' time.

"Tuesday the 29th?"

"Yes," confirms Mum, looking into her purse and appearing to reel back as if moths have just flown out. "We're all going to support Minnie. You're free, aren't you?" The way Mum says it, she's not asking a question, she's saying I'm bound to be free.

I think of the *Forest For Ever* exhibition clashing with *Macbeth* and I nod but I don't say a thing. Instead I watch as Mum bustles Velvet out the door, but then she turns back to me and says, "I think you accidentally left your teddy bear on our bed so I've put him back on yours. But it was nice to see him." Mum continues, "I noticed the walls in your bedroom. What happened?"

I mumble something about her wanting to decorate.

"Right," replies Mum, tucking her hair behind her ears. "I was thinking more about stripping them properly and getting a decorator in, but I can't be annoyed at you wanting to help."

"I'm a big help," I mutter despondently.

When the front door closes and Mum and Velvet have gone, taking a barking Sausage Roll with them, I throw myself on the sofa. Tiny bubbles of hurt and confusion burst inside me when I think of how Mum found me at the swimming pool. Truth is, I'm so grateful she did, but why didn't Mum tell me anything about it? There's so much I don't know about myself and the person I came from.

Eventually I rise from the sofa and wander into the bathroom and pull off my bobble hat and stare at my face, copper hair spilling forward. There's a crease of worry on my forehead and I rub my eye before leaning in to the mirror. My eyes are brown like conkers. Does my real mother have conker eyes too?

That's how it feels to be adopted. Your face doesn't look like anyone else's you know. You search it over and over, but you never get answers. So you imagine answers and you imagine your mother and sometimes it helps but not always.

Brrring-brrring-brrring. The phone chirrups cheerfully from the hallway so I pull my bobble hat back on and hurry towards it. When I pick up the handset there's so much crackling it sounds like popping candy on your tongue. But I do make out the words "Pegasus Park Adoption and Rehoming Centre".

"Hello," I mumble cautiously.

"Yes, you phoned and talked to us about adoption and rehoming. We're more than happy to help you."

Now there's more crackling on the line than popping candy on a pork chop with crackling.

"Oh, right. Mum's not here."

"Ah, sorry about that. I can call back another time."

The line fizzles and the woman thanks me for my time and says goodbye and I say goodbye. I only managed seven words in the whole conversation and those seven words nearly choked me. I stumble back to my bedroom and find my notebook in my school bag and I write:

IMPORTANT INFORMATION RECEIVED:
The rehoming is happening because the phone call proves it.

MUM: She's still in an odd mood.

DAD: He's being extra-nice to Mum and I think that happens when you're having a *baby*. They said so on the TV programme that Mum loves about babies. Yesterday I saw him rub Mum's back to cheer her up but she said he had fingers like a bunch of bananas. Dad said he was sorry his massage didn't appeal. Then he laughed but Mum had no idea why until he said "Peel" and "Get it?". (It doesn't work if you have to explain a joke.)

NEW THOUGHTS: There has to be an explanation as to why I was left at a swimming pool.

There's a sudden pang in my stomach when I think that I could go to the swimming pool, right this minute. The house is empty and it wouldn't take me long to run there and back before Mum returns with a gluten-free loaf. No one is around to ask where I'm going.

I look down at my school shirt, not realizing I've been crying for the past few minutes. There's a damp splash on the blue. It looks like a small swimming pool.

14

THUNK

In the ten minutes it's taken me to run to the pool, I haven't been able to stop thinking about my real mother. A soft drizzle begins to fall and covers me like a damp cobweb. The windows are steamy and a few people come out, their hair in wet ribbons, and they're laughing as if they haven't a care in the world. I bet they've all got a home with their real mothers. Quickly I duck into the shadows and make my way towards the back of the pool where the bins are. It's a place I've never been before.

Then I remember I *have* been here before.

I was here eleven years ago.

It makes my stomach drop.

As I settle into the shadows, I breathe in the scent of old chicken nuggets and damp moss and I feel so alone. My body is weak as a baby kitten as I lean against the brick wall. My feet manoeuvre around discarded tissues and food cartons from Good Buy, Mr Chips. It's a dumping ground, I tell myself. There's a shiver travelling through me and it makes my shoulders shake.

Slowly, I sink further down the wall until my bum hits the concrete and I pull my knees tight up to my chest. An icy breeze wraps itself around me and I hear laughter and it's getting closer and through the drizzle I can see a rainbow umbrella. It makes me think of Mum and how she says there's always a rainbow after rain. The umbrella comes closer and there's more laughter and it rises slightly and I can see a couple. The man kisses the woman and they smile at each other and for a second I think I recognize the man, but I can't place him. It bugs me for a minute, not being able to remember where I know him from, but then I realize I don't really care and the thought disappears into the drizzle. All I care about is my real mother. A stupid part of my brain thinks that she might just walk past in a minute, but I know deep in my heart that she won't.

"You're not coming," I whisper to myself. "You're not

coming back for me. I'm here waiting for you and you're not coming back." Crescent moons appear on my palms as my nails dig in and I have to swallow down a sob.

When my bum's completely numb I awkwardly rise up the wall again and trudge back home, glad of the rain making my face wet. That way no one can tell if they're raindrops or teardrops. Mum's back home when I return and she's putting the world's most expensive bread in the bread bin, saying it costs more than gold bars. Glancing up, she asks where I've been. "Nowhere," I mumble, wiping rain from my face.

"Nowhere?" echoes Mum. "Is that in Pegasus Park?" Her eyes meet mine and I'm afraid she can see into my heart and will know how I'm feeling. At this point I want to confide in Mum but when I search her eyes I swear they look sadder than a puppy dog waiting for a walk. I can't do it. I can't say where I've been and what I've been doing. I'm a superhero and I'm strong, I tell myself, even if I only half-believe it. My eyes are damp and I give my nose a swift wipe, and then I stare at my feet as if the world's most interesting comic is on my toes and I'm reading it.

"I went out for a walk. It's raining." The words eventually tumble out. "Does a rainbow always come after the rain?"

Mum seems surprised by the change of subject. "A rainbow always comes after the rain, but you can't always see it, if that makes sense." It doesn't. "Did you want to find one today? Is that why you went out?"

I shrug. There was no rainbow.

Mum tilts her head to the side and I can almost see the cogs in her brain beginning to move. "Is this about rainbows or you?"

"Things are changing around me," I whisper. "Every time I think I've got a glimmer of a rainbow, I get closer and it disappears."

"This is a tricky year," says Mum. "The last year of primary school always is. You've got senior school in September and that's a big step and it's natural to feel like your world is changing, but don't be afraid." I want to scream that this isn't about senior school, but I don't. "Sometimes change is a good thing. Otherwise everything would stay the same and we wouldn't move forward. And as we move, we learn and grow. You know, if you've got a problem it's always worth sharing it."

Changing the subject, I ask, "Was it a hard decision to adopt me?" I look up at Mum, gazing into her eyes for the answer. It comes within a millisecond.

"It was the easiest decision I ever made," replies

Mum, touching my shoulder. "It was also the best. Nothing would have made me let you go."

But mums do let you go, I tell myself. I look at Mum and I feel a golf ball squeeze into my throat. Mum smiles and I want to spill out everything I'm feeling. I want to say I'm happy she's having a baby but I'm sad that it means I've got to go. I want to say I'm scared about leaving behind the only home I've ever had. But the words still won't come. I think they're lost.

The following day I catch up with Tiny Eric in the playground. "You asked me why I needed good luck." The words burble out. "And I want to explain, because Mum said if you've got a problem it's always worth sharing, and I've got a problem." I take a deep breath. "So you know I'm adopted?" Tiny Eric nods. "Well, guess what? I decided I wanted to do my *Forest For Ever* project on my real family, so I found an envelope with my birth certificate inside, and my real name is Ace and that's got to be the name of a..." I pause.

"A superhero," says Tiny Eric. "That's why you really want to be one." Whispering, I tell Tiny Eric that he's right and that I'm looking for my real mother now because I need to live with her. "Whoa!" exclaims Tiny

Eric and he rubs his nose so hard I half expect a genie to shoot out in a puff of smoke.

"Whoa indeed," I reply, nodding my head. I feel the bobble on my hat move. When Tiny Eric asks why I need to live with her, I say, "Things have got complicated, because Mum and Dad are having a jelly bean. Mum said she wouldn't let me go, but mums do let you go. That's confusing to me. Everything is."

"Families are confusing," says Tiny Eric, nodding sagely. Then he adds, "Back up! A jelly bean?" Tiny Eric blinks and then scratches his head so much I'm beginning to wonder if he's got nits. I edge away slightly, because that's the last thing I need. "They're having a jelly bean. Seriously, a jelly bean? What flavour? You mean like a classic, or a sour, or those jelly beans that taste of stinky socks and vomit?"

I sigh, "Not a real jelly bean, you idiot. Jelly bean is just the name for the size of a baby. I saw it on a TV programme. Mum and Dad have to make sacrifices. We're packed together in our flat like sardines. So, I think I'm the sacrifice and I have to leave to make room for the baby."

I know Tiny Eric is interested, because he leans in towards my face. He asks how I feel and I say I don't *know* how I feel. Tiny Eric shakes his head and says,

"It's hard thinking you're going to live with someone else, especially if you don't know them well. What if you miss your bedroom?" I nod and Tiny Eric says, "And what if you have to go to a different school and you don't have your mates there and you worry about that and it keeps you awake but your mum says it'll be okay. Then she says you'd be changing schools anyway because you're going to a senior school." Tiny Eric has hardly paused for breath.

"Uh, okay," I reply. "I hadn't thought about the school and my mates, but now you've mentioned it I will." I pause for a second before adding, "I'd hate to be without you, Tiny Eric."

Tiny Eric rubs his eyes and mutters, "Conjunctivitis again."

After I've told Tiny Eric the whole story, he asks me what my next move is and I tell him I'm not sure. I explain that I've exhausted the Internet and haven't got any more clues as to where Rose Walker might be. "It's like finding a pin in a pigsty," I say sullenly. "And I've got so many questions for her."

"You know the area where you were born though, so we could try the local hospital to see if they've got any information on her. They'd have her address if she was a patient." When I say I never thought of that, Tiny Eric beams and says it's lucky that he did. Then the smile drops. "They keep files, you know. And if you're moving or changing doctors, you can have them. My mum's been trying to sort out our medical records recently." Tiny Eric swallows. "I bet they've got your mum's address."

"But would they tell me her address, if I asked? Could I be that lucky?"

Tiny Eric says, "Take out the four-leaf clover and stare at it."

I pull the drawing from my pocket and do what Tiny Eric instructs. "Um...it's not giving me the answer," I say, looking up.

"It's a four-leaf clover," says Tiny Eric. "Not a crystal ball."

While Mrs Chatterjee is talking about trust and getting us to fall back into each other's arms during our PSHE lesson, Tiny Eric and I make a plan. We agree that we'll text our mums to say that we're doing homework club after school and then we'll actually go to the hospital. Mrs Chatterjee is shouting that trust is a key issue in a relationship between two people. I tell Tiny Eric I trust him not to tell anyone what I'm up to and he nods. Tiny

Eric looks like he wants to tell me something too, but then Mrs Chatterjee shouts that Tiny Eric is supposed to be behind me and catching me if I fall back and we're not supposed to be gabbling away like two chimps at a tea party.

I fall back and Tiny Eric catches me. Then I straighten up again.

Nish falls back just as the bell goes. A second later he's in a heap on the floor and everyone is stampeding over him like bulls trying to get out of the china shop.

"What about giving me a superhero name too?" asks Tiny Eric as we hurry down the corridors towards the exit. "If you're Ace, who can I be? What about Lizard?"

"Taken," I reply, swinging open the door to the playground.

"Okay, how about Atom?"

"Taken."

"Okay, what about Storm Cobra or Wild Shadow of the Night or Pegasus Park Phantom, or how about Wings of Justice? Or how about Captain Encryptor?"

"Not taken," I reply. "Definitely not taken." This is clearly on account of it being total gobbledygook. Then Tiny Eric says we're missing something. "A mask? Pants?" I say, taking the steps two at a time. Tiny Eric looks at me in disgust as we walk through the playground and says he's wearing his. Then he says we're missing transport that befits a crime-fighting duo. I don't like to say that we're not actually fighting crime, all we're doing is trying to find out information that will lead me to my real mother. There's a big cough behind us and we both turn round and The Beast gives us a smile.

"How's that broken watch?"

"I'm still wearing it," I reply, looking down at my wrist. "And it's still broken," I add.

The Beast falls into the rhythm of our steps. "So, what are you doing now, are you going home?" When I say we're going on a mission, The Beast's eyes grow wide. "I like missions. I'm good with things like that. If you asked me about the missions of any superhero, I could tell you." The Beast waits as if hoping to be invited on ours.

Tiny Eric pretends to be hard of hearing and The Beast keeps trying to jump into our conversation without success. Eventually Tiny Eric says, "Don't you need to go and be with your mates from your class? You're not in our class." Other kids push past us, laughing, and The Beast glances at them. We part like the Red Sea as more kids surge through the playground.

The Beast looks at me across the crowd and a little part of me would like to ask The Beast about superheroes.

I didn't know The Beast was interested in anything like that, but now I'm certain it must have been The Beast at Comic Con. I smile, but before The Beast can smile back, Tiny Eric hisses, "You don't like The Beast, do you?"

"No," I say a bit too quickly. "Have you seen that holly bush in the far corner of the playground? I don't want to end up in there." I feel my face flush and The Beast looks at me and then away. I think The Beast heard me.

"Yeah, you wouldn't want to get into a fight with the Beast," whispers Tiny Eric, pulling me away. "Anyway, we've got bigger fish to fry at the moment." As I glance back, I swear The Beast is frowning at me, and I feel a tiny bit guilty about what I said.

At the top of Agamemnon Road, Tiny Eric stops in front of someone's garden and reminds me we need transport. "I present...the Binmobile," says Tiny Eric, waving his hands around. He might as well have announced that we are not crime busters, we are *grime* busters.

"I'm not sure this is the mode of transport I had in mind, Tiny Eric. I was expecting something sleek and black with go-faster wheels, not a wheelie bin." Tiny Eric doesn't answer me and I repeat what I've just said, and when I say it for the third time Tiny Eric reminds me his name is Captain Encryptor and he will only answer to that. It is Captain Encryptor who pulls the bin out and helps me into it and I'm thanking my lucky four-leaf clover that it is bin day and this one is empty. Meanwhile, Captain Encryptor clings onto the back and says this is an adventure and we'll be at our destination in double quick time. Captain Encryptor pushes us off and we're heading down Agamemnon Road.

Whooooooosh.

That's the sound of wind whistling through my bobble hat.

Whooooooosh.

That's the sound of wind whistling through my stomach.

Whooooooosh.

That's my life flashing in front of my eyes.

The houses are a blurry smear as Captain Encryptor and I, Ace, the-kid-nearly-peeing-his-pants, speed down the pavement in the Binmobile. An old lady who is in the way and in danger of being flattened by the speeding wheelie bin turns and runs in the opposite direction as fast as her legs will carry her, which is quite fast considering she's over forty-five and has probably had a hip replacement.

"The brakes," I shout as we hurtle to the bottom of the hill at breakneck speed.

"Yes," Captain Encryptor hollers back.

"It doesn't have any." I've just finished the sentence when the Binmobile slams into a wall and I become a human catapult, whizzing through the air before landing in a painful heap. Behind me I hear Captain Encryptor say that he didn't know I could fly but he supposes all superheroes can.

To say I'm annoyed is the understatement of the millennium. As we walk in the direction of the hospital, Captain Encryptor is saying that it wasn't his fault there was a wall in the wrong place and I'm saying that it wasn't the wall's fault that there was a bin hurtling towards it with two lunatics on board. Captain Encryptor asks where my sense of adventure is and I'm saying it's on the ground beside the wall, along with the contents of my stomach.

We head down past the precinct, past the shop where Velvet gets her sweets and along the street where the senior school kids hang out, and then past Sharkey's, which has a missing cat poster in the window. It catches my eye because it looks a bit like the cat I tried to save.

After ten minutes, Pegasus Park Hospital appears in the distance and I stop, feeling my breath catch in my throat. Suddenly everything feels different. I didn't know I'd feel this way, because I've passed the hospital lots of times, but this time something inside me has changed. A tiny part of me keeps saying my real mother was here and I was here with her and that makes my insides melt. The afternoon sun dips the hospital in golden yolk and I can see people scuttling in and out as we get closer. I inhale as we step inside and I feel a shiver ribbon down my spine.

The reception is the colour of mint chocolate-chip ice cream and I'm so busy looking around and imagining my real mother coming in here that I don't notice the small, polite cough. Captain Encryptor wanders over to the reception desk and the lady there looks at him and says, "Hello, sir, what is your name?"

"Captain Encryptor," says Tiny Eric. The woman jerks her head back and then asks if she can help.

Captain Encryptor snorts. "He is Ace and I am Captain Encryptor."

"They're our superhero names. I guess you want our alter-ego names," I clarify. "You know, like Bruce Banner."

"Who is Bruce Banner?"

"He turns green," I say, pretending to bulk up as I stand in front of the desk. "He was badly affected by gamma radiation that contaminated his cells."

"Contaminated cells?" The woman looks at us. "Is Bruce Banner in an isolation unit in this hospital?"

"I don't think so, although he's a physicist." The woman peers at us and taps her pen on the desk. "He's The Incredible Hulk, from the comic books – that's why he's got two names," I continue. "I'm actually Adam *and* Ace, but Adam will do. And I'm here to find out about my mother. Would you have her medical records and her address?"

"What's her name?" Exasperated, the receptionist's fingers dangle over the computer keys. "And what is she in here for?"

I swallow and all my senses tingle as I say, "Her name is Rose Walker and she had a baby here."

There's the *tap-tap-tap* of the computer keys and the receptionist peers at the screen and then peers at me. "Is it an unusual spelling?" I tell her it isn't, it's just Rose as in the flower and Walker as in Luke Sky. The receptionist looks at me and then *tap-tap-taps* again and asks, "When was she admitted to maternity?"

"Eleven years ago." I shuffle from one foot to the other. Annoyingly, Captain Encryptor asks if I've got ants in my pants and I say no, but I'm going to have fun kicking him in the bum in a second if he doesn't shut up and let me talk. Then I remind him that he nearly killed me after throwing me in a wheelie bin and Captain Encryptor says that was a load of rubbish and I agree and say it was.

Meanwhile, Mrs Receptionist Lady, who I have decided should be called The Glacier like an arch villain from this moment on, is giving me the full force of her frosty features. And I am giving her the full glare of whatever sliver of excellence I still hold after the bin incident. It's a stand-off. She purses her lips together and asks me to repeat myself and when I do she repeats it back, confirming that my mother was admitted to maternity eleven years ago.

"Uh-huh," I reply. It's like the mothership has landed and it all makes sense to her now. "Eleven years," I repeat. "But my other mother is having a baby now."

The Glacier thaws and lifts her fingers again and says, "Ah, so your other mother is in the hospital right now and her name is..."

"Sinéad Butters," I reply. The Glacier types it in and she looks at the screen and then she says, "Maternity," in a funny strangled voice and I go, "Yes." She leans in, squinting at the computer screen, then shakes her head for a brief moment. I feel like we're getting off track, so I say it's actually Rose Walker I want to find out about, and she looks at me and asks if that's the person who was here eleven years ago.

"That's right," says Captain Encryptor.

Exasperated, The Glacier says she can't help with someone's medical records from a birth eleven years ago and anyway medical records are confidential. Then she points us towards the door.

So we pretend to go to the door but we don't actually leave – and when the receptionist looks down at her computer, we rush past and down the hospital corridor. "Come on," says Captain Encryptor. "Maybe there are filing cabinets in maternity. Maybe her address would be there." He's pointing at a sign and saying that maternity is on the third floor. He flings open a side door and pulls me up the concrete stairs two at a time and we come out into maternity, floor three. "Come on," shouts Captain Encryptor. "We've reached our destination."

I stop.

I'm nervous.

This is where it all began for me.

This is where Ace, the superhero, was born.

15

BLAM

The maternity ward isn't mint-green like reception, it's the colour of sunshine and fluffy chicks and daffodils and it feels warm like a summer's day. As I wander down the corridor, the same thoughts keep tumbling inside my head: my real mother came here. I'm walking in her footsteps. I'm breathing the same air. I wonder if her hands were shaking like mine are now and if she knew she was having a boy? Had she picked my name? Did she think I'd be a superhero when I got older? Was she going to keep me and then something changed? As I'm daydreaming, I can hear someone further down the corridor walking towards us and they're talking about someone being in stitches and I don't think they mean laughing.

Captain Encryptor looks at me and I look up at him and then he opens the first door to our right and says, "We can hide in here until they've passed."

The room is a dim cavern and my eyes try to adjust to the darkness. Then I hear lapping water and a strange echoey noise surrounding me, almost like we're underwater. What's going on?

"It's Moby Dick," I hiss. "Remember when Mrs Chatterjee once talked about this book called *Moby Dick* and he was a giant whale. No superhero can beat Moby Dick in a fight. It's me against fifteen thousand kilograms of blubber." My heart has turned into a rubber ball and bounced up into my mouth. The whale sings around us and rivers of sweat burst from under my bobble hat. I'm about to scream when the lights come on and I'm dazzled.

Captain Encryptor is standing by the light switch.

Oh.

It seems there is a large birthing pool in the corner of the room and whale music coming from speakers above our heads. I recognize the pool from seeing one similar on Mum's TV programme. As I let out a puff of pure relief that I don't have to take on a whale, Tiny Eric peers out a glass porthole in the door and says the coast is clear again. It's time to go before we get discovered.

We walk down the corridors but we can't see any filing cabinets or files and it looks like we're not going to find my mother's address here. When we get back to reception The Glacier looks at us but then the phone rings, so we manage to get outside without her asking us where we've been.

As we're walking home I tell Tiny Eric I'm more cheesed off than a warehouse full of Cheddar. "Why does it feel like everything is so complicated?"

Tiny Eric furrows his brow. He thinks for a moment and his fingers tighten into fists. "I don't know." Tiny Eric shrugs. "Maybe it's because adults keep secrets and they do things that don't make sense. That makes things complicated and it annoys me so much. Everything does."

I stare at Tiny Eric, my eyes wide. Clearly something is bothering him, so I ask him what's wrong. At first he says there's nothing. For a while we continue walking and Tiny Eric scratches his ear while I look up into the clouds.

"You're right, there's a problem," Tiny Eric finally admits, shoving his hands into his pockets. "It's my mum and dad. They say we need to make changes but I don't want changes."

"What kind of changes?" I feel my hand reach out and brush his arm before I pull it away again. Tiny Eric says it's a long story and I say I like long stories even though I don't.

"They think we should move house." I blink because it doesn't sound like that big a deal. People move all the time. "But I don't want to because I like our house and our street. *Babcia* agrees that moving is the best idea but *babcia* doesn't know everything. They just keep saying it's for the best. But who is it best for? It's not best for me."

"Oh," I say.

"It's Dad." Tiny Eric brings his hands out of his pockets and runs his fingers through his hair. "He's got these plans. Dad's changed." His eyes glisten.

"Oh," I repeat.

I look at Tiny Eric and say nothing. I know he's probably just saying this about his dad because he's angry. Now I realize why he was drawing his dad as a monster and why he drew himself crying in the window of a new house. It's because he's annoyed with his dad's plans to move. But the thing is, Tiny Eric's lucky that he's got his mum and dad, and moving house is no big deal. At least he'll still be with his family. I want to say this but Tiny Eric is already stalking ahead.

I chase after him and thank him for coming to the hospital with me. "You're a great Captain Encryptor," I add.

"I'd rather be myself really. I don't want to pretend to be someone else," he replies. "Anyway, Captain Encryptor is a silly name." I don't remind him that he came up with it. Tiny Eric grins and then gives me a friendly punch to the arm and I give him a friendly punch to the belly, and we laugh as we wander through the housing estates of Pegasus Park. At the corner of Kink Street, Tiny Eric says this is his stop. We look down the street and there's a tall woman and a man standing beside her and he's banging a board into Tiny Eric's garden. It says *FOR SALE*. Tiny Eric pauses and then he says he'd better go because that's his mum and she'll be looking out for him. The weird thing is that Tiny Eric is a giant, but as he walks down the street he looks as small as a character from that book *The Borrowers*.

When I return home, Mum's at Bellybusters again and Velvet's at a party with her friend. Dad's alone in the kitchen and he's got the same wooden sticks and plastic on the table as he had that time when he said he was making a wish. He brings out some nylon string and sets that on the table too, alongside a piece of cardboard. I sit down in the seat beside him.

"What are you making exactly, Dad? You said it was a wish before, but I didn't know what you meant."

"It's a wish kite to be precise," replies Dad. "I was talking to a man at Comic Con about how to get them right. You're supposed to write a poem and tie it to the kite's tail and then fly your kite as high as possible to make the wish come true." Dad then disappears out of the kitchen before returning to the table with a ruler, scissors and a black marker pen.

"I used to wish on birthday candles," I offer.

"Did any come true?"

I reply, "Not yet, but they will."

Dad smiles and he says he's sure they will and then I feel my face heat up and I change the subject and ask about Granddad Fred instead. I wind some of the nylon string around a stick.

"He was a great dad," explains Dad. "But I suppose everyone says stuff like that. He didn't have the best start in the world but it didn't make any difference to him – because, you know, it's not always how you start the race in life, but how you continue running that counts."

I nod, but I'm not sure why we're talking about races.

Dad measures a red plastic bag and then cuts it using the scissors. "Granddad Fred was adopted."

I gulp. "Adopted?" I feel the watch, heavy on my wrist.

"Yes, as a baby. He never knew who his mother was. Don't look so surprised," adds Dad, taking two thin sticks and forming a cross.

"But, Dad..." I hesitate and then all the words spill from my lips. "Didn't he want to find his real family? Wasn't there always a little piece of him missing even if he was happy?"

Dad carefully opens the lid of the glue and shakes his head. "He thought about it for a while and he tried, but it didn't work out. But he was happy anyway." Dad smiles and says, "I loved my dad and I love you. Adopting you was important to me."

I feel my throat burn and my stomach flips over. Dad asks me if I like the watch. "It's an important watch because Granddad Fred loved it. In fact, he made it. He was always making things. He said the watch was like a beating heart for the whole family." Dad points to the clock tattoo on his arm. "That's why I have the clock on my arm. It reminds me of a beating heart. It reminds me of my amazing family."

My finger traces the heart-shaped kite that Dad's just made. He attaches the nylon line and a long tail and he gives me the black marker. As he gets up to put the scissors away, he asks me what I wish for. "Write what you want most and we'll let it fly with the kite and the wish might come true."

I think for a second, then I take the lid off the pen and write on a piece of paper: *MUM*. I don't meet Dad's eye as I write it because I feel sick. Inside it's as if I'm being stretched apart like a cheese string. Dad pulls me into a hug and he feels warm and safe and I don't want the hug to end but it does.

"It's great that your wish is for Mum. Mum would love that."

I mumble something but even I don't know what it is, because everything is all jumbled up in my head. I've written the word *MUM* on the wish kite but I don't know which mum the wish is for.

16

KABOOM

The wind on the top of the hill gently whips at my bobble hat and tugs at my coat. Dad strides ahead, saying how much he loves kite-flying and that it's a huge rush working with the wind, going whatever way it takes you. Pegasus Park is beginning to twinkle with lights as Dad tries to untangle the line of the kite, yanking the nylon string.

I look up into the twilight sky – orange gives way to inky blue and the tiny dot-to-dot of stars is appearing. Our hot breath makes white popcorn clouds rise into the cold air. For a while I forget about the jelly bean in Mum's tummy and being rehomed; I even forget I'm an extraordinary superhero and that I have to find my real mother. Instead, I'm just ordinary Adam and I'm with my dad and we're going to fly the wish kite together.

Once Dad has checked everything, we walk away from the kite, unravelling some line as we go. "You can fly this, Adam," Dad says. "Just like my dad let me fly a kite he once built for me. Guess what I wished for back then?"

"You wished for money?"

"Don't be daft. I wished for a Scalextric." Dad laughs and starts telling me how it was this brilliant slot car racing set. Dad tries to unravel more of the line and he runs backwards until he falls over some stones. I laugh so hard I have to stop myself from joining him in a heap on the ground. "Thank you very much, Adam." Dad hauls himself back up. "I never said I was a rock climber." For some reason that makes me laugh even harder and I'm clutching my stomach.

"Dad, would you like another child you could fly kites with?" I ask once I've got my breath back, trying to smile as if it's not an important question.

"I haven't thought about it," mumbles Dad, giving me the kite line. "Anyway, I've got you. And you're enough at the moment."

My smile drops. "At the moment, yes, but could that change?"

"Things are always changing. Life can be complicated, like the tangles in a kite string." Dad frowns and double-checks the line. "Being a parent isn't easy, but you always do your best for your children. Live for the moment, don't plan too far ahead and deal with whatever comes your way. Does that make any sense?"

Not really, but then the thoughts inside my head don't make sense either.

Dad tells me the wish kite is ready and hands me the line – I can smell the scent of green grass and salt on his skin. At first the kite drags along the ground and then Dad puts his hand over mine and the kite begins to lift. Up, up, up it sails, travelling on the wind. I follow it as it leads me along the top of the hill. Dad's laughing and shouting that I'm doing it and he knew I could. The heart-shaped kite dips and then rises up again and it's me controlling it. For once, I feel like everything's going right. The kite's flying and Dad's shouting that if life ever feels complicated for me I should talk to him. "I'm a great listener," he calls as I race further away. "I mean, I listen to Minnie moaning all the time. You can tell me anything."

"Okay," I call back, but then I think about my real mother and I think that I can't tell Dad about her. How could I? He'd think I've forgotten how amazing Mum is, but I haven't. The kite dips and rises again and then I'm distracted and it crashes to the ground.

"Kite down," shouts Dad, panting and running towards me. "We can fix it." He sits on the ground and takes the kite into his hands and then beckons me over to sit beside him. As soon as I do, Dad lies back and tells me to do the same and we look up into the sky as an aeroplane flies overhead. "I wonder where it's going." It glides above us, leaving a trail of vapour. "Do you ever look at planes and wish you were going on an exciting journey?" he says. I think that I wish stuff like that all the time.

Dad gets back up and fixes the kite and launches it into the air again. We both watch as it dances like a tiny heart on the breeze. "The wish is out there in the universe," says Dad. "It's soaring. Look at it fly among the clouds."

We follow the heart with *MUM* on it all the way down the hill and it takes us towards home as if it knows the way. In front of us I can see the tower blocks and I feel like I've had a great evening with Dad and I'm talking about comics and he's laughing. The moon appears like a pearl and I ask Dad if he thinks the Zorbitans will ever find The Grand Moon Master.

"I suppose so," says Dad. "If they persist they'll get there in the end." I smile but then Dad adds, "But I wonder what will happen when they do find him."

It's an odd thing to say and I'm quick to tell Dad that their hearts will glow and Dad says he knows that's going to happen, but what happens after that?

"They'll have a home with their creator. They won't forget what it was like before, but they'll all live happily ever after," I reply fiercely.

By the time we get home, Dad's told me a joke about how Superman's toilet is called the superbowl and I'm laughing – but then I see Minnie's got a face like thunder and Mum's trying to write out a plan of what we can eat for the next week. Minnie asks if we've been enjoying ourselves and it's obvious she's annoyed. That's when Minnie says it's a shame she wasn't invited. Dad says she wasn't here.

"You could have asked me," declares Minnie.

Dad looks perplexed. "Would you have wanted to come kite-flying?"

Minnie shakes her head and says she'd still like to be included so at least she could say no. Then she says I've had lots of outings recently, because I went to the Comic Con as well.

"He goes snooping about and everyone's all over him," says Minnie, tapping her lips with her finger. "Maybe I should try that. Why don't I go looking for something I'm not supposed to and then let everyone buy me tickets to Comic Cons and take me out for fun?" Mum is looking at Minnie like she's gone doolally.

"What are you waffling on about?" asks Dad, taking off his coat and resting the kite against the wall. Minnie flounces off to her room, saying that no one ever understands her, which is quite accurate.

"I was only telling the truth, so in your face, pizza base," says Minnie when I confront her in her bedroom. She reminds me that I'm not allowed to step over the red line or she might just have to subject me to terrible pain.

"*Pfftt*," I say. "What would you know about that?"

"I had my legs waxed once," says Minnie. "I know what pain is."

I hover at the red line as Minnie starts spouting about how I've been finding out about my mother and then letting Mum and Dad run after me.

"They're not," I say.

"You're a hypo," announces Minnie, and as I'm about to say I'm not a hippo, she says, "hypocrite, not a hippo."

There's no response from me because I don't have a clue what Minnie's on about. And even when she says a hypocrite pretends to be perfect but they're concealing what they're up to, I'm still clueless.

Next, Minnie begins counting on her fingers. "You've been at a comic thing, number one. And number two, you've been kite-flying. You also got Granddad Fred's watch and that's number three. Having the best treatment, I'd say. Even though you still haven't told Mum and Dad what you're up to. They're the best, you know, and they don't deserve to be messed around by you."

"That's ridiculous," I reply, leaning over the red line. "I was only out with Dad flying a kite. It's not a big deal. And you were at rehearsals so there was no way Dad could have asked you." I chew on my lip, knowing that Minnie's right about me not telling Mum and Dad what I'm doing. I am concealing it. "You weren't being left out on purpose," I offer, taking a step back.

"Really?" Minnie's eyebrows rise and she checks a hole in her navy tights. "You two are always doing things. Where are my trips out, just me and Dad? Why don't I get taken places? Where is my watch? It's like I don't matter."

Sometimes Minnie is a sandwich short of a picnic

when she's annoyed. But then the penny drops. "You're jealous," I launch back.

Minnie's eyes flare dangerously and she says she isn't jealous. "Anyway, I wonder how many trips you'd go on if Mum and Dad find out about you searching for your birth certificate and doing *your* family tree, not ours."

"They'd be okay," I reply cautiously.

"So tell them then," Minnie fires back. I pause, then shake my head. "You can't," she says triumphantly.

I wish I had better words to express how I feel, something moving and powerful that tells Minnie how important this is to me. It's got nothing to do with Mum and Dad, not really. It's to do with me and the part missing from my life. Maybe it seems stupid because I've always known I'm adopted, but now I'm older I do have choices. I can ignore the information I've found or I can use it to sort out the missing part in my life and make things perfect. Everyone wants a perfect life, right? Plus Minnie doesn't know that I *need* to find my real mother so I have somewhere to go when the jelly bean arrives – but I can't be the one to tell her about that.

"I think this conversation is closed," says Minnie, picking up her mobile phone. "Anyway, I've got to discuss my lines with my onstage husband. Callum's worried about some of his scenes." Minnie's fingers move across the screen. "And since I'm a great actress, I'm the person to help him with it. Close the door on your way out."

Back in my own room, I throw myself on my bed and look up to the superhero mobile Dad made me. It swings and flutters in the breeze from my window and my heart aches so much I feel like it might break. I had so much fun with Dad this evening that for a second I forgot I wasn't his real son. I forgot I was going to be leaving. We laughed for ages and talked about the Zorbitans and comics. I felt like I truly belonged.

Next door, in Mum and Dad's room, I can hear gentle sobbing and I know it's Mum. This time I don't think my teddy bear is going to sort it out. There's a sniffle and a pause and I get up from my bed and listen. As I'm about to go to Mum's room, the sobbing stops completely and I wonder if I imagined it. Why would Mum be crying when having a baby is supposed to be the happiest time of your life? That's what the TV programme said.

17

Tiny Eric stops me in the playground and says he's sorry we didn't find my real mother's address at the hospital. Then he says he's been thinking big thoughts.

"Ooh, well done," I reply, laughing. "Keep it up."

Tiny Eric says I'm very funny and without hesitation I say I take after my dad. Then I feel a strange pang in my stomach as I remember I don't know who my real dad is. Tiny Eric says he got home last night and started working on a picture. But not just any old picture, he tells me. "This one is going to help you find your real mother. I had the idea when we saw that missing cat poster in Sharkey's window."

"Um, how does a missing cat poster help me?" I blink back my confusion. "I don't have a missing cat."

Tiny Eric taps me on the bobble hat. "Hello, is anyone in there? The bobble hat's on but there's no one home." He tells me he knows I'm not missing a cat, but I *am* missing my real mother, and if we put up a poster then everyone in the area will keep an eye out, or maybe she'll even see the poster herself.

"Yes, but there was a photo of the missing cat," I respond. "I don't know what my real mother looks like."

"That's where I come in," says Tiny Eric, his eyes glittering. He pulls out a poster from his school bag and holds it up in front of me. It says: I'M TRYING TO FIND ROSE WALKER. I THINK SHE LIVES IN PEGASUS PARK BUT IT MIGHT BE SOMEWHERE ELSE. I'D LIKE HER TO GET IN TOUCH. SHE IS PROBABLY IN HER THIRTIES OR FORTIES. PLEASE CONTACT YOUR LOCAL SUPERHERO ON: 0123 457 900

"That's my mobile number," I say, pointing at the poster. "It's a great idea. But, like I said, I don't have a picture to include."

"I've left a space," replies Tiny Eric. "Do you ever watch those police dramas where they draw an image of the person they're looking for?"

"My real mother isn't a criminal," I blurt out.

"I know," says Tiny Eric, bringing out a pencil. "Keep your hat on. But it's the same idea. Someone describes the person they want to find and an artist draws the image and puts that out there. It's genius."

Thinking about it, Tiny Eric's right. It *is* genius. Why didn't I think of it? I'm the genius around here. Tiny Eric tells me to sit down on the playground wall and then close my eyes and describe what I feel about my real mother. When I shut my eyes at first I can't see anything but darkness and I tell him I can't do it. "There's nothing," I mumble. Tiny Eric urges me on, saying I don't have to see her in my head, just imagine her warmth and then describe how I feel.

"Do it from the heart," explains Tiny Eric.

Slowly a picture begins to form inside my head. "She's nice," I whisper. "And she's got this smile that lights up her whole face and makes her eyes sparkle. There are a few crinkles at the sides that make me think of crinkle-cut chips. She's got dimples on her cheeks. One, two." I grin and my closed eyelids flutter. "And her nose turns up like a funny ski jump." After a few moments of describing how my real mother looks, Tiny Eric tells me to open my eyes.

"It's incredible," I say, staring at the drawing. "I'd

love a real mother like her. She looks warm and kind and smiley."

"She does," says Tiny Eric, holding up the finished poster. "Shall we put it in Sharkey's window after school? If it works for missing cats, it's going to work for you."

I'm so excited I can hardly think straight.

At three thirty I'm vaulting the tables and dragging Tiny Eric with me, which isn't easy since it's like dragging a double-decker bus along with your teeth. We rush straight out of the school gate and down Agamemnon Road and then we pass Good Buy, Mr Chips and we're at Sharkey's. There's a tiny *pip* as we swing open the door and we walk straight to the counter and Sharkey gives us a smile.

"We'd like to put an ad in the window," says Tiny Eric, passing his poster over. Sharkey rubs his chin and says we have to pay. I nudge Tiny Eric because I've got no money. Sharkey says it'll be fifty pence and Tiny Eric begins scrabbling about in his pocket, bringing out an HB pencil, a photo of a building with the word *szkoła* on it, a marble, a half-chewed sweet and a photo of him with his mum and dad. The family photo is torn and I'm about to say he needs to stick it back together when he brings out fifty pence and puts it on the counter.

Sharkey takes the money and looks at the poster and says it's a good drawing but not that good really. I swear he mutters, "Nothing like," but then he shrugs and says, "It'll be in the window for a week." As we leave the shop, I spot Minnie and her friend Sienna outside Good Buy, Mr Chips. Minnie has her nose in a carton of chips and a battered sausage.

"Don't tell Mum I've been eating junk," says Minnie when I reach her. I shrug and I'm about to say something, but Minnie carries on telling Sienna about how she's dating Callum now because they couldn't deny their onstage chemistry. "It was serendipity that we were thrown together in the Scottish play." Minnie bites down on the battered sausage and chews for a while before saying. "You're good as a witch too."

Sienna stops eating, a chip dangling from her lip.

Minnie continues, "Yes, I was just saying to Callum that you're so realistic. You don't even need any different make-up, just that black eyeliner you always wear. And I swear that Mr Bravo was impressed at how witchlike you were."

Sienna doesn't appear to have an answer to this. And as it's all about as riveting as watching an invisible dog scratching his invisible fleas, Tiny Eric and I begin to mooch away. As we go I hear Minnie saying she needs to go into Sharkey's and get some chewing gum because Mum will smell grease on her breath if she doesn't.

Tiny Eric says he's confident that the poster will work and he reminds me to keep believing and keep staring at the four-leaf clover.

"I've been staring at it so much recently it feels like it's welded to my eyeballs." I laugh as we turn the corner and saunter down the road. When Tiny Eric takes the next turning with a wave, I continue on my own. That's when I hear someone grunting behind me and the *click-clack* of heels.

"You've changed, Adam Butters," says Minnie, catching up with me. I smell a puff of mint from her breath.

"Huh?" Sometimes Minnie is so random I've got no idea what she's on about. "I haven't," I reply, looking at her. "I look exactly the same as I've always done." We walk together towards Pegasus Park Towers.

"I'm surprised your nose hasn't grown to twice its length, Pinocchio." When I pull a face, Minnie adds, "Because you're telling lies. You didn't use to tell lies the way you do now." Minnie's eyes narrow. "I don't know who you are any more."

"Neither do I," I spit as I follow Minnie up the stone steps leading to our flat. "That's the problem." After that Minnie shuts right up. I think I might have won this argument. But she hasn't finished with me yet.

Looking at me straight on, Minnie says, "Oh, you're so clever."

"Yup," I reply smugly.

Fire sparking in her eyes, Minnie blusters, "But you're not as clever as me." I'm about to say that I am when Minnie goes, "Nice sketch, by the way." Seriously, I have no idea what she's on about now, although that's nothing new.

"The drawing of Mum, stupid."

"Oh, right," I mutter, but I don't have a clue what planet Minnie is on. I did draw an alien last night, but that was nothing like Mum, unless Minnie thinks Mum has one eye in the middle of her head and goes by the name of Cyclops Galactica. Anyway, I tore it up straight afterwards. I bet Minnie has been snooping in my bedroom on the quiet. When I get in, I'm going to booby-trap it with bits of Lego on the floor. If you stamp on Lego you always scream out.

Minnie tosses her hair over her shoulder and nearly blinds me as it whips my eye. Then she turns the key in the lock and opens the door to the flat. And as I'm walking in behind her, she shuts the door in my face.

I might be wrong, but I think Minnie won that argument.

The next couple of days pass and there's no response to the poster in Sharkey's window, and I've got so tired of staring at the four-leaf clover that I've had to take a break from it before my eyeballs begin bulging like they're bursting out of a squishy mesh ball. Minnie has stopped speaking to me completely, which is a bonus. We only communicate by angry looks. And Velvet has offered me Sausage Roll twice in twenty-four hours. I haven't heard Mum crying again but I did see her with misty eyes, and when I opened my mouth to speak Mum hushed me, nodded, and said yes, conjunctivitis.

It's Saturday evening when my world turns upside down. Minnie's rehearsing at Callum's house and Mum's bathing Velvet. Dad tells me to come and look at the latest copy of the Zorbitans comic. I'm leaning over the pages when I feel my bum vibrate. I reach into my pocket and pull out my phone. There's a message from a number I don't recognize.

Beside me Dad laughs and says that the Zorbitans are trying their most hare-brained scheme ever in this strip. I swallow and feel my eyes begin to sting like a jellyfish as I stare at the text:

I saw the poster. I'm Rose Walker. I'm sorry but I do not live in Pegasus Park any more. I was just visiting. I've left now and I don't know when I'll be back. Take the poster down and stop looking. Stay with your family and be happy. Don't text me back. Goodbye.

It's as if I'm in quicksand and it's caving in and I'm falling and the sand around me is slipping and Dad's not aware so he doesn't reach out to help me. Instead he's going on about how the Zorbitans will try everything. My real mother can't be saying goodbye when I've only just found her. It's like maths – it doesn't make sense to me.

I tell Dad I've got homework to do and turn and walk towards my bedroom. He says, "On a Saturday night? Are you feeling well?" I don't answer. To be honest, I can't. I don't have any words. My last hope has melted away like a Malteser on a tongue.

18

WHOOOSH

It is dark inside
my bobble hat.
I don't want to come out.

       I'll stay here while the world is

              falling

                    down

                         around

                              me.

And even though
I have Mum and Dad
I can't tell them how confused I am
because I love them

and I don't want to hurt them

even though I'm hurting.

And I can't look to my real mother

because I don't know her

and she doesn't know me

and she doesn't want to get to know me either.

Where do I go now? Where can I call home?

I'm afraid of not having a family

and a home.

I'm afraid of it because of what happened to me when I was a baby.

And I'm afraid that I'll

never find the missing part of me.

Not ever.

19

KER-RASH

On Monday morning I feel like I'm carrying the weight of a baby orang-utan on my shoulders. After the text on Saturday evening I went straight to my bedroom and tore up the drawing of the four-leaf clover and scattered the pieces on the floor like confetti. It hadn't brought me any luck and I was angry that I'd wasted so much time staring at it. When I get into the playground I tell Tiny Eric that the poster worked. "It did?" he says brightly and he claps his hands together. "I knew it would."

"Only one problem," I say, staring up into the sky to stop my eyes watering. "I got a text on Saturday from

Rose telling me to forget about her. So that's it." I shrug and then look at Tiny Eric. "It's over. She didn't want me then and she doesn't want me now. I tried so hard and I wanted it so much. I *needed* it so much."

Tiny Eric blinks back his confusion and says he doesn't understand and I say I don't either. "But you're a superhero and you're excellent. You've saved a life. And where are you going to live now?" I tell him I thought I was special but I'm not and I don't know where I'm going.

"Could I live with you for a bit?" I look at Tiny Eric. He coughs and says it might be tricky. He'd like to but... "I know," I reply, shrugging. "Don't worry. You might be moving house."

Tiny Eric says I *am* special and it'll be okay, but my ears tune him out, like when Velvet puts on her favourite TV channel and watches the same programmes over and over again.

I can't concentrate when Mrs Chatterjee says our trees are almost finished and the show is coming up so we need to do the last bits. I'm not listening when she tells us to tie whatever new tags we've got onto the branches. Even when she talks about how the *Pegasus Park Packet* are thinking about encouraging other readers to look into their genealogy, I don't care. My tree is sitting in the corner and only has a few tags on it, whereas Nish's has loads.

Mrs Chatterjee says she has a new surprise. "Whichever tree impresses me most is going to stay in the school reception for the rest of the year so everyone can see it. You'll be a star in school and I imagine your parents will be very proud."

"Who cares?" I mumble. Being a star isn't that great. I've tried. And my real mother wouldn't be proud anyway. She wouldn't want to know. The text proved that.

On the way home from school, Tiny Eric says I can't give up on my real mother and I tell him I didn't give up on her, she gave up on me – there's a difference. "Don't let her," exclaims Tiny Eric fiercely. "You've got to try again. Don't ever give up. Text her back and tell her you want to see her. Texts aren't the same as meeting someone. If she saw you in real life, she'd change her mind. Tell her how you feel. Say you've saved a life – that's amazing with a capital A."

After some persuasion I agree to text her back and say that I'll tell her I've done something special, but not exactly what it was. "She might want to know all about it."

Tiny Eric is right. I can't give up.

Hi, I'm glad you got in touch with me. I'd love you to ring me or meet me as I've done something incredible I think you should know about. You have my number. Please contact me again.

I send the text and I can imagine my real mother hearing her phone bleep and seeing the message from me. She'll understand how important it is to me that I meet her. She'll change her mind. In fact, she might even be reading it now and wiping away her tears of joy. She'll text me straight back and tell me she made a mistake and she's sorry and I'll forgive her because she's my real mother. Plus, she'll want to know why I've done something special and what it's all about. The text will come before I get home from school.

It doesn't.

It'll come before I get into school the following day.

It doesn't.

I try not to feel too miserable with a capital M, because at least she hasn't told me to get lost again. This means there is still a tiny sliver of hope. Anyway, my real mother must be busy working. I bet she has an important job and that's why it's taking some time. She'll be desperate to get back to me.

Still no reply.

She isn't.

The next day, when I'm walking home from school, I send another text. I know I told myself I wouldn't be too pushy, but I can't help myself, not when this means so much.

Hello, only me. Yes, that sounds casual. *I've sent you a couple of texts.* True. *I know you're probably busy but we should meet up.* Okay, meeting face-to-face is important even if you are busy. *Please contact me again.* I think about putting a kiss at the end of the text but then think no, no, that's too much. So I put a smiley face instead. Then I hit send and continue walking down Agamemnon Road, whistling.

Minnie's outside Good Buy, Mr Chips again and I'm about to walk past her with my nose in the air since we're not talking, but then I notice she's been crying.

How do I know? Because she looks like a panda, with her cheeks totally black from runny mascara, that's why. She's shovelling a load of chips into her mouth between sobs. When I stop she says, "I've got no appetite." I'm about to say she's having a laugh, only it's obvious she isn't. "It's Callum," she splutters. "He's been cheating on me and I swear it's that witch, Sienna. Oh, he told me he isn't, but someone's been texting him behind my back and he won't let me see the messages and he keeps saying he doesn't have a clue who they're from, but I'm sure they're from Sienna."

"Oh," I say.

"Double-crossing witch," says Minnie, wiping her cheeks. I reel back as the black smears reach her chin – it looks like she's got a goatee. "She knew I fancied Callum and that we were meant to be together. Then she gets her claws into him when my back is turned. *Pffttt.*" Minnie eats another handful of chips. "I'm going to waste away," she says, looking faint. "This is the heartbreak diet."

I like the sound of the heartbreak diet because it would mean I wouldn't have to eat so many vegan stews, which are playing havoc with my insides.

Minnie sniffs. "How am I going to play my part with Callum on the stage? I'm going to have to..." She gasps. "Act."

All the way home Minnie's saying how life is so hard and why can't everything go right for a change? "How could he reject me? I'm gorgeous," she snivels, without so much as a smile. "My life is over. No one rejects me." When I ask Minnie if she'd consider quitting the play, she turns to me and says, "No way. No boy is ever stopping me getting the applause I deserve. I'm not a quitter, not ever. Winners don't quit."

For once I think Minnie has a point. I can't quit on my real mother either. Superheroes are not quitters. No matter what happens. As we near the flat, Minnie turns to me and says, "It doesn't feel good to be rejected."

"I know," I reply as we wander past Mrs Karimloo's flat and then up the stairs past Mr Hooper's. It's only when Minnie stops outside our door and says that she's going to text Callum and tell him she's not very happy that I get an idea.

"I've got to be straight with him," says Minnie. "I'm not taking this lying down."

"You're standing up," I reply shortly.

"I'm not taking it standing up either. I'm going to tell him I'm annoyed and then offer him another chance. He'll have to eat humble pie."

"I'd love some pie," I say.

Later that evening I fling myself on the sofa like a lazy starfish and switch on the TV. Mum's got a pile of books from the library on the table. There's one on how to eat greens and feel good and one called *Health Means Wealth*. Picking the book up, I idly flick through it until I come to a thin slip of paper Mum's been using as a bookmark. I feel like my insides have turned to icicles. My eyes do a double take. Because on the bookmark, in neat, precise letters, Mum has written:

Possible names

Bailey
Max
Charlie
Jake
(Jack)
Oscar
Teddy
Sam

There's a circle around the name Jack.

This means the jelly bean is a baby boy. I snap the book shut, push it away and retreat into my bobble hat where I can hide. Somehow, knowing it's a boy makes everything worse. I've been their son all this time and it hurts like a sledgehammer on a nut when I think of another boy taking my place. Jack Butters. Jack Butters. Jack Butters. Why does that sound better than Adam Butters? Why does that name sound right? Why, when I say my name, does it sound wrong?

Who knows how long I'm under the hat. That's the thing about the hat. Time stands still in there and nothing matters. I can feel the heat of my breath and hear my heart going *ba-doing, ba-doing, ba-doing*. Over and over I keep trying to tell myself that it doesn't matter that the jelly bean is coming and it doesn't matter that it's a boy or that his name will be Jack, because I'm texting my real mother. I'm going to be okay, I tell myself.

Then, from nowhere, I feel a hand on mine. There's a light squeeze. Dad sits beside me and asks what I'm watching on TV, which is ridiculous since I'm under my bobble hat. Slowly I pull it back up.

"Do you like the name Jack?" I tug on my earlobe as Dad switches channels. "Is it better than Adam?"

"You mean like Jack Frost from the Marvel comics? I love how Jack Frost can manipulate snow and ice. And then there's Adam Strange from DC Comics."

"I'm not talking about superheroes. I mean Jack is a good name for a jelly bean." I stare at Dad, searching his eyes. Dad holds my gaze and gives me his I-don't-have-a-clue-what-you're-talking-about face, which isn't all that different from his usual face.

"Er…for a jelly bean, I'd prefer hot buttered popcorn or tutti-frutti as a name," says Dad.

No baby should be called Tutti-frutti. Dad has lost the plot. I shake my head and slump back on the sofa. When Dad goes into the kitchen to make tea, muttering about how he'd like a box of hot buttered popcorn right now, I text my real mother again. I beg her to meet up. It's getting urgent now. I know it's not big or clever to beg, but finding out the baby is going to be called Jack makes everything feel even more real. Winners don't quit, I tell myself over and over again. And superheroes are winners. After a moment I send her a heart emoji, and when she doesn't reply I send her a broken heart emoji.

When Dad comes back into the room he sets down his mug of tea and says, "I know Mum's health kick makes us all dream about sweets – Lord knows I've been thinking of salty chips and egg-custard tarts sprinkled with cinnamon – but if you're desperate for a jelly bean I could sneak out to Sharkey's and buy some. Just don't tell Mum."

"I don't want a stupid jelly bean," I mutter. "If the jelly bean was here now I'd have to go straight away and

I don't want to. Don't you understand how I feel?" A rocket fires up my chest.

Dad looks confused. "Maybe we'd better not talk about jelly beans."

"Maybe we'd better not," I reply.

After school on Thursday I'm walking home and I send Rose one final text asking for anything, any tiny crumb of interest, a little speck, one little word, anything at all. There's no reply and when I reach Sharkey's I've worked myself up so much that when I see the poster in the window I go inside and tell him to take it down and rip it up.

"Okey dokey," says Sharkey, leaning on the counter. "Your time is up anyway unless you want to pay another fifty pence for a second week."

"There's no point. She contacted me and said she didn't live here any more." The words feel like barbed wire in my mouth.

Cool as a cucumber in a fridge in Iceland, Sharkey replies, "She'll be in Switzerland, I suppose." He arranges some Mars bars on the counter and then shuffles a few magazines, before setting them down again in a neat pile. "She'll not want that interior design magazine she sometimes buys then. No one else in Pegasus Park will want it either, so I suppose I could cancel the order."

Pow! There's a bang inside my head when I realize what Sharkey's saying. I blink so much I think I've used up all my blinking for the week. I echo what I think I've heard – that Rose Walker is in Switzerland – and Sharkey answers in the affirmative, saying she lives there for months at a time. Then he says if she's not in Switzerland, she's in that big blue house on Maltman's Hill because she also lives in Pegasus Park.

"Mrs Sharkey would love a house like that. It's grand," says Sharkey, whistling through his teeth. "Rose Walker's husband is a banker though. He doesn't sell chocolate and quick noodles."

My mouth is open so wide you could fit an extra-large pizza in there and still have room for the Ganymede moon. "You know Rose Walker?" The words stutter out like tiny guinea pig droppings. "Why didn't you tell me when we brought in the poster?"

"You didn't want my opinions," says Sharkey. "Anyway, I didn't understand the poster and I said so, because there was this drawing of…"

But I don't hear what Sharkey is waffling on about because I'm already out the door. It feels like I've got wings on my feet and they're carrying me towards Rose – towards my real mother, a new home and a new beginning.

This is going to be better than when Dad gave me a rare comic featuring a make-your-own Ariadne out of washing-up gloves and said I could keep it. Who cares if Rose didn't text me back? Maybe she was busy. Maybe she was in Switzerland, like Sharkey said. But now I can go to her house and even if she's not there at the moment I can return another day. In fact, I can keep returning until I meet her. My feet barely touch the pavement as I run towards Maltman's Hill. I've passed this area before, but we don't go there much because the houses are really posh and we don't know anyone who lives there.

But you do, I tell myself.

Your real mother lives there.

You'll live there soon too.

Maybe you'll visit Switzerland like an international jet-setter.

As I get closer, the houses get larger and the streets get wider and the roads are twice as big as the roads around the tower block. Trees line the pavements and the houses are all different and the colour of sherbet sweets – pale lemon, raspberry, pink – and there's one big blue house in the middle and I can feel my gut bubbling like it's got its own internal fizzing machine and I know it's the one. It's Rose's house. As I walk towards it I can hear a piano tinkling through the open downstairs window. Rose might be inside after all. Expectation travels up my spine and makes me shiver slightly. Slowly I saunter past, whistling. Then I turn and walk the other way, whistling. I turn again and stroll past humming and then I turn again and begin to sing. I can do this, I tell myself. I can knock on the door and tell her who I am.

Everything is going to be okay. The four-leaf clover worked after all. I was wrong to destroy it thinking it wouldn't. Suddenly the piano stops and I see a curtain twitch and I run away down the alley beside the house. I pause, my heart pounding and then I laugh like a hyena being tickled with a feather. What's the point in running away when I've been waiting for this moment?

The fence at the side of the property is high but not too high for a superhero like me. I pull myself up to the top of it and peer over into the back garden.

"It's like blooming Buckingham Palace," I mumble, my eyes wide. The garden is full of plants and one little rose bush with a single rose on it. It makes me smile. A rose for someone called Rose. It's nothing like the dark smudgy drawing I did. There's a pale grey summer house the colour of a pigeon at the bottom of the garden and the doors are wide open and I can hear the yapping of a little dog. The piano starts again and the music ribbons around me and then it suddenly stops. It takes me a few moments to pluck up the courage to go towards the front of the house again, and as I reach the end of the alley I see a black car pull out of the front drive and zoom away, small gravel stones spitting around me.

My jaw hardens as I realize that if it was Rose inside, she's gone now.

All the way back to the flat I could kick myself for not going to the door sooner. But I won't kick myself because that would hurt and anyway I can go back tomorrow. A superhero like me doesn't give up that easily.

20

ZOOM

I'm so excited about knowing Rose's address that I hardly slept a wink last night. Minnie said I looked different this morning and I said it was because the world was a beautiful place, and then she said it wasn't a beautiful place because it was full of useless men. Dad raised an eyebrow and said she wouldn't want any pocket money from her useless dad then, and Minnie screamed that she was talking about Callum and she couldn't do without the latest red lip gloss called Dragon. Mum told everyone she'd turn into a dragon if we didn't stop arguing and then said she has an appointment this morning while we're at school.

"At the hospital?" I ask.

Mum looks at me. "Um...yes, how did you know that?"

I shrug and say appointments are usually at the hospital so I took a guess. I'm not telling Mum I saw the letter from Pegasus Park Hospital in her drawer calling her in for a scan. And I can't say I overheard her talking to Grandma. Mum looks at Dad and he shakes his head and Mum says it is a quick appointment and she'll be back by the time we're home. She smiles and hands me a white jellyfish on a plate. She puts one each in front of Velvet, Minnie and Dad too.

"What the blazes is this?" Dad's in shock.

Mum says, "It's an egg-white omelette."

"You're yoking," replies Dad.

Ignoring the joke, Mum says she isn't. Dad pokes his fork into the centre and it wobbles and he jerks back. He says it's alive. Mum isn't laughing. She stands up from the table and says she's working her fingers to the bone making sure we all eat well. "You want to be fit and healthy on the insides, don't you? A healthy body is important and I should know." Mum's eyes go misty again and as I open my mouth she looks at me and says, "Yes, yes, yes, conjunctivitis, I know. I'll mention it to the doctor along with the million other things I'm asking." Mum flounces towards the door, then turns and says, "And it's not just healthy eating, everyone. You need exercise too."

"Extra fries, you say?" Dad asks with a grin. Mum glares at him and leaves, slamming the kitchen door.

At school I can't stop daydreaming about meeting my real mother. Even when Mrs Chatterjee tells us to make any last touches to our family trees for the *Forest For Ever* project, I'm still imagining what it'll be like to tell her I'm Ace. Tiny Eric is putting the last leaf on his tree and his fingers are all glue and he's peeling it off like sunburned skin. He turns to me and says he can't believe my real mother lives on Maltman's Hill. Only rich people live there.

"In a massive house," I reply. "She's got a nice car too. It's black and much better than the Binmobile." Tiny Eric laughs and says the Binmobile was special. "Yeah," I reply. "Special in that it didn't have brakes. I can't believe I found out where she lives, Tiny Eric." I feel excitement and nerves bubble inside my stomach. "If you hadn't drawn that poster it would never have happened. I'm going to go back and this time I hope she's inside and if she is I'm going to ring the doorbell and then *WHAM!*"

Everyone turns to look at me. Clearly I said, "Wham!" a little too loudly. Mrs Chatterjee says she's glad I'm either talking about an '80s boy band or happy about the project, but either way my tree is still looking quite bare. I put my hand up and say it won't be bare for long, and I hold up three new tags where I've written that my real mother has a big house on Maltman's Hill and she's got a black car and she plays the piano (okay, so I'm not one hundred per cent sure it was Rose playing the piano but that's not going to stop a superhero who wants a gold star for this project).

"Good, I'm glad you've got more tags to add," says Mrs Chatterjee. "Please tie them on your tree. The exhibition is on Tuesday, so today and Monday are your last days to finish up." I put the tags down and pick up my glue pot as Mrs Chatterjee continues, "I hope you've given your family the invite."

Holy doughnuts! Mine is still lying in my school bag. I didn't take it out. When I go to my real mother's house, I must take it with me. After she's answered the door and hugged me, I'm going to tell her about the project and she's going to say she'd be delighted to attend. Oh, I can see it all now. It's going to be the best moment. *And* I'm bound to be on the front page of the *Pegasus Park Packet*. I haven't forgotten about that. I'll be famous. I'll tell the reporter I'm Ace and my real mother will nod. "He's Ace," she'll confirm. "And I'm lucky that he lives with me now."

"Wake up, Adam," says Mrs Chatterjee. "You're spilling glue."

It takes ten minutes to peel it off my trousers, while Nish is busy shouting that it looks like a seagull has pooped on me and Tiny Eric says if a seagull poops on you it's good luck and then he goes on to repeat that he knows all about luck.

I clear my throat and lean over towards Tiny Eric and whisper, "Talking about good luck...I feel bad and we shouldn't keep secrets so I've got to tell you this... I tore up the four-leaf clover drawing. I'm sorry. I got angry and I thought it wasn't working and I got rid of it and then I had all this good luck and I feel rotten because you helped me." I squint, waiting for Tiny Eric to get mad. Instead he says it doesn't matter.

"You believed," explains Tiny Eric. "So you don't need it any more. You've got enough good luck to carry you on."

"You could draw me another one."

"I haven't got my green pencil on me."

"Bring it in."

"I've packed it away," says Tiny Eric.

I look at him and say, "How hard is it to unpack your

pencil case?" Tiny Eric shrugs and it looks like it's very hard.

At lunchtime Tiny Eric and me are sitting in the dining hall eating our sandwiches (mine look like they're filled with porridge, although Mum insisted it was home-made hummus) when The Beast sits down beside us. The Beast has egg sandwiches and they stink and Tiny Eric wants to move but I say we should stay. Tiny Eric gives me a look. To be honest, I'd like to talk to The Beast about superheroes, but it's hard to know what to say because I've never talked to The Beast properly before. No one talks to The Beast. To start some sort of conversation, I stretch my hand across the table to show the watch. "It's still not working," I say.

The Beast looks pleased, which doesn't seem quite the right response to my watch being broken. "Oh, right," says The Beast, sausage fingers brushing my wrist. Tiny Eric shakes his head in horror. "But it looks good," The Beast goes on. "The strap is going to snap though, you should get it fixed. I could get my uncle to look at it for you. He could fix the strap." The Beast takes a bite of egg sandwich and follows it with a slurp of juice.

"Maybe," I reply, twisting the watch this way and that.

I give it a little flick with my fingernail and then I hold it up to my ear. There's still no ticking.

Nish appears and says Mrs Chatterjee wants someone to help her clear up the art stuff in the classroom. When I ask him why he can't do it he says he's got a broken arm. I look at his arm and say it doesn't look broken, and Nish asks me if I've got X-ray eyes.

"Like Superman," says The Beast.

I'm about to talk to The Beast about heroes when Nish looks at me directly and says, "Mrs Chatterjee asked for you."

Tiny Eric shrugs and The Beast takes another bite of sandwich as I get up from my chair and walk towards our Year Six classroom. Gingerly I knock on the door and Mrs Chatterjee shouts for me to come in. "You wanted me to help clear up," I say, shuffling into the room.

Mrs Chatterjee smiles and nods. "I'd love a bit of help." Her chandelier earrings swing as she rises from her seat and points towards the glue pots, telling me to put on the lids and sort out the paintbrushes. "They go in the tubs," says Mrs Chatterjee.

After a few moments of clearing up together, Mrs Chatterjee asks me how I'm getting on now the *Forest For Ever* project is coming to an end. She doesn't look at me, just carries on picking up bits of rubbish and throwing them in the bin.

"It's fine," I reply, throwing brushes into the red tub. I stack paints and then try to scoop up small mountains of stray silver glitter. Mrs Chatterjee shuffles some sheets of paper and says she brought me in because she thought I might like a little chat.

"It's just there were a few tags on your tree that were a little confusing to me."

I blink. "It's okay, miss. I understand them," I say. "To be frank, family trees can be complicated." If you say "to be frank" it sounds like you know exactly what you're talking about. Dad always says it to customers about broken locks. To change the subject, I show Mrs Chatterjee my watch. "Mum gave me this – it's a watch from my Granddad Fred. He was important in our family. Only the watch doesn't work."

Mrs Chatterjee peers down at the watch, saying that it's lovely and she's glad the project made me think about my granddad. With a smile, she asks if I'd mind putting the scissors away in the drawer and I offer to take the glue pots and tubs to the stationery cupboard too. I put everything away in the right place and when I come out of the cupboard Mrs Chatterjee says I've been very helpful and offers me a gold star.

I nod, wiping my glittery hands on my trousers.

Mrs Chatterjee smiles and reaches into her drawer and at the top I can see the register and there's a bright green Post-it note beside the name *Eric Kowalski-Brown* and that's Tiny Eric. I see the date *29th* and the head's name, and there's an address, but I don't think it's Kink Street. Perhaps Tiny Eric's parents have found their new house. I hope it's near me. Mrs Chatterjee pulls out a gold star, closes the drawer and sticks it next to my name on the board. As I'm leaving the classroom, I turn back and say, "My tree is going to be the best tree in the forest. I'm going to be proud of it."

Mrs Chatterjee nods and says, "That sounds perfect."

"I'm going to bring my mother to the exhibition," I add. "I'm just not sure if she can come yet, but I'm going to ask her."

"Why haven't you mentioned it to her already?" Mrs Chatterjee looks perplexed and her eyebrows form a long quizzical slug.

"I'm waiting until everything is perfect, and it will be."

As I leave the classroom I swear Mrs Chatterjee is so touched by what I've said that she's dabbing her eyes with a tissue she's picked up off the table. To be frank, I don't have the heart to tell her that was the tissue Nish was cleaning his glue brush with.

21
BIFF

Superheroes don't get scared, I tell myself as my finger presses the doorbell on the blue house in front of me. I can't hear a piano playing this afternoon, but inside there's a tiny *yip-yip-yip* from the dog. The doorbell tinkles and I know someone is in there because I see a shadow behind the frosted glass and my mouth dries up and my legs feel weak. It's stupid, but I want to run away again, and then I tell myself that I'm being silly.

This is your mother, I say inside my head. *You can't be scared of your mother, you spanner.*

Without warning, the door swings open.

There's such a whoosh inside my body it feels like

I've trapped lightning in a bottle and stashed it in my stomach. Stars suddenly glitter in front of my eyes and I blink so much I swear my eyelids think they're getting a surprise workout. A woman looks at me and I look at her and it feels like I might collapse at her feet like an unconscious octopus. Eventually I see her mouth move and I think she's said "Hello", but I'm so happy she's speaking to me that I forget I'm supposed to answer back.

"Hello, can I help you?"

My mother is amazing – not only can she speak, but she says more than one word. I know I'm gaping but I can't help myself, because I'm thinking about all the birthdays when I wondered who my real mother was, and now I'm looking at her. She's got a bob and her hair is the same copper colour as mine. And she has conker eyes.

"Your hair is like the finest spun copper thread," I mumble, thinking aloud. Rose tilts her head and her brow furrows and I cough, trying to pretend I didn't say something so stupid. As I lean in closer for a better look, Rose leans back, only a tiny bit, but I sense it. Suddenly I'm annoyed she doesn't recognize me. She should know I'm her son instantly.

Rose clearly doesn't, because she asks what I want.

I want a home with my real mother, I'm screaming inside, but on the outside I say, "You sent me the text and I've been looking for you. I've texted you lots of times."

"What text?" Rose looks at me and she's confused. "I didn't get any texts on my phone. That's strange." Finally she smiles and I can tell she's recognized me and this is it, she's about to say she's happy to see me. "Oh, you're here for charity. You're collecting, aren't you? I'll go and get my purse." I tell her I don't want money and then she asks if I've come to the wrong house. "My neighbour has a boy about your age, maybe you want them."

"No, I want you," I say quietly, shifting my weight from one foot to the other. "Are you Rose Walker?"

She says, "Yes, that's me."

Somehow this isn't going exactly how I imagined it. I thought our eyes would lock and she'd know who I was and welcome me with a hug. It's up to me to say it and I clear my throat and inhale. "My name is Ace."

There's an awkward silence as Rose repeats, "Ace?" There's a tiny flicker in her dark eyes and then she smiles brightly. "I don't think I know anyone by that name."

I feel her move to close the door, so I say my name

louder: "I'm Ace. *Your* Ace. You must know me," I say, more quietly now. "Look at me closer." Rose stares at the bobble hat I'm wearing and for a second I think about taking it off to show her we've got the same hair colour but I don't. At this moment I need my security blanket, as Mum calls it. I want to feel safe. Rose shakes her head, until I say quietly, "I'm your son."

In movies, this is the bit where the world goes into slow motion and the two people smile at each other and maybe they're distant to start with but then they run through a meadow towards the other person. And they throw their arms out and they're just about to meet and that's when your heart feels like it's going to soar...

Unfortunately Rose doesn't watch the same movies as me, because she leans out and grabs me by the elbow. The thread of my daydream snaps. However, I don't mind, because now I'm inside the blue house. I'm in my real mother's world and it feels incredible to be here. The hallway is bigger than our whole living room. Looking down it, I can see a brilliant white kitchen and out into the garden all the way to the pigeon-coloured summer house, and I want to go out there and sit in a chair, reading my favourite comics. The dog I heard earlier appears and snoops around my feet, sniffing my leg.

"Stop, Bonbon," says Rose. She slowly runs her fingers through her razor-sharp bob. "I don't know where you've come from or how you got this address, but you shouldn't be here. People might have seen you."

At first I'm confused – what difference does it make if anyone saw me?

"How did you find me?"

I glance down and see that Rose's huge diamond ring is throwing a tiny rainbow across me. It makes me think of Mum and I wish she was here to help me say the right words. Mum always has the right words. When I explain I put a poster in Sharkey's window, she says she knows the place because she occasionally picks up an interior design magazine there.

I'm trying to think of things to say to fill the silence and I suddenly blurt out, "I'm a superhero." Rose blinks, which isn't the reaction I wanted. I try to explain it to her: "You called me Ace and I thought that sounded like a superhero's name and I thought how superheroes make everyone happy and I wanted to do that." I don't mention how I wanted to make Mum happiest of all. This doesn't seem the right time. I swallow. "I even saved someone's life."

I thought this would sound more spectacular than it does. If I told Mum and Dad I'd saved someone's life,

I'd be swallowed up by hugs and kisses and Mum would be straight on the phone to the whole family, and then she'd ring the paper herself to say that her son was the best son in the universe. Instead, Rose says, "That's nice," and she adds that my mother must be proud.

I want to scream: *YOU ARE MY MOTHER. I WANT YOU TO BE PROUD.*

Rose softens and says, "This is complicated and I'm not sure what to say. I wasn't expecting you to come here. You're not supposed to be doing this. Does your mother know where you are?"

I shake my head. The words *You are my mother* keep going around my head like they're on a carousel. "I found my birth certificate in a drawer where Mum keeps lots of keys. You see, Dad has a key-cutting business." I know I'm coming up with more waffle than an American diner but I can't help myself. "And they don't know anything about it. But they're busy anyway. Mum's having a baby. It's a boy." Rose says it'll be lovely for me to have a baby brother. "Do you have any other children?" I ask. I say "other" because I mean "other than me".

Rose dips her head. "My husband and I don't have any children because we didn't want any."

"Oh," I manage.

There's an awkward pause. Rose looks really uncomfortable and I feel a wave of disappointment swell inside me. Slowly Rose reaches up and rubs her eye and then looks at me as if she's got nothing else to add. But it can't end here, not after everything I've done to find her. I mumble something about how much I wanted to connect with her and how I've got questions that need to be answered. I say I can't leave until they are. There's a tiny twitch in Rose's right eyelid. With a sigh she asks me what the questions are and I inhale.

Why did you abandon me?

Why didn't you take me back?

Who is my dad?

Why did you call me Ace?

Did you love me?

I ask the first question and Rose replies, "I'm not sure I'd say 'abandon'. I did what I felt was best for us both." I mutter that I think leaving a baby at the swimming pool is kind of "abandoning". Rose's eyes narrow slightly and she shakes her head and I get the feeling she's not going to discuss it further because she repeats she thought it was for the best. When I ask why she didn't keep me in the first place, Rose says, "I was young and alone and I tried to be a decent parent for a few weeks but it was terrible and I knew you'd have a good life without me. I'm afraid your father is long gone. He didn't want to know." That's question three answered without me even asking it. Whoever my dad was, he's not here now.

So I'm straight in with question four: "Why did you call me Ace?"

Two tiny circles of red build on Rose's cheeks. "When I was pregnant I lived near a shop. I'd go into the shop and buy spaghetti hoops."

"Was there a hero in the shop?" I'm a bit confused, but I must be named after a hero who saved the shop from a burglary or something. My stomach is a windmill. What's even better is that my real mother loves spaghetti hoops as much as me! I can't get the words out fast enough. "I love spaghetti hoops too," I squeak before she can explain any further.

Rose nods and then continues, "I'd go into the shop all the time, like I said. And it was because I craved spaghetti hoops." I tell Rose I know about cravings because I've watched Mum's baby programmes. "Yes, so as I was saying, I didn't eat much else." I'm not sure I understand yet what this has got to do with my name. "You asked me why you were called Ace...well, that was the name of the shop. It was called ACE, short for Alec's Cavern of Everything. I thought it would do as a name."

"The name of a shop?" I blink. "Where you got your spaghetti hoops? The shop was called ACE?"

It takes a second...

Phoom!

It feels like a kick in the guts from a wallaby when I register that Ace is not a superhero name at all. I was never destined to be excellent. I was named after a shop that sold spaghetti hoops. All I can think is that *I'm* like a spaghetti hoop – nothing special, just one hoop in a whole can of hoops; one hoop that you can't tell from another.

I'm almost dizzy with shock and Rose is staring at me and she says they were nice spaghetti hoops, if that helps. It doesn't help when she adds that she's never eaten them since because she got so sick of them after eating so many.

Bonbon barks and Rose bends down and picks him up, cradling him and smothering him with tiny kisses. He snuggles into the crook of her arm and Rose coos, "Oh, baby. Did you miss your mummy when you were in the garden?" I blink back my envy. How come the dog's getting kisses and cuddles? Why is she calling the dog her baby and herself its mummy? She hasn't said that about me yet and I *am* her baby and she *is* my mummy. I can't believe I feel this way about a dog.

The phone rings and Rose looks at it and then at me and then back at the phone, which doesn't stop ringing, and she eventually picks it up and says, "Hello."

There's silence and I don't know what's being said on the other end.

"Sorry, someone's just come to the door."

Silence hangs over us again. I swallow, thinking Rose is going to tell the person that I'm standing here. She'll say her son is standing in front of her.

"Oh, it's no one."

No one. Did Rose say I was *no one*? Surely she didn't mean it. I stare at her as she makes smacking kissy noises down the phone and then says, "Bye, see you later," before hanging up.

Rose says her husband will be home soon. I put my hands in my pockets and somehow it doesn't seem like the right time to ask Rose if I can come and live here with her and her husband, a man who isn't even my dad.

It is obvious Rose is ready for me to go as she's edging nearer to the door, so I quickly blurt out that I'm working on a *Forest For Ever* school project about my family tree. Shyly I say, "On *our* family tree." Bonbon skitters down the hallway and into the kitchen and Rose's eyes follow him. "We're having an exhibition on Tuesday – would you come and see my tree, please?

Please..." I can hear myself pleading and Rose is awkwardly shuffling, but she's making all the right noises about the project sounding fascinating. I pull the ticket from my school bag and hand it to her. "We could be on the front page of the *Pegasus Park Packet* if our story is the best. And I could come and get you that evening of the exhibition to take you there."

"Right," says Rose, looking at the invite. "You mean this coming Tuesday?" When I tell her yes, she nods and smiles. "I'll see what I can do," she adds.

"I'll come and get you anyway," I say. "I don't want you to get lost finding the school."

I grin as Rose pushes me towards the door. She smells of coconut and I imagine she's like an expensive tropical island – not that I know what that smells like, because Mum and Dad always take us on camping holidays. I want to hug her goodbye but it doesn't feel right. Instead I reach out my hand to shake hers. But my hand is covered in silver glitter – I see it glint – so I pull it back again quickly. Then before I know what's happened I'm back out on the street and the door has closed behind me, without time for a hug or a handshake or anything.

As I walk down the pathway I have a sudden urge to see my mother again. I run back and push my finger against the doorbell. Bonbon barks and Rose opens the front door and I pull off my bobble hat, letting loose a shock of red hair the exact same colour as Rose's. I hand my hat to Rose, telling her to look after it for me until Tuesday evening.

"I'll get it back then," I explain. As Rose takes the bobble hat, looking a little confused, I tell her it's important and that I'd never give it away unless the person was really special to me. Rose frowns and stares at it as if I've handed her a burst balloon. One hand moves to her temple and she rubs her head. She tries to give me a smile but it doesn't quite reach her eyes. I stare at her. *This is your mother*, I tell myself. My stomach flips over. I glance up at the house. *This is going to be your new home on Tuesday*, I add.

Suddenly I think of 53 Pegasus Park Towers and Mum. I didn't mean to think of her but she pops into my head. She'll be at home now, making dinner. It'll be something good for us and it'll taste horrible, but Mum will tell us she's keeping us healthy. Velvet will be playing with Sausage Roll and Minnie will be talking about "damned spots" which are mentioned in the Scottish play.

I snap back to myself when Rose says she's got to go because her husband will be home soon and they're going out to dinner with friends. There's an edge to her voice and it feels like she's in a mega hurry. With the most cheerful wave I can muster, I walk down the path again. When I glance back once more, hoping to give Rose a final smile, she's already gone. She'll keep my bobble hat safe though, I convince myself. She's my mother and she understands me. Mothers always understand their children, don't they?

As I wander down the street, I realize three things. The first thing is: if Rose didn't text me then who did? And the second thing is that I forgot to ask Rose: *Did you love me?* Then I think, *Of course she did.* The third thing is that glitter sticks to your hands like concrete.

22

SPROING

"What happened to you?" squeals Minnie as I open the flat door. "Where's your hat?"

Mum joins us in the hallway and Velvet too and they're all looking at me like I'm an alien who has just landed their spaceship at 53 Pegasus Park Towers. Mum says it's nice to see my hair for a change and she asks where the hat is and I say I let someone borrow it. "Someone at school?" asks Mum. I shrug and avoid answering, which is easy because Velvet is interrupting and asking if she can touch my hair, like she's never felt hair before.

"It's soft," says Velvet, giving my locks a tug.

"Like Sausage Roll's fur."

"I'm getting my hat back," I add quickly, comforting myself. "I just let the person borrow it, not have it for keeps. No way can they have it for keeps. But they're special, they'll look after it."

Minnie says I've actually got a normal-sized head when she was sure it was the size of a pea under there. Mum tells her to shush and I tell her to butt out of my business.

"I'm not a goat," says Minnie.

Minnie can't spoil this moment for me though. My real mother will come to my *Forest For Ever* exhibition next week. I'm going to go and pick her up to take her there. She was interested in it, I know she was. And I know seeing me on her doorstep was a big shock, because she wasn't expecting me – I understand, it's been eleven years. But she's going to come to the exhibition and then I'll move in with her and Bonbon and, bit by bit, it'll be perfect.

"Goats can't be the Lady in the Scottish play," adds Minnie and she begins talking about spots and then she says this is going to be the performance of a lifetime. "Just you wait until Tuesday – then I'll be worthy of an Oscar, or putting my hands in concrete on Hollywood Boulevard."

"Is that where they're re-concreting the pavement around Hollywood Parade, near Pegasus Park High Street?" Mum manages a little smile. "You don't want to put your hands in that."

Ignoring her, Minnie continues, "Just make sure you don't applaud Callum. He's dead to me."

"If he's Macbeth he's dead to everyone, I think," adds Mum. Then Mum's going on about what a fabulous family outing it will be. Yeah, witches and murder – seems like a great evening out to me, I tell myself. We could eat healthy popcorn while we watch the slayings.

"You can't get out of this," says Minnie, squinting at me. "I need all the applause I can get."

"What if I've got a bellyache?" I say cautiously.

"It doesn't stop your bum sitting on a chair," replies Minnie. She thinks for a second and shakes her head. "If you need the toilet, they're right beside the stage." When I say I might have a headache, she says she'll give me a headache soon, because she's going to bop me on it, with a plank. "You're coming," says Minnie finally, her eyes bulging like two tightly squeezed hard-boiled eggs. "Everyone in this flat is."

"Sausage Roll?" Velvet grins.

"If that dog barks in the middle of my performance

I'll personally find him and take away his rubber dog toys."

Velvet shakes her head and says Sausage Roll is going to stay at home.

That evening my mind is all over the place and I keep thinking about Rose and her red hair and how she used to eat spaghetti hoops. Everything is so muddled I can't even concentrate on watching TV and when Minnie turns it over to her model programme I don't argue.

Minnie's phone bleeps and she looks down and tuts before staring back at the TV. "They didn't stick out their booty either," shouts Minnie. "Knock off another point." The phone bleeps again and Minnie looks at it. "Oh, shut up, Callum. I gave you another chance and you're still getting texts from Sienna and then denying it." There's another bleep and Minnie says it's Sienna and she's not going to text her back. She throws down the phone in disgust – but when I glance over at her, her eyes are glittering like crystals. The phone bleeps again and Minnie says, "Ignoring you and ignoring your stupid texts." Then she stops ignoring and begins texting.

I'm trying to watch the girl with the big teeth getting

a makeover and she's wailing that she doesn't want a shaved head. "Wear a bobble hat," I mumble. "I would if I could."

Minnie gets up from the sofa and goes to the toilet. I hear the door slam and the sound of gushing water and then the squeak of the toilet roll holder. Her phone bleeps again and I get up and go to silence it – and that's when my heart leaps into my mouth and stays there. I stare at the text message that's just come through. There's a name and number beside it. I recognize that number. At first I'm confused. It's the number that Rose supposedly texted me from. "Why would *you* send me a message pretending to be my real mother?" I seethe.

I drop the phone and march out of the living room. I barge past Minnie in the hallway and she says I need to look where I'm going. "Losing your bobble hat has gone to your head," she spits.

"Playing Lady Macbeth has gone to yours," I reply, opening SPAM HQ's door and then slamming it behind me. When I drop onto my bed I pick up my own mobile phone and look at the message from "Rose Walker" and I can't believe who is really behind it. It's definitely the same number I've just seen on Minnie's phone. "Why would you hurt me? You don't even know me," I whisper and then I chuck the phone across the bed and it skips across the surface like a flat stone on the ocean.

That night I dream I'm in a swimming pool and it's dark and Rose is there, but she's talking on the phone and it feels like I'm drowning but she doesn't notice and someone has to throw a giant spaghetti hoop to save me. When I wake up I can tell it's still the middle of the night because my room is in blackness. Then I hear Mum's bedroom door open and Mum tiptoes down the hallway. I hear the bathroom door open and close and then the toilet flushes and the tap gushes. Mum sniffs and then blows her nose and there's another sniff and silence for a few moments. After a while, I hear my bedroom door creak open and a tiny triangle of light puddles into the room. I give a pretend snore as Mum whispers, "I love you, Adam. You're my heart." I can feel my own heart beating inside my chest and it feels so loud I'm surprised Mum doesn't think I've got a kettledrum in my bedroom.

My door is softly closed.

I'm in darkness again.

"You didn't," says Tiny Eric in school on Monday.

"Oh yes I did," I reply with some pride. "I walked right up to the door and rang the bell and she answered." I swallow deeply.

"Did she look like you imagined?"

"Kind of. She has the same hair as me," I reply, combing my fingers through my hair. Tiny Eric says I look good without the bobble hat and then asks what the house was like. "It was nearly the same size as Buckingham Palace. Only it was blue and didn't have a flag. There weren't any guards either and no balcony and no corgis. There was a dog called Bonbon. I think it was a Chihuahua. It yapped a lot. She said he was her baby."

Tiny Eric's eyes widen. "So, nothing like Buckingham Palace then. What happens next? Do you move there? Is she going to give you your own bedroom? Will it be full of comics? Will you take your own stuff from the flat?"

I hadn't thought of any of those things. I hadn't even asked if I could live with her.

I pause. "I'm going to bring her to the *Forest For Ever* exhibition. And after that I'm going to ask if I can come and live with her. She'll have seen the family tree by that stage and it'll be perfectomundo. That's the right time to ask. I didn't want to rush into it." Perfectomundo,

250

man oh man, why did I even say that? I sound like Dad when he has no grasp of English.

When the bell goes we head towards class. I grab Tiny Eric's arm and say, "There's one more shocker. Rose never sent me a text saying goodbye – and you'll never guess who did. Wait until you hear this..."

Tiny Eric nods all the way to the classroom as I tell him what I found out. And then he stops and says, "Why though? Why lie?"

"I don't know," I shrug. "I don't understand it at all."

In class, Mrs Chatterjee says we need to check our trees and put any last bits on them before they go in the exhibition for tomorrow. I finish off mine by sprinkling it with more silver glitter. Minnie always says "more is more". Mind you, she's usually talking about make-up.

"This is looking good," says Mrs Chatterjee, leaning down and looking at me. "Your mum is going to love it." Then she wanders over to Tiny Eric. She doesn't ask him about his tree, which is totally empty, except for lots of leaves. Instead she leans down and whispers something to him, and then she rests her hand on his shoulder before moving on. It makes me stop throwing glitter around.

I lean over to Tiny Eric and whisper, "You haven't got much on your tree. How come?"

"My tree is broken," says Tiny Eric. When I say it doesn't look broken, he explains, "That's the thing. The tree looks okay but on the inside it isn't. And some of the roots are cracked. I don't think I'll be able to make it better."

"I could help," I say, trying to wipe glittery dandruff off my blazer shoulders. "I've nearly finished mine."

"You can't help," says Tiny Eric. "No amount of glitter is going to sort this out."

At the end of the day, Tiny Eric and me walk through the playground. He looks down at me and says I've been a great *przyjaciel*. When I ask him what that means, he smiles and says, "Friend."

"You're a great przy-ja-wotsit too," I say.

Tiny Eric gets conjunctivitis again, then swings his school bag over his shoulder and says he's got to hurry home this evening because he's got lots to do. With a wave, I say, "Bye then."

But instead of saying goodbye back, Tiny Eric salutes and says, "You're a superhero, Adam."

At the time I didn't think anything of it, but as I'm walking home now I remember he said something else. He said I'd *been* a great friend. Why didn't he say I *am* a great friend? Tomorrow I am going to tell him about his tenses. Just like Mrs Chatterjee once said to me.

23

THWACK

Next day is the *Forest For Ever* exhibition. The classroom clock ticks from 8.50 to 9 a.m. Then it's 9.04 and there's still no sign of Tiny Eric. He didn't tell me he wasn't coming in today, but I did think he was acting a bit strange yesterday. Last night I couldn't get it out of my head that he said we'd *been* good friends and I wanted to text him, but Sausage Roll needed a walk in the local play park and Velvet made me take her too and we got carried away having a who-can-swing-the-highest competition and I forgot all about it.

Mrs Chatterjee is calling the register and I'm first and I shout, "Yes, miss!" She glances up at me and then keeps running down the names. Nish Choudary shouts, "Yes, miss!" and after that there's a constant drone of "Yes, miss!" until she calls out Belle Talbot and finally closes the register. I look around and no one except me seems to have noticed that she didn't call out Tiny Eric's name.

All morning I keep looking over at Tiny Eric's desk and there's something strange about it. At first I'm not sure what, but then I realize his pencil case has gone and when I sneak a look inside the desk, his books are gone too. I gave him a badge from Surelock Homes once. It was a promotional thing and Dad brought home loads of them. That's gone too. There's nothing left. It's like Tiny Eric has disappeared.

At lunch, The Beast squeezes up beside me and pulls a peanut butter sandwich out of a red lunchbox and takes a big bite. Between chews The Beast says, "You're like Batman without his mask." A chunky finger points to where my bobble hat was.

"Do you like Batman?" I ask, opening a packet of kale crisps.

I peep inside the bag before offering one to The Beast. I watch as The Beast sniffs the green crisp, then takes a nibble before spitting it back out, saying, "Ugh! They're awful." I agree, laughing. The Beast continues, "I love Batman and Spider-Man and The Incredible Hulk and the Zorbitans. I love all the superheroes."

My eyes widen. "I didn't think a..." I cough, spraying kale crumbs everywhere, as I think twice about what I was going to say. "I didn't think a person like you would love the Zorbitans. I love the Zorbitans too. Did you see the latest issue?" The Zorbitans actually found The Grand Moon Master, but their emerald hearts didn't glow and that's how it ended. Dad said it was a comic "cliffhanger" and I said I didn't like comic "cliffhangers".

The Beast vacuums up a chocolate biscuit, then says, "I wanted the Zorbitans' hearts to glow. It was a swizz. I bet their hearts *did* glow, but we just didn't see that bit. It'll be in another comic."

I nod – The Beast has a point. Surely their hearts did glow, but it was after we'd turned the last page. "You're right," I say. And The Beast smiles at me. The Beast has quite nice teeth, if you look closely.

After lunch, Mrs Chatterjee asks us to get out our trees because we're going to put them in position in the school assembly hall for this evening's exhibition. I wait until everyone else has pulled their trees out of the cupboard and then go in for mine. Tiny Eric's is still sitting in the corner and I pull it out too, saying to Mrs Chatterjee that we need to include it in the exhibition even if there aren't any tags on it.

"He might be able to come tonight. Maybe he's feeling better," I say hopefully.

"Ah, that's a lovely thought, Adam." Mrs Chatterjee perches on the edge of her desk. "But I'm not sure Eric will be there tonight. Class, I think I should let you know that sadly Eric won't be joining us in this class again." There's a shocked silence. Nish looks over at me and I feel a rocket of worry launch from my stomach. "Without going into all the details, his mother has decided to move back to her parents' house in Poland for a while and Eric will be going to a local school there."

Tiny Eric's gone? He's moving house to Poland? And he's got a new school already? I saw that word written on the photo he brought out of his blazer pocket, so it must be true. My eyes begin to burn and I have to look up at the ceiling to make all the water dribble back into my eyes and down my throat. And it feels like I'm battling conjunctivitis too as my mind races over everything.

I look up at the wall where Mrs Chatterjee has put

Tiny Eric's drawing of his dad and it hits me like a whack from Thor's hammer. It was Tiny Eric's dad I saw that evening at the swimming pool. I knew I recognized him from somewhere – the classroom wall, that's where. It would all fall into place if there wasn't something else troubling me. The woman he was kissing wasn't Tiny Eric's mum.

It all makes sense to me now. That's why Tiny Eric drew his dad as a monster the other week – he'd been let down. It was about so much more than moving house.

I want to hide in my bobble hat and feel safe but it's not there and my head feels cold as I slump onto the desk. Tiny Eric isn't allowed to go. I don't want to lose him, because he helped me find my real mother. It was his four-leaf clover drawing and his poster that made it happen. He is my friend. I knew something was wrong but I was so tied up in myself that I didn't see how sad he was. How can you not see that your friend has problems too?

I've got to put it right. Being a superhero means recognizing when others need you, and even if I failed before, I've got to do something for Tiny Eric now. I raise my hand.

"I want to sort out Tiny Eric's tree. It can survive and be okay. It just needs some love."

Mrs Chatterjee nods. "What a lovely idea, Adam."

Nish puts his hand up. "I'll help him."

One by one, everyone in the class puts their hand up. "We'll help."

Overwhelmed, Mrs Chatterjee says, "Children, you are wonderful and I'm proud of you. What a good deed to do for your friend. You all deserve a treat. Remember I said the winner of the best tree would get some sweets? Well, I've got enough sweets in my bag for everyone in the class, because you're all wonderful." Mrs Chatterjee reaches into her handbag under the table and brings out a big bag of liquorice. "Don't all rush at once," she says, opening the bag.

No one rushes all at once, but I get up and go to the front and take a brown one and try to convince myself it's chocolate. Smiling, I go back to my seat.

"You've got a black tooth," shrieks Nish as I chew the liquorice and swallow it down almost whole. "You're like a pirate."

Everyone wants one then and we're all black-toothed pirates as we repair Tiny Eric's tree. I write lots of nice things about Tiny Eric and I tie them on. Nish works on more leaves and he makes them look realistic, with veins and everything. Eventually the tree's upright and everyone looks at it and gives it a round of applause.

Tiny Eric's tree might have felt empty without the tags but now it is better, because it is a family tree and we've been his family, at least for a while.

Mrs Chatterjee looks at all the trees and says we've done ourselves proud and we're going to go to the assembly hall now and put them up, ready for tonight's exhibition.

In the hall she consults her clipboard and begins calling out names and pointing to spots on the floor where she thinks the trees will look best. I'm in the centre and Tiny Eric's tree is going to be beside mine. Mrs Chatterjee finds a black sack behind the curtain on the stage and brings it out. She rummages around inside it and snakes of fairy lights slither out. "Let our families shine," says Mrs Chatterjee, trying to untangle the lights.

Five minutes later we're all trying to untangle the lights and Mrs Chatterjee is muttering about tangle monsters and how you put fairy lights in a bag untangled and then they come back out all chewed up and knotted. Eventually we get the fairy lights sorted out and we put them all around our trees and Mrs Chatterjee switches them on...and it's magical.

"Each tree represents a family. Each tree is a guiding light in the world. They all shine in their own way. And although the trees are separate they are connected by light and love and humanity. And perhaps sometimes it can feel like the trunk of a tree has split, but the tree will still flourish in the end. It can take a while for the damage to fade, but with love and water, green shoots will come again." Mrs Chatterjee looks at Tiny Eric's tree and nods.

As we're leaving the assembly hall, Mrs Chatterjee pulls me to the side and asks if I've enjoyed the project. I tell her I have and she continues, "I know your mum will be very proud when she sees your tree. It's so good I bet she'll have tears in her eyes."

"Yes, miss," I reply. "We're coming together. I can't wait for you to meet her."

Mrs Chatterjee pulls a face. "I've met her," she says. "At parents' evening, remember." Then she shouts at Nish for not closing the door. "Were you born in a barn?" Everyone laughs.

Minnie is waiting for me at the gate after school. "I thought I'd come and get you. We finished our dress rehearsal a bit early today. It was the last one before tonight's big performance." Minnie looks at me and then combs her fingers through her hair. "Adam, tell me the truth."

I swallow.

"You want to come to my play, don't you? You've not mentioned it once." I puff out some relief. I shrug and Minnie continues, "It's just that I haven't really spoken to you properly for ages and I thought it might help if we talked. I mean, we used to talk." She clears her throat as we head down Agamemnon Road. "I always wanted a brother, you know," she says.

"You did?" I find that pretty hard to believe.

"Yes, when Mum and Dad were getting you I was really excited. That's what Mum says anyway – I can't really remember. But that's because it's like you've always been part of the family. And when you arrived you and me gave each other presents, because Mum said you should give a gift to a new baby and the new baby should give you one. She said that was fair." Minnie hoists her school bag back up onto her shoulder. "You got me a doll."

"I can't remember," I reply, chewing on my lip. To be fair they don't taste great so I stop.

"That's because Mum bought it, silly." Minnie laughs. "You were just a baby, so you could hardly trot off to the toy shop and buy me a doll. I think it was Mum's way of making things nice. Mum's like that."

"I know."

"Do you know what I gave you?"

I shrug. "A toy?"

Minnie smiles and the wind catches her hair and it flies up like brown ribbons. "I gave you a bobble hat. To be fair, I don't remember it either. But that's what Mum told me she bought from me to you. Mum said you looked beautiful and the bobble was almost as big as you. When you got older you wanted to wear a bobble hat all the time and Mum kept buying them, and then it sort of became your security blanket. She told me off once when I was making fun behind your back, and said it was fine for you to wear the bobble hat until you didn't need it."

"I'm getting it back," I reply. I feel my cheeks burn.

"Right," says Minnie.

"I'm going to be wearing it later."

"Adam, you're happy, right?"

Minnie is being all weird and nice but I still can't bring myself to talk to her about the stuff I really need to. And she's no better than me, because she's skating around everything like a world-champion figure skater. "Yes," I reply. "I'm happy."

"You're happy with us, I mean."

I swallow and the wind ruffles my hair and it feels strange being without my bobble hat. Clearing my throat I reply, "Yes, I'm happy with you."

As we walk on in silence, I feel Minnie pat my shoulder and then drop her hand.

"One more thing," says Minnie. She stops and turns to look at me. Her eyes are like muddy pools and her jaw is set. "I'm sorry."

I shrug, not knowing what to say. Somehow shrugging seems easy.

We don't speak again, not even when we reach the tower block. The lift is broken and we walk up the concrete steps. We pass Mrs Karimloo's place and wander down the corridor and then up another flight until we reach our flat. Minnie turns the key in the door and repeats, "I'm sorry, Adam."

Minnie never apologizes for anything. "For what?" I ask, my voice tight as an over-blown balloon.

"For not being a good sister to you. For not noticing you were fed up. For trying to mess things up for you because I'm selfish. For never wanting you to leave us."

I want to say *You are a good sister* and *I forgive you*, but I'm too choked up to speak.

24

PHOOM

"Okay, kiddoes. I'm glad you're both home. We've got to get everything sorted out if we're going to make this play in time. So, Adam, get cleaned up. Minnie, do whatever it is you do when you spend an hour in the bathroom. Break a leg or whatever it is. Oh, and before I forget we've got a little surprise for everyone after the play." As Minnie opens her mouth to ask what it is, Mum laughs and puts a finger to her lips as if she's not telling. As Minnie goes into her bedroom and slams the door, Mum adds, "And, Velvet, can you please stop lying on the floor playing with Sausage Roll, I've just put you in a clean top." Velvet looks up from the kitchen floor and then says she has to play with the dog or he'll get sad.

"I'll get sad if I have to go and iron another top," exclaims Mum. She's clucking about like a hen looking after its chicks. "I've texted Dad and he's on his way and will be back in about five minutes."

The words wrap around me and I feel my chest tighten. After Minnie's triumphant play and after all her applause, Mum and Dad are going to sit us down and tell us about the jelly bean. Then they'll say they're making sacrifices. After that I'll be told I've got to go and that they're rehoming me. If I hadn't found my real mother, this would have been a disaster. But I'm okay now because I can live with Rose and I don't need to be rehomed with a stranger. I think for a second: Rose *is* a stranger. But then I shake the thought away.

The front door opens and I hear Dad shuffle into the hall and shout, "I'm home." Velvet runs to meet him and I hear her telling him she loves him and then she's stampeding back down the hall. The bedroom door opens and Minnie is shouting that Velvet can come in but not to disturb her. Dad saunters into the living room and as I follow him he looks at me and says, "Argggghhh! I still can't get used to you without the hat."

I shrug and pull at the threads on the cuff of my school jumper. "I'll get it back," I mumble.

"So, are you ready to go and see a crazy, loud woman who wants her own way? And while you're there, do you want to see Lady Macbeth too?" Dad laughs.

"Adam." Mum peeps into the living room. "You're not getting ready. Hurry, we haven't got for ever." I tell Mum I want to stay in my school uniform. "Why? You don't need to wear a uniform to Minnie's play."

I can't tell Mum about my exhibition and I don't think Mrs Chatterjee would be happy if I turned up in my jeans and a hoodie. "I thought it would look smart," I lie.

Mum's eyes glitter and she comes into the living room and ruffles my hair and says I'm very thoughtful. She doesn't suspect a thing. She doesn't know I'm going to make an excuse and leave them when I get to Blessed Trinity. I thought I could pretend to have tummy pains and then I could go to the toilet. They'll be so caught up in the play they won't notice how long I'm gone. I can text them every so often pretending I'm in the toilet, but really I'll run to Rose's and take her to my exhibition instead. The play is bound to go on for hours.

"You're the best son in the world," says Dad. "What would we do without you?"

"You'd have a new arrival – that little surprise for us." I can't believe I've just said it out loud. It's like my tongue doesn't even belong to me.

Mum and Dad look at me and then at each other like they're playing a ping-pong game. What they don't do is deny it's true. "How did you know?" Mum's voice has dropped to a whisper. "Don't let Velvet and Minnie in on the secret yet because we're going to tell everyone after the play. It's going to be amazing, isn't it? Are you happy? We are." Mum takes Dad's hand. "We've waited for this for ages."

"It's a boy." I think of the list of boys' names that I found in the book. "You're going to call him Jack."

"Yes, it's a boy." Mum grins. "We've got to find him a little space in the flat. But we haven't decided on a name – we thought we'd let you all name him instead. Oh, what a wonderful addition he'll be to this family."

There's a cold hard ball of ice inside me and my brain begins spinning like a top. I don't want to name the jelly bean because he's taking *my* little space. Plus, it looks like Mum and Dad are beyond thrilled because they're sharing jokes and smiling. For the first time ever, I feel totally left out of this family – like I don't belong here.

They've already moved on. This proves it. Mum and Dad are thinking of their son. Not me. I knew I'd have to go but now the time is here I want to puke. Dad is smiling at me as though someone has jammed a melon slice in his mouth. Then he says it's going to be exciting having another little scamp in the flat. In that second my ears turn to fuzzy felt but I see they're happy and that means they must be happy that I'm going and Jack the jelly bean is coming. It hurts that I tried for so long to be a superhero and make Mum smile and now it's the jelly bean that's making her truly happy.

"I don't care about him," I yell, and Mum's jaw hits the floor. "What about me?" My voice is so high-pitched all the dogs in the neighbourhood have probably pricked up their ears.

"What *about* you?" Dad's face is blank. He rubs his hand over his head. "What are you talking about?" He isn't even pretending he's bothered, he's just staring at me as if I've gone wackadoodle and he hasn't got time for this.

"Oh, Adam, it's a lovely thing for us all. Things have been hard recently and this is a new beginning." Mum's reaching out to me. Her hand is warm but I shrug it off. "We thought it was a nice surprise." She looks wounded, like I've trampled on her toes in stilts.

Minnie appears at the living room door. She looks around at everyone, then says, "Awkward."

"Don't be so silly," says Dad. "Nothing is awkward. Now, are you ready for the play? We can't wait to see you being a star." Dad's bustling about again and it's obvious the conversation is almost over, but I can't let it go. I'm like a dog with a giant dinosaur's bone between my teeth. "Go and get ready, Adam," warns Dad.

I feel swallowed up. "All this is because of a 'jelly bean'!" I spit the words out. "You were going to let me go over that jelly bean – well I've got better things to do anyway. I don't care about the jelly bean, because I've got my own life to live." I want my bobble hat more than ever because I've got nowhere to hide and Mum and Dad are staring at me and Minnie is laughing and saying, "Jelly bean, what jelly bean?"

The laughing bangs inside my head like a drum and when Dad mouths, "Jelly bean?" and holds his hands up in confusion, I can't control myself any more. I rush forward and pummel him in the stomach with my fists. His mouth makes a big O. And I hear myself shouting, "YOU'RE NOT MY REAL PARENTS! YOU CAN'T TELL ME WHAT TO DO!" The words burn like balls of fire inside my mouth and I can't believe I've said them out loud and I see the pain in Mum's eyes and I know I might as well have punched her too, only with words.

If I don't belong to this family then I don't want Granddad Fred's watch any more – they can have it back. I grab at it on my wrist and pull. The strap snaps and I throw the watch on the floor. It lies at my feet. Without waiting for anyone to speak, I run to the front door, open it and slam it hard behind me, before dashing down the stairs, my breath bursting through my mouth.

I punched Dad like he was a supervillain. I punched him hard and I hurt Mum with words and I threw away the watch that was supposed to remind me of the family and then I ran away. Superheroes shouldn't really run away, but then again, dads aren't supposed to be supervillains.

I'll move into Rose's house immediately, I tell myself, straight after tonight's exhibition. I'll explain that I can't stay at the flat any more. I'll get my bobble hat back too. My feet clatter down the last flight of steps and I'm out into the evening. *It'll be okay*, I tell myself. The whole way across the grass I soothe myself, and by the time I've reached Agamemnon Road I'm convinced that Rose will hear my story (I won't tell her I punched Dad) and she'll love me. Mothers always love their kids, deep down. She'll get to know me and she won't be able to help herself because I'm so loveable. And I'll be so nice to Bonbon and if Bonbon loves me I'll have to stay.

"It's going to be awesome," I mutter, trying to forget what just happened at home.

When I see the blue house I feel a swirl of happiness and I stand in front of it, just inhaling. My stomach bubbles as I crunch over the gravel and I pull my hand from my pocket and press the gold doorbell. I can hear it tinkle inside. I'm already prepared with a big smile. After a few seconds the smile drops and I press the doorbell again, and then the smile is plastered over my face again, waiting for Rose to throw the door open. I press the doorbell again and again and then I hold my finger on it for ages.

My phone bleeps.

Adam, I have no idea what the problem is with jelly beans. But come back and we can chat about it. We all like jelly beans, if that helps. I won't ring in case you're still annoyed, but text me. Love Mum x
PS We're heading off to the play now but we can meet you at Blessed Trinity.

I don't answer, because all Mum's saying is she likes the jelly bean – she doesn't understand and I'm not going to try to make her. My fist bangs on the front door and there's a horrible ripple of worry washing over me but I try to ignore it.

At the house next door there's the spit of gravel as a car pulls up and a woman gets out. "You okay there?" She looks at me with my fist still on the door. My knuckles are red but I nod and then bang again, and I pretend to ignore the woman as she pulls some plastic bags from the front seat of her car. Slamming the car door, she looks over at me again and says they're not there.

"They're out?" My fist drops. I feel it throb. "When will Rose be back?"

"Probably in six months," says the woman. She smiles and sets her bags on her front step. The woman must be joking, so I snort and start laughing, and then ask her when Rose will really be back. "Okay, it could be seven months or even a year," she tells me. "They tend to rent this property out." I realize she's serious. The laugh dies on my lips and I feel my legs go weak and wobbly as a newborn giraffe's. "He's got a job in Switzerland and they live there mainly. They do pop back occasionally to sort out this house."

Pop back? They really live in Switzerland for up to a year? That's what Sharkey said too, so I know she's telling me the truth. My tongue feels thick and it's hard to swallow properly. "Are you joking about them having left? I've only just spoken to Rose and given her my bobble hat." I know the woman isn't kidding but I have to ask. She shakes her head and says she's not. The world goes blurry around me and I have to steady myself against the wall.

"What's your name?" The woman is squinting at me now, suspicious of what I'm doing hammering on the door of someone who hardly lives here.

"Um," I say, my mouth draining of saliva.

"You must have a name. Perhaps I could try and let them know you called."

I swallow. "Yes, I have a name." I pause, thinking about how Rose said I was named after a shop that sold spaghetti hoops. Ace wasn't such a brilliant name after all and instead of being proud of it I don't want to be Ace any more. My heart heavy, I say, "Just call me Spaghetti-Hoop Boy."

The woman cocks her head to the side as if she's heard the words but she can't understand, and then I turn and stagger across the gravel. When I reach the pavement I take off running away from the blue house as fast as my feet will carry me. The wind whooshes in my hair and I feel the prickle of it in my eyes as I run down Maltman's Hill towards the centre of Pegasus Park.

When she was on the phone I remember my real mother telling her husband that I'm no one – and maybe she's right. Perhaps I'm even less than Spaghetti-Hoop Boy. Maybe I'm no one.

No one

No one

No one

No one

No one

No one

25

KRASH

You're no one, because the jelly bean is going to take your place at home and your real mother has abandoned you for the second time, I tell myself. Rose would say she hadn't "abandoned" me again but she has. The tears come and I can hardly see, so I let my feet carry me wherever they want to go. One tiny conversation with a woman I don't know and my family tree has been chopped down and destroyed. There's no *Forest For Ever*. There's not even a tree left.

I feel as if I don't know where I'm going or how I'm going to get there. Even if I reach a safe place, I don't know that I'll survive what's happened. I'm as wobbly as a jelly on a trampoline. "You left without saying goodbye, Rose! How can you do that to me again? I was going to show you the tree and move in and be friends with Bonbon. I was going to make you love me. And you have my hat!" I shout into the wind.

A wave of sadness almost swallows me. Five minutes ago I thought I had a future with my real mother. I thought I could live in the blue house. I thought I'd have a new home. I'd be safe. But I'm not. I hoped that I could forget about the past and my real mother would hug me and tell me she was sorry she left me by the swimming pool and that her home was my home. And I'd say it was okay because I'd already forgotten about the past and we were speeding towards our future. But there is no hope now because it's all exploded and I don't know if I'm Ace or Adam or Spaghetti-Hoop Boy or no one.

No one, I say to myself again. *You're definitely no one.*

I run down the road towards nothing, no future, no Rose, no idea where I'm going. Inside I'm screaming but no one can hear. Weaving through tooting traffic, I run down Kink Road where Tiny Eric lives, and I hope I can find Tiny Eric and I'll tell him not to leave and he'll help me and I'll help him. But outside his house the *FOR SALE* sign has changed to *SOLD* and the curtains are pulled and I know he's not there either. Tiny Eric has already gone.

The sun dips between the clouds and the air cools and I feel myself shiver. How could my real mother do this to me again? The question spins around like a conker dangling on a string inside my head. I wanted her to want me so much that I'd forget about having to leave my family. Deep down I believed that Rose could replace my mum when my mum had a new baby to replace me. For some reason I thought a little part of me that was always missing wouldn't be any more. I was wrong. There was just one problem – she never wanted me in the first place. My real mother was never a mother.

I stagger towards the flats, my heart broken like a Christmas bauble stomped underfoot. Beyond me I can see Pegasus Park Towers and that's when my phone bleeps again. It's Mum saying that I'm not at Blessed Trinity and she's getting worried now.

If you don't want to come here, Adam, please go home and wait for me there. X

My old home is at the top of the tower block but as I ascend the stairs I realize I can't go there. It's not my home any more. This is worse than my worries about being rehomed with strangers. I can't go to the flat and my real mother's home isn't my home and it's never going to be.

Through a river of tears, I notice the flat that used to belong to Mrs Karimloo and I remember what Dad said. Glancing around to make sure no one can see me, I bend down and lift the flowerpot. There's a flash of silver. The old front door key is there, just as Dad said. She must have forgotten to take it with her. I pick it up and turn it over in my hand and then I push it into the lock, my heart thundering. I twist it and the door opens and I sneak inside. The tears come now – I want my bobble hat back. I want my mum back. Is it so awful to want what everyone else has? I want to be normal and things to be perfect. I wanted to find the missing part of my life...but will I always feel like there's a hole inside me?

There is nothing but quiet inside the flat. I suck the air through my teeth as I wander down the dark hallway and into the living room. There are no curtains and through the window I see Pegasus Park laid out below like a small Lego town. That's when I scream: "I don't understand what's happened to me!" And the words are so angry that it startles me and and I'm exhausted by all the emotions pouring out.

Quiet, tired, broken, I slip down onto the floor and lie curled up in the dust. There's a small bleep from my phone and I don't even bother to look at it. I close my eyes and Rose creeps into my mind and I have to force my eyes open again to stop her. A few moments later the phone bleeps a second time and I weakly pull it from my pocket and stare at the message.

Mum here. I'm coming to you. Velvet says she's sending Sausage Roll in front because he'll lead me straight to you. She says he's a bloodhound. Did you ever know he was a bloodhound? No, me neither. x

There's a silly smile on my lips because that's just like Velvet. She did say Sausage Roll was special and I figured that was because he was invisible, but trust her to say he was a bloodhound all along. I love Velvet. The smile falls again.

Outside I can hear a police siren slicing the air and I huddle deeper into the shadows. The cold early evening light dribbles into the room and dust dances around me like tiny sprites at a ball. All these thoughts gallop through my head and I find myself whispering, "What did I do wrong when I was a baby? What did I do wrong the second time?" A sob builds up in my chest and it gets so big it spills into a wail and my eyes feel like they've been stung by a scorpion. Tears spill down my cheeks and I don't stop them.

Look at me, I'm not a superhero. I'm no one.

No one wants me. *I* don't even want me. I hate who I am, but worse than that, I don't even *know* who I am.

Everyone in my class will be at the school now for the *Forest For Ever* exhibition. They'll be chattering like monkeys at feeding time and Mrs Chatterjee will be ticking the list to make sure we've all turned up. The *Pegasus Park Packet* reporter will be there. I pull my arms from my blazer and try to hide inside it, but it's not my bobble hat. It's not safe. I wish I'd never given my hat away, because it was my security blanket. Stupidly, I gave it to someone who didn't even need it and didn't care about what it meant to me. It was from Minnie and it made me feel like I was part of the family. I was in Minnie's gang, the Butters' gang, and I was safe and no one and nothing could ever hurt me again.

That's gone now.

I'm not in anyone's gang.

I pull the blazer from my head and wipe my damp cheeks with the corner of my sleeve and then I curl up again like a tiny prawn, my head resting against the wooden floor. There are noises from above me and I can imagine all the families in the flats around me having fun and I want to join in but it seems so far away. There's a creaking inside the flat and I squeeze my eyes tight. *Shh...* I tell myself. There are monsters all around.

When you don't have your mum, you notice the monsters.

Outside another siren comes and goes. I gulp the stale air and it's hard because my chest feels tight, like there's a rhino sitting on it. At first I take tiny gasps, because I've got this – I know how to breathe. It happens without you thinking about it. But now that I *am* thinking about it, it seems difficult. This time I only take half a breath and sweat begins to build on my upper lip. The next breath is a full one and I feel relieved, but the breath that comes after is a half, and another half breath comes after that, and it feels like I'm sinking down through the floorboards.

I don't know how long I'm lying there, but it's long enough to feel frightened and surrounded by monsters. My eyes are squeezed so tight now I can see tiny floating spaceships behind my lids. As I'm wishing I could evaporate like candyfloss in your mouth or slip through the floorboards, I hear footsteps outside. They come close and then they clatter up the steps to the floor above. I hear a door slam and then a few moments later it slams again.

My tears are warm and I let them soak into my hair.

I hear footsteps again. They're close.

The front door creaks and then I hear footsteps inside the flat's hallway and I can barely breathe. The steps are careful, slow, and then they stop. And I stop too – I stop moving, stop breathing, stop everything. It feels like even the world has stopped.

"Hello," whispers the tiniest voice.

It's a monster and it's found me. You should never answer a monster. The floorboards creak as I move my elbow.

"Hello." The voice dribbles into the room. "Is anyone there?"

No, there's no one. I'm no one.

26

ZOING

The voice comes again, soft like a song. "Hello? Adam, are you in here?" It's Mum and her voice cracks as she whispers, "Oh, Adam, please don't be lost. I can't lose you. I found you once, please let me find you again."

My heart stops galloping and my muscles relax almost automatically the second I realize it's her voice. I can't even see Mum yet but the black blanket of fear is falling off me and I know it's being replaced by Mum's blanket of love. The smell of damp begins to disappear and is replaced by the scent of sunshine.

The footsteps begin to move again. "Adam, if you're here I want you to know how much I love you."

"I love you too," I whisper.

I unfurl from the floor and Mum rushes into the room and she sees me in the corner and falls down beside me, and she's saying she's so glad she found me and she was worried sick and I shouldn't have run off like that. She said she tried the flat and when I wasn't there she panicked until she remembered what Dad said a while ago to her about Mrs Karimloo's flat being empty.

Mum can see me so I'm not invisible even if I feel like it. Mum can see me inside and out too. "Why are you here, alone in the dark?" When I don't answer, Mum continues, "Okay, you don't have to speak if the words won't come. Let me talk to you instead, because sometimes it's time for a mum to speak up." When she says the word "Mum" the tears spill down my cheeks and Mum uses her thumb to wipe them away.

"I *am* your mum, so I'm allowed to say that. You said we're not your real parents, but where it counts, deep down in here..." Mum's fingertip moves to her chest where her heart is. "...I know we are."

I look up at Mum, maintaining eye contact. "I'm sorry for what I said."

Mum tells me there's nothing to be sorry for. Then she says, "I guessed you might be here because I knew you'd never go far from home, and Dad told me he'd mentioned the key was under a flowerpot to you. Pegasus Park Towers *is* your home, Adam, even if you don't think so sometimes." More tears come as I think about the jelly bean and how my room here will be his and how I envy him because *I* want my room.

Mum brings a tissue out of her pocket and hands it to me and I give my nose a big blow. "I thought things weren't right recently," she says.

"What do you mean?" I murmur, winding my school tie around my fingers.

"You weren't Adam somehow," says Mum, "and I couldn't put my finger on it, but something felt different. I felt like I'd lost my Adam and I wasn't sure exactly where he'd gone. It was as if you stopped being you and started being someone else – someone distant."

I breathe in and scratch the side of my head where all the tears have made my hair damp and my skin tickle. "I wanted to be a superhero." I pause. "A superhero called Ace. I wanted to make you happy – I wanted to make *everyone* happy."

Mum nods and she doesn't look surprised. It's pretty hard to surprise Mum, even if you put cling film over the toilet or a pretend spider in her bed. "I see. How did you find out your name?" I tell Mum I searched for the envelope I wasn't supposed to look at until I was sixteen. "Ah," says Mum, but she's not angry. "It *was* your envelope, but I just felt it was better for you to see it when you were a little older, that's all. I wasn't keeping it from you."

"I was called Ace, Mum."

"I know."

"I thought it was a special name for a special boy."

"It is. You are a special boy."

"But it's not." I grimace. "I'm not."

"It's the name your birth mother gave you. It is special and you are special and don't let anyone make you think differently."

"I wanted to find her and I wanted to be excellent too. Because if I was, everyone would..." The words stutter out: "Be happy." Mum's eyes are full of worry and she asks me what happened. "I found her name out from the birth certificate. At first I just wanted the information. Then I saw my name and thought I was destined to do good deeds like a superhero. I wanted to be the best and I wanted to prove it."

Mum smiles. "And did you prove it?"

"I wasn't all that good at being a superhero. I tried to save a cat and help old people, but it wasn't as easy as

I thought. Then one day I pulled a boy back from stepping out into the road and saved him from getting hit by a car." Mum's eyes are wide and her mouth pops open. "Yeah," I whisper. "I did. And then I found out where my real mother lived." Lived. I said *lived*, not *lives*. I got the tenses right. I swallow. "And I went to tell her I was Ace."

I can barely look at Mum now because I can see the glitter in her eyes. She reaches for another tissue in her pocket and blows her nose too. "And what happened then?"

"The name Ace didn't mean a thing. It was just a stupid shop where she bought spaghetti hoops."

Mum stares out the window into the distance, and it's obvious she's thinking, and the glitter is still sparkling in her eyes and her nose is redder than Rudolph the Red-Nosed Reindeer's. "Of course you're allowed to look for your mother and I want you to know I understand. As a mother myself, I know how important it is and how much you needed to do that." Mum sighs and I see her chest rise and fall. "I only want what's best for you and so even if it means me losing a bit of you, losing my Adam, I won't get in the way of you connecting with your mother."

"She didn't want me," I whisper. My heart flutters as

though it's full of broken-winged moths. "I thought everyone loved a superhero, but she didn't love me."

"Oh, Adam." Mum's voice wraps me in a blanket of softness.

"She lived in a big house with lots of rooms but there wasn't even a tiny corner for me. I thought I'd have a home with her. And I was going to take her to my *Forest For Ever* exhibition that was on tonight at the school. She was going to come. Only she didn't. She walked away from me, just like she did the first time."

Mum jolts and tilts her head to the side. "Hold on. Did you say there was an exhibition at your school?"

I nod. "I knew it was the same night as Minnie's play and I wanted my real mother to come and see the family tree I'd done. I wanted her to be proud and take me home with her. I wanted to live with her."

Teardrops spill onto Mum's cheeks and the light from outside catches them like sunlight on raindrops. "Oh, Adam. You wanted your mother to take you home?" Mum wipes the tissue across her face. "You gave her your bobble hat. She was the special person."

I nod.

"Okay," whispers Mum.

"But she disappeared to Switzerland and took it with her. Or she threw it away. I don't know. It's gone anyway.

She didn't want to give me a home. She didn't want me at all."

Mum looks so sad and she takes my hand in hers and says, "I don't have any magic words to take away the pain. There's no real medicine for a sore heart." She smiles, adding, "Except love, and I've got plenty of that." Mum's hand squeezes mine. "I'm sorry that you've had a hard time finding your mother and I know you're feeling like you've lost her again. But I don't want you to feel like you've got *no* mother. Mothers come in lots of different shapes and sizes. Sometimes a mother isn't even the person who gave birth to the child."

My shoulders rise up to my head and drop again. "But I wanted her to love me. I wanted it to be perfect, because meeting your mum should be."

"Perhaps the time was right for you, but not for her."

"Oh, I didn't think about that. Do you think another time might be the right time? How will I know when that is? Will it be next week, or next month?"

Mum looks directly into my eyes and says, "That's a question I can't answer, but the door isn't closed for ever. Things change, people grow and people change too. Don't let the spark inside you go out. Not yet. And in the meantime..." Mum clears her throat. "Would you consider letting me step in and be your mother? I know

I'm not the mother you were hoping for right now, but I love you more than you'll ever know."

"Why would you want me?"

Mum coughs. "What do you mean?"

"I didn't think you'd want me. I've punched Dad and I've run away and I've tried to find my real mother and I wanted her to give me a home because I knew I was losing my home with you. Anyway, you've got the jelly bean to think about. That's why I started to take down my comic wallpaper for you. I wanted to help. It's okay. Don't worry. I know you can't fit me and the jelly bean in. I understand. I'm not yours and the jelly bean is."

Mum looks confused and she stares at me and asks me why I'm mentioning jelly beans now. "What is this jelly bean thing? You'll have to explain it to me, because I'm so confused."

I clear my throat and try to focus on a spot on the ground so I don't have to look at Mum. "You've got a jelly bean. I heard you mentioning it to Grandma on the phone." When I glance back up there's a flicker in Mum's eyes and she swallows and I see her hands trembling as she pushes her hair behind her ear. "I know 'jelly bean' is a name for the size of a baby in your tummy. And I heard you talking to Dad about the sacrifice and the flat being small. So I know I'm going to have to make room for the baby – I know I'm the sacrifice you have to make. I saw an appointment for a scan in your bedside drawer too, and you'd torn out an ad about rehoming me." I look down again as Mum gives a tiny snort of surprise. "I'm sorry," I continue. "I know I wasn't meant to see any of it. I was looking for a key. I didn't want to spoil the surprise of the new baby, but I knew I'd have to go."

Mum's face is serious and she tells me I mustn't worry, but I'm already worrying. "You're right. I have had scans. I'll explain the rehoming part later, but it's something completely different and, yes, it's a surprise. There *is* going to be an addition to the family, but, Adam, you're not being rehomed! You're not leaving the family – you *are* our family." Mum squeezes my hand once more and looks directly at me. "And I'm not having a baby."

This doesn't make sense. What about the jelly bean and the conversation and the scans and the surprise? I didn't imagine any of those things – they really happened.

"On the phone to Grandma I said it was the size of a jelly bean." I nod at Mum and she continues, "But I wasn't talking about a baby, although I know people sometimes call the babies in their tummies jelly beans. This was more like a lump."

The word "lump" makes me shiver. It doesn't sound as good as "jelly bean" did. It sounds painful and worrying and it's making my heart thunder and my throat dry up. *Lump, lump, lump*, I tell myself. I don't like it. I don't want Mum to have a lump. Now I wish it *was* a jelly bean. This time I squeeze Mum's hand.

Mum tells me not to panic but I ignore her and start panicking. "The lump is in my breast and it's small but it's there and growing. That doesn't mean you need to worry because it's still early days, and I've spotted it quickly and I've been to the hospital and they think it might be okay, but it needs removing. They have to check the lump to make sure."

"A lump?" My head is spinning around like a washing machine. "You've got a lump, not a baby? I got it all wrong!" My mouth spits out, "You're not going to die, Mum, are you? Please tell me you're not going to die." I can't bear it. I can't have wasted time chasing my other mother while my mum was ill.

Mum thinks about the words and then slowly says, "I don't have any intention of going anywhere without a fight. You see, I've got everything to fight for. I've got Dad, Minnie, Velvet and you. I'm not planning on dying any time soon. And I'm sorry if I've been weepy or moody, but it was a lot to take in."

There's a river coming from my eyes and Mum can't get tissues out of her pocket fast enough, and she tries to stop it but the river keeps flowing and I'm saying I can't lose her and she can't die, and she's shushing me and saying that she's doing everything she can to take care of it. She's promising that she's in safe hands and that the doctors are looking after her.

"But I'm frightened, Mum. Everything has changed and it's scary."

"I understand that you're scared," soothes Mum. "But sometimes it's the things we don't know that are the most frightening. Whereas when we know there's a problem and we can step up and try to do something about it, that's not as scary. It's like I told you – after the rain there's a rainbow. You might look out the window and think everything looks grey and miserable, but then the sky clears and the rainbow appears and you realize things are better and you're happy."

"I still want that rainbow," I sniff.

"There is going to be one," Mum replies fiercely. "There always is. It's the same as day following night and the stars appearing in the darkness. The world keeps turning."

"I want my bobble hat back now. How am I going to be safe without it?"

"Because even without it, you're part of this family and no matter where you go and what you do, we will be looking out for you." Mum puts a damp tissue into her pocket. "And, Adam, I've never said this before but I want to say it now...I'm grateful to your mother." Mum sees the shock on my face and puts her finger to my mouth to stop me arguing. "I am, because she gave me the greatest gift I've ever had. She gave me you, when I'd been waiting for you all my life. If she was here I would hug her and thank her for giving me the chance to share my life with you."

I've never considered it like that before, but Mum's nodding and smiling and saying I'm incredible, that I'm special, that she loves me.

"But that sounds like a superhero," I whisper. "And I'm not one. I never was Ace."

Mum inhales and pauses before saying, "You don't have to be a hero to be super, Adam. You just have to be you." For a moment I can hardly breathe and Mum nods. "Being you is quite enough and there is no need to prove anything, because I love you without any proof. I love you because you're you. I love you for changing my life and I love you because you're mine and nothing will change that. You're my son, Adam, and you're my heart."

What happens next is that the room feels a bit brighter than it did before. It's as if the darkness isn't so black, as if the monsters have disappeared, and Mum leans towards me and says that, no matter what happens in the future, we will always have each other. Mum says that I'm stuck with the Butters' family for ever.

I whisper, "Mum." Then I do something I'm not expecting. I reach out my arms and Mum looks at me, a little confused. Then she smiles and reaches right back and she pulls me into the biggest hug of sunshine and I feel my heart beat in time with Mum's heart. I think of how Mum always says she holds me in her heart and I know that's where I am now. This is my home and always will be. And we don't say anything, because sometimes words aren't necessary. All I know is that I've found my real mother and she was here with me all the time.

27

CRACK

The following day Minnie says she's moving on from being an actress and has decided to be a singer instead. She's going to audition for a school band called The Peanut Butter Zombies. She says she doesn't mind that I didn't come to see the play yesterday. "Callum was totally rubbish in it anyway. He kept overacting. He couldn't even die properly. How can you be rubbish at falling over and pretending you're asleep? It can't be hard because Dad pretends to be asleep all the time when Mum asks him to do anything. Anyway, I don't care about Callum any more." Then Minnie says she's been keeping a secret from me and she's been feeling bad about it.

"I know the secret," I reply. "It's about the text."

Minnie looks down at her hands. Her nail polish is chipped. "You knew?" I tell her I guessed because when her mobile phone bleeped I saw a text and I recognized the number straight away. I'd already memorized the number, because it was so important to me. "Why didn't you say? You could have told Mum and Dad that I was being horrible." I just shake my head. Minnie goes on to tell me that she saw the poster in Sharkey's window and knew what I was trying to do, and so when she was at rehearsals with Callum she borrowed his mobile phone when he went to the toilet and texted me, pretending to be Rose and telling me to forget her. "Then I wiped the message from Callum's phone. He didn't know anything about it."

My eyes lock on to Minnie's.

"I know," sighs Minnie. "You thought you were texting Rose and when your replies came back I thought Callum was being all secretive and getting texts from a girlfriend. I told you not to text back so I didn't think you would. Callum wouldn't even let me see the texts or I would have known it was your number. It was a stupid mix-up. But it was all my fault and I've got you a present to make up for it." Minnie disappears into her bedroom and then comes back clutching a plastic bag.

"I gave you this gift when you were a baby and I'm giving it to you again. I want you to feel safe and I know it's not *the* bobble hat, but it's almost as good."

I tell Minnie thanks and I look at the bobble hat. "I love it," I declare, my fingers running over the pom-pom. "But would you mind if I didn't wear it? I've worn one for years and it's always made me feel safe, but now I *do* feel safe. The truth is, I never really needed a safe place because my safe place was already here with my family. I just didn't realize it and now I do."

Minnie grins. "Woo-hoo, get you!" Then she says she's a poet and didn't know it. A second later her eyes cloud over and she says, "I really am sorry about the text. It was a horrible thing to do. I'm a bad sister."

I say, "You're not."

"I am," replies Minnie, pushing her fingers through the plastic of the bag. "I've been jealous of you for ages. Ever since you got interested in comics and you and Dad were always together. I felt left out and I was angry because he was *my* dad." Minnie looks ashamed. "Everything Mum and Dad taught us – that we are all equal and family – went out the window. I felt like you were more special than me and I envied you."

"Me?" I'm shocked mainly because I was the one who envied Minnie.

"Dad always looked like he had so much fun with you. And he's not interested in fashion shows and make-up. Those were the things I wanted to talk about." Minnie shakes her head and then sighs and says that's no excuse though. "I wished you'd never come here and I kept wishing you'd go away." There are tears in her eyes as she continues, "Then I saw you that night of the storm and you were in Mum and Dad's room and I found out you'd discovered your birth certificate, and suddenly instead of wishing you'd leave I wanted you to stay more than anything. I couldn't imagine being without you. You're my brother."

I nod, my eyes watering. "Conjunctivitis," I whisper, wiping them.

"That's why I told you to forget your real mother and why I sent you the text. It was selfish but I wanted you to stay and I was scared your real family would be better than ours. I even imagined you'd get a new sister who'd be so much nicer than me."

"I understand," I whisper. "But finding my mother was something I had to do. Part of it was because it felt like a piece of me was missing. It's sort of like when you lose a jigsaw piece and you really want it so you can complete the picture."

Minnie tilts her head and then disappears to her

bedroom again before returning and sitting down. "Open your hand. This is for you."

Minnie's palm brushes mine.

In my hand sits a tiny heart, a small jigsaw piece. "I found this under my wardrobe yesterday and it reminded me of that jigsaw I once gave you. It's yours."

And in that moment I know my picture is complete.

I've got used to knowing my real mother is in Switzerland with Bonbon. I've squished her into the tiniest corner of my mind. Of course, I'd be fibbing if I said I never thought about her once in the last month. I have, because it's impossible to forget that I met her. But every time she pops into my head, I keep thinking she gave birth to me but she wasn't a *mother*. Because it's taken me a while to understand that a real mother is the person who tucks you up in bed, tells you stories, wipes away your tears and your snot, cleans up your sick after you've had too many fruit squashes – a real mother is the person who loves you. That wasn't Rose. My real mother has always been Mum. Mums don't just carry you in their tummy; they carry you in their hearts for ever.

Mum says a letter from Switzerland turned up at Dad's work this morning. She told me that Rose must have found out that Dad had a key-cutting business and looked up the address. My heart pounded and my hands were trembling and I knew it was me who told her. Dad wouldn't have been hard to find as he's the only key-cutter in Pegasus Park.

"Don't be worried," said Mum. "I'm here for you, if you'd like to read it." She peeled the envelope open and pulled out a letter. There wasn't a lot of writing on it and Mum's eyes bobbed from left to right. "Would you like to read it?"

I shook my head.

"Well, I'll tell you a little bit of it. She says she's sorry she left so suddenly but they had work commitments. She says she'd prefer it if you didn't try to contact her, as her husband doesn't know about her past. I'm sorry, Adam." Mum folded the letter and didn't say anything else about its contents, and I didn't ask.

I pretended I wasn't bothered. I was so not bothered that I didn't eat much dinner. I was so not bothered that I didn't watch TV. And now I'm in my bedroom, still trying to pretend I'm not bothered. There's a little tap on my bedroom door and Mum comes in carrying a box. "I'm sorry about the letter, poppet. I know you've been fretting about it, but like I said before, perhaps it just isn't the right time for her." Mum sits on the bed beside me and hands me the box, and when I ask what it's for, Mum says, "It's a memory box. It's a place to store the things that are important to you. Open it and see…"

I lift the lid and inside is my birth certificate, one tiny white bobble hat that Minnie gave me as a baby and a photograph of the family flying a kite when me and Minnie were little. Dad has me on his shoulders. Mum is fussing and making sure I don't fall, while also trying to hold onto baby Velvet, and Minnie is just sticking her tongue out and holding the kite.

There's something else in the box – a tiny photo, and Mum says it's of Granddad Fred.

"And a baby," I add.

"It's his grandson," says Mum.

"They look so happy," I reply.

"Don't you know who it is?"

"You said – it's Granddad Fred. And he's holding his grandson and, look, his grandson is playing with the watch," I reply. "Is it Uncle Jon's son?" Mum turns the photo over and asks me to read the writing on the back.

"A very proud Granddad Fred and his wonderful grandson, Adam." There are big tears in my eyes and Mum squeezes my hand.

"Put anything you want in there. It's for memories of the past and for new memories you make with us.

You can mix all your memories together and what you'll get is something wonderful. Something that is unique to you. This is your life, Adam. It might feel a bit muddled up, but one thing will always be there in the centre of that muddle and it's us. Dad says he told you about it not being how you start the race but how you continue that counts. It's up to you how you do that, but wherever you go and whatever you do, your family will be right there behind you."

I let the tear fall but it's not a sad tear.

Another thing that happened recently is the dog. It's not an invisible dog either and it does bark and it chews the sofa. The dog arrived the day after Minnie gave me the jigsaw piece. There was a knock on the front door and when I opened it there was a dog sitting there and then it trotted inside and I shut the front door and it promptly weed on the floor. Mum wasn't too impressed and I said I was sorry and that it must belong to one of our neighbours.

Then there was another knock at the front door and I opened it and Dad was standing outside with a big grin on his face. He said he'd knocked the first time but hid to surprise us.

Dad looked down our hallway and said, "He's arrived," and Mum said, "He has," and that if Dad could clean up the wee that would be lovely. Then she handed Dad poo bags and said they were his as well.

It turned out the dog didn't belong to a neighbour because it was ours. It also turned out that the dog was the surprise that Mum and Dad had been talking about for ages. It was the dog that needed a bed, a blanket and a toy. And it was the dog that needed a space and that they had to make sacrifices for. None of that was anything to do with the jelly bean. And the collar and lead they gave Velvet for her birthday was a clue, but we didn't pick up on it. Also the slip of paper I found in Mum's drawer was the number for a *dog* adoption and rehoming centre, because that's where the dog was coming from. All that time I was convinced the surprise was a baby and that it was a boy, and I was sort of right, because it was a baby boy dog. I added everything up but got my calculations a bit wrong. Velvet was so happy about the dog that she laughed and cried and then she weed a bit too, but Mum didn't mind when she blamed it on the dog.

We also said goodbye to Sausage Roll. Velvet said she was sad to let him go but it was the right time. Mum asked if she was sure and Velvet said she was, because Sausage Roll was here to make us happy and he had.

"Ah," replied Mum, smiling.

"Yes, he found Adam when we lost him."

Mum broke out into a laugh and said that was right.

"Okay," said Velvet and she opened the front door and waved goodbye to Sausage Roll. "He was a special dog," she whispered. Our new dog, which we christened Dog Star, licked Velvet's hand.

"Yes, he was." I squeezed Velvet's hand and she squeezed right back and then I remembered the dog had licked it first and I took my hand away. Meanwhile Mum gave Velvet a biscuit and she forgot all about Sausage Roll.

28
BOOM

Mum's got surgery this week and I've tried not to worry but I can't help myself. This is the time I want to be a superhero most of all. I want to zap the lump with a blaster and I try to imagine killing it. When I say this to Mum she smiles and says thank you for the offer but in this case perhaps it might be wiser for the surgeon to take a look at it. She explained that they're going to give her a general anaesthetic and then they'll use a vacuum to suck out the lump. Mum called it a lumpectomy.

"I thought vacuums sucked up things you don't want," I said.

Mum smiled and ruffled my hair. "They do and I hope this special vacuum works for me. Once the lump is removed they'll send it for testing."

"I'm frightened," I told Mum, and I was. Think about it. You've found your real mother at last and you never want to let her go, but then something as tiny as a jelly-bean-sized lump comes along and threatens to make her sick and it's scarier than any villain out there. Mum said she was frightened too and it was okay to feel that way – that we shouldn't deny our feelings or bottle them up, and that getting them out was important. "You can't leave me," I whispered and I felt selfish but I couldn't lose my mum.

Mum wrapped her arms around me and pulled me in close and I could smell sunshine again and she was warm and I felt safe. Mum's heart was beating and I could feel mine beating in time with hers. Burying my head into her body, I felt stupid for ever thinking the jelly bean was a baby and guilty for ever thinking I was going to need to find a new home. Deep down I think I knew Mum and Dad wouldn't do that to me, but I was so confused about everything.

Before this I never thought someone I loved could die. I was living inside a big bubble, thinking about the mother I didn't have instead of the mum I did. Now,

I'm sitting with Mum and it's the night before she goes into hospital and there are so many things I want to say to her and I can't remember any of them. But somehow it feels like she already knows how I feel, because she reaches her hand out and squeezes mine.

I squeeze back immediately.

We don't talk for ages. When we do, Mum tells me how proud she is of me. She tells me that she reached out to me once and I gripped her hand and squeezed it. "I needed you just as much as you needed me," says Mum. I look at Mum and ask her how that's possible because I was a baby without a mum so surely I needed her most. "You might think that," replies Mum. "But I needed you too. I knew I wanted a baby and at the time I was having a few problems and it didn't happen and so we'd planned to adopt. We already had Minnie and we loved her so much our hearts felt like they could explode. When I found you it was like I'd found an angel and I knew I loved you too. Exactly the same way I loved Minnie." Mum's eyes fill up with tears and she looks away. "Never think that you owe me anything for finding you, when it's really the other way around. I owe you for letting me be your mother. You've brought me so much joy. It's immeasurable."

I squeeze Mum's hand again.

"It's just like the joy Granddad Fred brought to your great-grandparents too. That's what the watch was about – something to symbolize that connection and joy you both have brought to our family." Mum reaches into her pocket and pulls out Granddad Fred's watch and I feel my face burn.

"I'm sorry I threw it at you. I was angry. I didn't mean to throw it away. I love this watch."

"You didn't throw it away," soothes Mum. "We understand that you were hurt and confused, but this watch still belongs to you. You saw the photo. You were holding it. So while I was looking after it for you, I took it to a repair shop in town and got the broken strap fixed and I asked the man there if they could try repairing the watch itself. I said we'd tried before and it was worth giving it another go. But he couldn't fix it. He showed it to this girl and she smiled and said it was lovely. I told her it was special and she agreed. She said it probably belonged to someone nice and I said it did. Anyway you can still wear it, if you want, but it doesn't go. Perhaps it never will."

I put the watch back on my wrist where it belongs. The new strap looks nice but I wish I'd never pulled it off in the first place. I'm never taking it off again.

The next afternoon Mum prepares to go into hospital and her face is as pale as tracing paper. I want to say lots of things to her but all I can do is make a heart with my fingers and Mum makes one back with hers. Minnie gives Mum a kiss on the cheek and Velvet clings on to Mum and Dog Star is licking Mum's shoes. Minnie's eyes are red-rimmed and as Mum pulls away Minnie bites her lip. Grandma is here to look after us while Mum is at the hospital, and she gives Mum a hug as she leaves, and then Grandma goes into the kitchen, telling us a cup of tea will help. But we don't move from the window. Instead we watch the Surelock Homes van drive away with Mum and Dad inside. Rain splatters on the window and it looks like the sky is crying for us. I feel so sick that I nearly fall onto the floor, and it's Minnie who holds me up by hooking her arm in mine, and then Velvet hooks on too, and we three stand at the window for the longest time.

Minnie looks at me and says she has a question that's been bothering her for ages. "You know that poster you put in the window of Sharkey's?" I nod. "Why was there a drawing of Mum on it? I never understood that bit, seeing as you were looking for Rose." I blink. "It was how I imagined my real mother. I closed my eyes and thought about the mother I wanted most in the world and I described her and Tiny Eric drew her for me."

"Well, it was a drawing of Mum," says Minnie. She smiles and stares out the window into the distance.

And I realize she is right.

At the time Mum's supposed to be out of surgery, I look out of my bedroom window far across Pegasus Park and in the distance, on the horizon, I swear I can see a tiny flicker of a rainbow. It disappears after a moment but that doesn't matter. It's just enough for me to know that Mum's okay – that there's a rainbow after the rain and even if the sky is dark there are still stars.

I touch the window with my fingers and trace a rainbow on the glass.

When Dad gets home he tells us Mum is comfortable and he'll pick her up in the morning. I tell him we have to fly the wish kite and Dad says it's a bit late to be going out to make wishes. Minnie and Velvet look at me and ask what the wish kite is.

I tug on Dad's sleeve as I explain, "You write a wish poem on it and let it float high into the sky, don't you, Dad? That's what Granddad Fred told you when you wished for a car."

"You wished for a car?" Minnie looks at Dad. "You

wished for a car and ended up with an old red van. What went wrong?"

Dad laughs. "I wished for a Scalextric and I got one. And no, Minnie, before you wish for the contents of a make-up counter, I don't think that'll work. Since there are four of us, we need to combine our wish tonight, if we're doing it."

We look at each other and Dad takes Minnie's hand and Minnie takes mine and I take Velvet's and Velvet takes Dad's. *Four hearts*, I think. *Four hearts combining to make one, like a four-leaf clover*. Dad gives us a moment to think what we want to wish for and then says we'll go around the circle and ask each other.

I think of Mum in the hospital and when Dad starts he says what I'm thinking: he wishes Mum will come out healthy and happy. Minnie looks at Dad and she agrees. "Same, Dad," she says. "I miss Mum already."

"I want Mum back at home. She's my heart," I say.

Velvet thinks for a second and says, "I want a ribbon for Dog Star's hair." We all glare at her. "And I want Mum home so she can put the ribbon in his hair."

I tell everyone to wait and I run into my bedroom and come back with a sheet of paper, and I say I've already written a wish poem we could attach to the kite. I tell them I wrote it for homework about my real mother and now I know that's definitely Mum. Dad says he wants to hear it and Velvet nods. Dog Star is biting his tail so I'm not sure he's too bothered. With a trembling voice, I read:

I know your heart's a special place
That I can call my home
No matter what I do or say
I know I'm not alone
And if I have got worries
I know that you will care
You'll wrap me up in lots of love
I know there's plenty spare
And if I had a wish tonight
I'd make that wish for you
For you're the only mum I need
You're my perfect mum come true.

The heart-shaped kite soars through the night sky and the wish, which has been tied to the ribbon, goes with it. Stars twinkle and it's as if each star listens to the wish and blinks in agreement. Dog Star barks at the moon like he's a werewolf, which is ridiculous because he's a schnoodle (a schnauzer poodle mix) and Dad says that he thinks Granddad Fred is looking down at us too. I look up into the sky as the heart kite sails this way and that and I imagine Granddad Fred is up there, and my heart feels so full of love that it could burst. It's only when Dad says we need to get back that we bring the kite back to Earth.

"I think our wishes will come true," says Dad. Then he winks. "I didn't really wish for a Scalextric with Granddad, you know."

I look at Dad.

"I wished to be happy – and I truly am, because I've got my family." Dad smiles and says, "You're my perfect son come true." He pulls me into a hug and then gives me a punch on the arm. I think I preferred the hug, to be honest.

Mum comes home the following day and she's tired and sore but she's alive. "I'm still here," says Mum. "You can't get rid of me that easily."

Minnie grins at me and Velvet's jumping up and down and so is Dog Star, although he doesn't seem to know why.

"Now," says Mum, "we can put it all behind us and move forward. We are the Butters and we're strongest when we stick together."

Mum wasn't able to give us hugs for a few days but

it didn't take long before she was back to normal, and we found out the lump was benign, which meant it was okay, then life got back to normal too (well, normal for us anyway, because we're not really normal at all, especially Velvet). School was the same as before. Mrs Chatterjee knew why I hadn't turned up to the exhibition, and ever since then she'd check I was happy and tell me I could talk to her if I wanted to.

The only thing that was different was that I couldn't completely forget about Rose, because in real life you can't just switch off your thoughts. Nothing is perfect, no matter how much you'd like it to be. But I've been thinking since everything has happened. I've decided that it's okay to think about my other mother sometimes and it's okay for life to be imperfectly perfect, because that's good enough. If my brain had a big switch with the words ROSE WALKER on it I might have flicked it off, but since that's not possible I just live with the fact that she's in Switzerland and that I'm no longer looking for her because I found everything I needed right in my own flat.

Last night Mum said that if I ever needed to write a letter to Rose, maybe in the future when things might have changed, she still had the envelope from Switzerland with the address and she'd keep it safe for me. I said I did need to write a letter but not to Rose. I needed to write a letter to someone who was very special to me once, someone who I didn't spend enough time with, and when they had problems I didn't notice because I was so wrapped up in my own and I felt bad about that. Sometimes you forget that others have problems too.

Dear Tiny Eric,
I'm still missing you. You were the best friend I ever had. You were a hero too. I know that now because there are heroes everywhere and sometimes they come in disguise. They come in the disguise of looking ordinary (when really they're extraordinary). Dad told me that once but I didn't understand and now I do. True heroes are all around us. There were heroes at the hospital helping my mum recently too when she had an operation.

I hope you're happy. I looked at your drawing of me as a superhero last night and I know I said you didn't draw me as a superhero but you did, didn't you? You just didn't tell me. All those squiggly words at the bottom didn't make sense but last night I looked them up.

Już jesteś superbohaterem!

You're already a superhero!

It was clever, Tiny Eric. If only I'd understood it before. You drew me as myself because you already thought I was great. I think you knew so much more than me. You helped me learn to believe with your drawings. You said the drawing of the four-leaf clover would bring me luck and it did, but I had to believe. It just took me a long time to believe in the most important thing of all: me. And not just me, but who I really am, and not who I thought I should be or who others thought I should be.

Anyway, everything is okay now, although I still have to put up with Minnie. But that's not going to change. I'm sorry your mum and dad have split up. Mrs Chatterjee said you were going to Poland, so I bet you're with your babcia now. Perhaps you're eating little pigeons (ha ha). I hope school is fun. Perhaps you've even made a new friend there. I hope so. Everyone needs a hero like you in their life.

Another thing, I'm never wearing my bobble hat again. I know, I know. My bobble hat was a safe place and I loved it and when I was worried I'd go inside it and stay there for a while. I gave my old one away, but then Minnie got me a new one but I don't think I need it. So now I'm giving you my bobble hat. It's lucky - wear it and believe, but believe in you.

I'd better go now because the bell is ringing and it's lunchtime. Mrs Chatterjee allowed me to write this letter just before the break. Mrs Chatterjee is okay, sometimes. I'm not going to tell her that though.

Goodbye,

Adam ☺

P.S. I'm including the front page of the Pegasus Park Packet. Remember we did our Forest For Ever project and someone was going to feature in the paper? Well, that someone was you. I wrote about how you were a superhero to me and how superheroes come in all shapes and sizes. Mrs Chatterjee said it was brilliant and passed it on to the paper. She also put your tree in reception so everyone could see it. She said your tree was special because it branched out and reached everyone in the class. She said we'd never forget you because your tree was the tallest and most upstanding in our forest.

Mrs Chatterjee takes the letter and says Tiny Eric will be very happy to get it. "And what's this?" Mrs Chatterjee looks down as I hand her my bobble hat. "Are you sending this to Eric?"

"Yes," I reply. "I want Tiny Eric to have it."

"That's lovely," says Mrs Chatterjee, smiling. Then she adds that's she proud to have me as part of her school family and she'll make sure that Tiny Eric gets this lovely letter, the newspaper clipping and the gift. The school have his new address in Poland, she tells me. And she's certain he'll be very glad to hear from me. "Now, scoot," adds Mrs Chatterjee. "You've only got twenty minutes of break left before you're back in the classroom for maths." Mrs Chatterjee pulls a scary face and I scoot right towards the door.

Outside in the playground, everyone else is playing together. Even though it's been a month since Tiny Eric left, I still don't have a new best friend even though I've got lots of mates. But as I sit on the wall by myself, I hear a little voice say, "Who is better, Batman or Superman?"

"Batman," I reply, looking up.

"Why?"

"Well, he doesn't have any superpowers but he still saves the day."

"That kind of makes him sound ordinary." The Beast

sits down beside me and offers me a sweet.

"Maybe," I reply, taking one. I pop it into my mouth. "But that's what all the real superheroes are. Look around you."

The Beast looks around. "What am I looking at?"

"The superheroes," I exclaim.

"Where?"

"Every person here in this playground is one," I say and I feel myself swell up inside. "We all are. You're a superhero because you're you. I'm a superhero because I'm me. We all might look ordinary but we're not, we're *extra*ordinary. I've learned that recently."

"You're clever."

"I know," I say, laughing. I happen to glance down at Granddad Fred's watch and I can't believe it but the cogs have started moving. "Look," I say, pointing the watch towards The Beast. I grin. "The watch is working again. Mum said she took it to a shop to get it repaired and they couldn't fix it, but they must have done something because look at it now."

The Beast says, "I know about your mum because she came into my uncle's shop. I was there. I saw the watch and I knew it was yours but I didn't say so. After your mum had gone my uncle replaced the strap but he couldn't fix the workings. He tried everything he could but he said he couldn't get the heart of the watch fixed. I asked him if he was sure it wouldn't go and he said he was sure." The Beast peers into the watch and sees the cogs rotating. "Maybe it was you who mended the heart of it." The Beast grins. "It had to be you." As The Beast turns away I say I'm sorry we weren't friends before. The Beast says it's okay and maybe one day we could be best friends.

"You won't throw me in a bush though?"

The Beast laughs and says, "Oh, right. FYI that day me and my friend were playing superheroes and pretending we could fly and she tripped and fell in a bush."

"A holly bush," I say.

"Yes, that was unfortunate," replies The Beast. "And not exactly superhero behaviour. But it wasn't my fault and I did try to help her back out."

The bell rings and The Beast starts to walks away from me.

I shout, "Hey, we can't be best friends until I know what your name is."

"It's Eve," replies The Beast.

"And I'm Adam," I say, laughing. I was never Ace because Ace didn't exist, except on a piece of paper.

My name is Adam Butters and I love comics and the

Zorbitans and I loved my bobble hat for a while but now I don't need to hide in it. I love living on planet Earth, top floor flat, number 53, Pegasus Park Towers. I don't smell of dogs any more but if I do it's because we have one and I love him too. He's part of our family. I love my little sister Velvet and I guess I love Minnie too, even though she still annoys me. I miss Tiny Eric every day but I love having a new best friend. Eve isn't in my class but we meet up every lunchtime to talk about comics. Sometimes we swap them, and we're going to the next Comic Con together. I still like sunshine, rolling down hills, and my teddy bear, but I don't eat spaghetti hoops. I love my mum and dad. They've always believed in me and accepted me for who I am, not who I thought I should be. But most of all I love living here with my family and there isn't anywhere else in the universe I'd rather be.

JUST CALL ME LARA...

Lara's debut novel, *A Boy Called Hope*, has been shortlisted for lots of prizes, including the Waterstones Children's Book Prize and the IBW Book Award, and won the Sheffield Children's Book Award 2015 and the Salford Children's Book Award 2016. Her second novel, *The Boy Who Sailed the Ocean in an Armchair*, was shortlisted for the Blue Peter Book Award and nominated for the Carnegie Medal.

Lara was born and studied in Northern Ireland, before moving to London. She loves tap-dancing, daydreaming, eating chips, wearing glitter and writing. Not necessarily in that order. What's more, she has just found her first four-leaf clover and feels very lucky.

Follow Lara on Twitter @LaraWilliamson
and find out more at: larawilliamson.com

If you could have a superpower, what would it be?

I'd love *lots* of superpowers. But if I had to choose, first on the list would be the ability to fly. Recently, I had a dream that I was a superhero and I could fly to the tops of skyscrapers. Oh, it was brilliant; exactly as you'd imagine. The wind was in my hair and I felt exhilarated and I was zooming everywhere until the alarm went off and I woke up. When I realized I couldn't fly at all I spent the rest of the day sulking.

If you could give yourself a superhero name, what would you choose?

Lara was the mother of Superman so I'm pretty happy with my name already but if I had to choose another one

I'd be "Glitter Assassin" and then I'd spray villains with glitter bombs that exploded from my hands. *POW! POW!* If you've ever tried to get rid of glittery particles you'll know that they stick to you like glue. Imagine all those mean, miserable villains covered in sparkles that wouldn't come off. It's a fabulous thought, but fiendish too.

And what would be your superhero motto?
Secretly I'd like to borrow "Kazoo" from Adam but as it's already taken I'll go for "Persistence pays off". That's my real life motto and I use it all the time. Not so long ago I had this dream of writing a book and getting it published. It didn't happen immediately but like all the best dreams I kept telling myself that persistence would pay off. And the more I said it, the more I believed and the harder I worked. I never gave up on myself, or the motto, and *WHAM!* the dream of getting published became a reality.

What was your inspiration for Adam?
I wanted Adam to think he was ordinary and to believe he needed to change and be extraordinary to be loved. But what Adam didn't know is that he wasn't ordinary at all. He was already extraordinary but he needed to go

on a journey to discover that. Shhh.... Come closer and I'll tell you a secret. Like Adam, *you* don't need to change who you are for anyone. Being you is enough.

In the story Adam writes a poem about his mum for the wish kite. If you were writing a poem for your kite what would you wish for?

I'd wish to step inside a book,
to meet old friends and take a look,
at worlds beyond this earth I know,
to Narnia with land of snow,
to Faraway Tree with slippery slide,
adventures with the Famous Five,
midnight feasts – I'd have a few,
I'd solve a crime with Nancy Drew.
To Oz I'd go without a care,
and Secret Garden? See you there.
I'd talk to spiders all the day,
I'd chat to Wonka on the way
to midnight gardens and the rest
to live in books would be the best.

Do you feel sad to leave your characters at the end of a book?

Adam wanted a tiny backward glance from his mother in this book. Without spoiling the story I feel like when I say goodbye to my characters I give them that one last little backward glance before we separate. I can't resist acknowledging them, knowing that we shared a story and that it's okay if we both walk away as stronger people. By that last page, even if it's bittersweet, I recognize it's time to let them go, and when I do, I know they're the true heroes in the story, they're kind, thoughtful, loving and they're going to go on and be amazing in many ways (even if we don't get to read about them).

ACKNOWLEDGEMENTS

There are many superheroes without whose help,
support and enthusiasm I couldn't have written
this book.

Superhero: Madeleine Milburn. **Superpower:** loyalty,
all-round loveliness and calm in the face of any storm.
Reads like lightning too.

Superheroes: Cara Lee Simpson, Hayley Steed.
Superpower: multi-tasking brilliance.

Superhero: Thérèse Coen. **Superpower:** rights
negotiating, support, and cycles at the speed of light.

Superhero: Rebecca Hill. **Superpower:** eyes like lasers
that see straight through a manuscript and find the
heart and then make it beat stronger. Rebecca is a
champion and I'm glad I'm on her team. Kapow!

Superhero: Anne Finnis. **Superpower:** super-sharp
eye for detail, passion for plot and the ability to
support an author when they feel the manuscript
might beat the living daylights out of them. Holy
doughnuts, she's ACE!

Superhero: Katharine Millichope. **Superpower:** designs powerful, dynamic, out-of-this-world covers that make you go WOW!

Superheroes: Becky Walker, Sarah Stewart, Anna Howorth, Amy Dobson, Stevie Hopwood, Sarah Cronin, and Will Steele at Usborne. **Superpowers:** reading, editing, publicising, designing and being all round dynamic. Go Team Usborne!

Superhero: Carlos Aón. **Superpower:** making the cover come alive. Boom!

Superheroes: Marvel, DC and Action Comics. **Superpower:** creating inspirational superheroes – Superman, Batman, Spider-Man, The Incredible Hulk, The Thing, Thor, Captain America, Adam Strange, Jack Frost and Jack Power and many more that we love.

Superhero: Melissa Roske. **Superpower:** you're a wonder, woman!

Superheroes: Graham, Mum, David, Josie, Geraldine, Dessie, Peter, Joe and Ally. **Superpower:** being the best family in the entire universe.

Superhero extraordinaire: Millie. **Superpower:** being a hero because you're you. And that's enough!

Also by LARA:

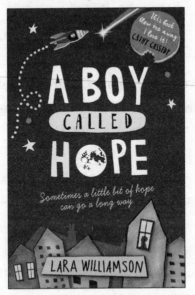

Since his dad ran off with the lady from the chip shop, Dan Hope's life has gone a bit strange, what with his sister acting mean and Mum's new boyfriend keeping secrets. And now – even stranger – his dad has turned up as a presenter on TV.

So Dan decides to sort out his messy family, starting with getting his dad back. But as one genius plan after another goes pear-shaped, Dan fears that his wish will never come true...until he starts to realize that your real family aren't always the people you share your name with.

ISBN 9781474922920

Praise for A BOY CALLED HOPE

Shortlisted for **Waterstones Children's Book Prize 2015**
Shortlisted for **Independent Booksellers Week
Book Award 2014**

"Warm, heartbreaking and hilarious in turn...a fabulous
book about love, families and making sense of life."
The Sunday Express

"A beautifully written and heartfelt novel that made
me laugh and cry in equal measure."
Waterstones Booksellers' Children's Books of the Year

"*A Boy Called Hope* will tug at your heartstrings and
probably make your eyes all leaky, but it's such a great
book for huddling under a blanket with."
The Mile Long Bookshelf

"Lovely, heartwarming, funny read. I laughed out loud,
and I may have shed a tear or two."
Michelle Harrison, author

Also by LARA:

Becket Rumsey is all at sea. His dad has run away
with him and his brother Billy in the middle of the night.
And they've left everything behind, including their
almost-mum Pearl. Becket has no idea what's going on –
it's a mystery.

So with the help of Billy and a snail called Brian, Becket
sets out on a journey of discovery. It's not plain sailing,
but then what journeys ever are?

ISBN 9781409576327

Praise for
THE BOY WHO SAILED THE
OCEAN ON AN ARMCHAIR

Shortlisted for the **Blue Peter Book Awards 2016**

Nominated for the **CILIP Carnegie Medal 2017**

Shortlisted for **Independent Booksellers Week
Book Award 2016**

"A touching, funny tale."
The Sunday Express

"An entertaining read with a serious and
absorbing story at its heart."
Books for Keeps

"Prepare to laugh, cry and simply marvel."
Lancashire Evening Post

"I am incredibly excited to read more of Lara's work
in the future."
Book Monsters

For more supersonic stories go to:
WWW.USBORNE.CO.UK/FICTION